Merry Christmas.

Judy Bancroft

2019

The House on
Christmas
Street

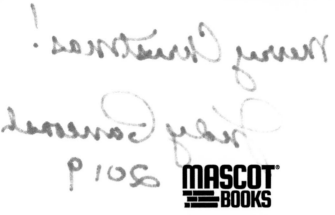

www.mascotbooks.com

The House on Christmas Street

For more information, please contact:
Mascot Books
620 Herndon Parkway #320
Herndon, VA 20170
info@mascotbooks.com

Library of Congress Control Number: 2019911870

CPSIA Code: PRCP0919A
ISBN-13: 978-1-64543-243-2

Printed in the United States

This book is dedicated to the hundreds of decorating enthusiasts across the globe who have used my song, "The House on Christmas Street," in their displays, thereby giving joy to thousands of people I may never meet. I am eternally grateful.

The House on Christmas Street

**Written by
Judy Pancoast**

Inspired by a script
written by Rick Hautala

It's got forty-seven thousand twinkling lights
And Santa Claus up on the roof;
Dasher and Dancer and all the other reindeer-
Rudolph's up there, too!
With a band of merry snowmen dancing on the porch,
And a couple of carolers singing by the lamp-post
Over near the front door;
It's where everybody meets;
It's The House on Christmas Street!

The House on Christmas Street

Music & Lyrics
By
Judy Pancoast

Chapter 1

"**What are those** fools doing out there in this heat? She's going to have that baby right in the driveway if they aren't careful!"

Muriel Michaud was talking to herself, something she found herself doing a lot these days. She peered out of her bedroom window at the young couple across the street, as they struggled to get an oversized carton out of the back of their minivan. The Nadeaus were quite the sight—the woman looked about ten months pregnant with baby number three, and really shouldn't have been doing anything strenuous. Her string bean husband had climbed into the van, and was pushing the carton out as she tried to grab its other end.

The job was proving nearly impossible because of her huge tummy. This was a disaster in the making.

Muriel didn't consider herself a busybody, but ever since she'd retired from her teaching position of thirty-five years, it had been harder and harder to fill the empty hours. After all, one could only sweep the kitchen floor so many times a day, and she wasn't the kind of person to while away the hours in front of the TV. Her people-watching had begun innocently enough, but now nothing was more fascinating to her than watching the comings and goings of the folks in her neighborhood.

Franklin Street was her street. She and her husband Raymond had bought their two-story Colonial in 1959, when they'd been married only three years, and they'd raised three children there. It was a perfect middle-class neighborhood in Kennebec City, a small Maine city named for the river on which it had been settled. Even today, most of the modest houses from that time were still the same; they were decently spaced with nice lawns and gardens, some with front porches.

Muriel conjured up an old memory of Franklin Street and fell into a reverie. The road was lined with trees before Dutch elm disease got them, and the neighborhood was full of life. In the summer, it was children riding their bikes, playing kick the can or dodgeball, and mothers strolling their babies or just standing in their yards, chatting over the fences. On the weekends husbands washed and waxed their cars in the driveway, radios blaring. Muriel could almost smell the evening barbecues that had everyone smacking their lips, as the smell of delicious food on the grill filled the air. Come winter, the kids took their sleds and toboggans to the hill at the empty lot down the road to go sledding. Back then, most mothers stayed at home, and year 'round you could hear them calling their children for lunch. It seemed like just yesterday...

In recent years, though, the character of the neighborhood had changed. All the original neighbors had either died or moved away— all but Eileen Ferris next door, who had lived there even longer than they had. None of the new families had time for socializing. Women were working, and gone were the days of moms in pairs strolling their babies around the neighborhood, or inviting each other over for coffee. Muriel had once been one of those young mothers, and she'd had a lot of friends her age in the neighborhood. That was a lifetime ago.

Muriel sighed as she refocused on the present, reaching through the white lace curtains to crack the window open.

Labor Day in Maine was shaping up to be hotter than usual, and the cicadas were buzzing their heads off. She couldn't remember it having been this hot since that summer she took the kids to the beach nearly every day. When was that? '74? '75? All the summers when the kids were still kids seemed like one big jumble. The slight breeze that sometimes came through the front bedroom window was warm and sticky now, instead of fresh and cool. The heat was made even more disconcerting by the volume of the Nadeaus' bratty four-year-old twins. Or were they five, now? Muriel wasn't sure.

The couple finally had the unwieldy box out of the van. Muriel leaned forward and squinted to read the bold writing on the side of the box: BROYHILL.

The Nadeaus were making their way slowly to their front porch, Esmerelda waddling forward and Andy stepping gingerly backward until they finally turned and began to side-step. The boys, who'd liberated themselves from their booster seats, were running around the yard screaming. Muriel gasped as their pregnant mother stumbled and yelped, the carton slipping out of her hands and falling to the driveway. Andy put own his end of the box and rushed to help his wife. She sat on the porch steps and mopped her forehead with the back of her hand.

"Phew!" said Muriel. "That was a close one."

The Nadeau family was the newest addition to the neighborhood, having moved in about two years earlier. Muriel had heard they'd moved up from "Taxachusetts" so Andy could get his Master's Degree at the University of Central Maine. He was a lanky guy, given to wearing baseball caps. Muriel suspected he was probably bald under those caps. Esmerelda was barely five feet tall and quite round now, even though she wasn't due until…was it December? Muriel couldn't recall. Word was they'd met in her homeland, the Dominican Republic, while Andy was doing some kind of teaching there.

The twins were just toddlers when they'd moved to Franklin Street, and now she was expecting again. God forbid it would be another set of twins, although it sure looked likely. Either that, or she was the type to put on a lot of weight when she was eating for two.

Esmerelda had recently cropped her thick, black hair into a pixie. Smart idea; she wouldn't have much time to take care of her coiffure with a job to hold down and three kids running wild. Muriel had no idea what the young woman did for work, only that she packed the kids into the car every day and they didn't come back until around supper time. *She must have them in some kind of preschool.*

Ray strolled into the room and started rummaging through the oak dresser, still in his pajamas. "Well, it's about time," said Muriel.

"What's that?" he said, examining the brightly colored shorts he'd just pulled out. Although seventy-seven, he stood up to his full five-foot-eleven and moved with the grace of a much younger man. He had a sharp sense of humor and loved to chuckle at what he called his wife's "antics," but she guessed that was part of why he seemed so young. He also had a frustrating propensity for going outside and working in the yard when Muriel was trying to make a point about something. As a result, the Michauds had a beautiful perennial garden, a small topiary, a backyard brick barbecue with patio, a man-made pond, a shade garden, and a perfectly manicured lawn that rarely had an autumn leaf touch it for more than a day. Muriel would have given up all that beauty for a husband who listened to her.

"I said it's about time. The Nadeaus have finally brought a crib home, and it looks like a pretty expensive one, too. Says 'Broyhill' on the box. Those don't come cheap. Do you suppose his parents bought it for them? God knows, *he* probably couldn't afford it."

"Think I should go over and give 'em a hand?" said Ray, observing the scene from over his wife's shoulder before ambling over to the closet and pulling out a short-sleeved shirt.

"And throw your back out? I don't think so. I don't know why they had to get rid of the perfectly good cribs they had. Recalled because the kid's head could get caught in them. I never heard of such a thing."

"Who told you that?" Ray sat down on the green-and-pink floral comforter to pull on his socks.

"Oh, I have my sources," Muriel replied. "She's gonna hurt herself out there working in this heat. Or go into early labor. She should lie down and let that good-for-nothing husband take care of things."

"Now, just what makes you think he's good-for-nothing?"

"Just look at him! Almost thirty years old and still in school? What's he need a Master's in Chemical Engineering for, anyway? You did fine at the mill for over forty years without one. If you ask me, he should have a decent job by now...especially with two little ones and another one—or two—on the way."

"How the heck do you know all this stuff? I don't believe you've spoken one word to those people in all the time they've lived here."

"Like I said, I have my sources."

"Well, your sources ought to mind their own beeswax," said Ray, as he left the room and disappeared down the hall.

Muriel took in a breath, intending to yell after him, when suddenly Andy Nadeau looked straight up at her, smiling and waving, as if he knew she'd been watching all along. She quickly pulled back out of sight, paused for a few seconds, then cautiously peeked out again. Through the screen she could hear Andy, his attention now on the wild boys, yelling, "Matty! Ricky! Will one of you please get the front door?"

One boy had spied a squirrel and was chasing it across the lawn, while the other, apparently scared of the squirrel, ran screaming toward his mother. They acted as though they hadn't heard their father at all, and Andy ran up to open the door himself.

"Spoiled, if you ask me," Muriel muttered, just as an unfamiliar car came slowly up the tree-lined street and stopped directly in front of the opposite house.

Muriel was intrigued by the magnetic sign on the driver's side door, proclaiming in bold, red lettering: *FLO, FLO, THE REAL ESTATE PRO*. Florence Hackett, Kennebec City's number one realtor, and star of countless TV commercials, stepped out of the car and began to wave madly, flashing a bright, white Pepsodent smile. She looked just like she did on TV.

She was dressed for success in a bright yellow power suit, and would be impossible to miss even if she weren't gesturing like a fool towards the wood-paneled station wagon pulling up behind her car. With her bleached-blonde hair, she looked like a walking lemon.

40 Franklin Street was a white, Cape Cod-style house, trimmed in blue, with a peaked roof and two dormer windows staring down on the neighborhood. The window boxes and carefully selected shrubs and flowers around the front porch gave it a cute and cozy appearance. Added in the eighties, the one-story addition on the side opposite the attached two-car garage distinguished it from the other Capes on the street.

The house was set farther back from the road than the other homes, and had huge front and side lawns. Muriel envied the privacy a big front lawn provided. The house sat on nearly an acre of land, with a field behind it; she envied that, too.

She still thought of it as the Wyman house. The original owners had been like second parents to her when she and Ray had moved in with their little Nancy all those years ago. When she was seventeen, Muriel had lost her mother to breast cancer, and she craved the help of an older woman in the matters of being a housewife and mother.

Ed and Lucy Wyman had long since moved to Florida and passed away, and the house had changed hands twice since then. It had been on the market for two months now, empty ever since Tom Webster's company had transferred him to California. He and his family had left in June, driving away in their SUV or SVU, or whatever the heck they called that thing. And while the car was full—jam-packed with luggage, children, and dogs—the house was left empty and bereft.

Muriel missed the Websters. They rarely closed the blinds, and she'd invested so many hours spying on them, she'd felt like part of the family. Now, here she was, peeking through the curtains and watching this new family spill out of their car and onto the lawn.

The man looked like a regular enough fellow —six feet tall or so, slightly pudgy, with the beginnings of a bald spot showing through his wavy brown hair. His khaki trousers were a bit saggy in the behind, but his polo shirt appeared freshly ironed and fit snugly over his belly.

The woman, presumably his wife, strode right up to Florence, not waiting for her husband to catch up.

Must not have any kids. Not with a figure like that.

Just then, one of the car doors popped open, and out bounced a pretty teenage girl in denim shorts and a yellow tank top. Her chestnut ponytail gleamed in the sun as she ran to catch up with her mother, and Florence ushered the two of them into the house. Instead of joining them, the man remained on the lawn, staring at the house and its surroundings. He seemed to mutter to himself as he strolled around the property, apparently inspecting the eaves. Then he walked back to the curb, turned, and framed the house with his hands as he scanned the front, looking up at the roof.

He made his way around the house, disappearing for a moment until he emerged from the other side. As he approached the front, he stopped and turned his attention to the struggle next door.

Without hesitation, the man strode briskly across the grass over to the Nadeaus' home.

Aha! Muriel thought. *That's going to be the deal-breaker. Why would anyone want to buy a house next door to that zoo?*

Chapter 2

Don Cassidy could see that the skinny guy on the porch was having some trouble maneuvering a carton, and his wife looked altogether too pregnant to be lifting any boxes, especially in this heat. Their two screaming boys weren't helping matters. One was tugging on his mother's skirt, and the other was yelling nonsense and chasing a squirrel with a stick.

"I got the other end," said Don, taking the porch steps two-at-a-time and reaching for the carton.

The man looked up. "Oh! Thanks!"

The woman seated on the front steps ran her fingers through her hair, pushing it back off her face, damp with perspiration. She smiled at him without saying a word, absent-mindedly rubbing her huge tummy with the other hand. The boys had taken off to chase the terrified squirrel around the side of the house.

The pair lifted the box between them easily, and carried it inside the house.

"Mister, you're a godsend. The nursery is just at the top of the staircase."

Don's heart pounded away as he trudged up the stairs, carrying the bottom end of the box. Thankfully, the door to the small, brightly painted room was, indeed, right at the top of the stairs. After gently putting down his end of the box, he reached into his pants pocket and pulled out a handkerchief.

"I'm Don Cassidy," he said, mopping his brow. "My wife and I are looking at the house next door."

The two men shook hands. "Andy Nadeau. Great to meet you."

A few minutes later, they were banging through the screen door and back onto the porch.

"Esme, this is Don," said Andy. "He and his family are looking at the Websters' house. They're moving up from Florida."

"Usually, people move the other way," she said, taking his offered hand. "It gets pretty cold here in the winter." She'd moved from the stairs to an Adirondack chair on the porch, and was fanning herself with a newspaper flyer. Wind chimes hanging from the porch roof made a half-hearted tinkle in the warm breeze.

"Yeah, but we thought it would be nice to have four seasons for a change. Besides, my wife—Maggie—she's originally from Portland, so we've been looking to get up here for a while. I've never had a real white Christmas, you know?"

"Oh, you'll get plenty of white with your Christmas around here! Just remember…sometimes it's white in April, too!" Esmerelda laughed. "Would you like a glass of ice water or a soda or something?"

Just then, one of the boys came screaming around the corner of the house, with the other only a few steps behind.

"Mommy! Mommy! Ricky slugged me!"

"Did not! Stop lyin', Matty!"

The tussling twosome clambered up to the porch, jostling Don as they pushed past him. Matty hid behind his mother's chair, using her as a shield.

"You started it!" said Ricky.

As one, their parents interrupted, "STOP IT!"

Miraculously, both boys clammed up, Matty glaring at Ricky from behind the security of his mother.

Don observed the scene with a wry smile. Friends and relatives had pestered him and Maggie for years about having another child, but they were happy with just the one. He was especially annoyed by the suggestions that he "needed" to have a son. He loved being Daddy to a girl, and enjoyed teaching Jenny how to sink a basketball just as much as he'd enjoyed playing dolls with her when she was little. As he watched the boys bicker and push their parents' patience to the brink, he silently affirmed the "only child" decision.

"Well, I guess I'd better get back over there," he said, heading for the stairs. "Nice meeting you folks."

"Hope we'll be neighbors!" yelled Andy. "I owe you!"

Don made his way back toward his wife, now standing on the front walkway having an animated conversation with the realtor.

"Mr. Anderson over there," she said, pointing toward the white Colonial to the left side of the house, "is a professor at the University. He lost his wife about a year ago...awfully sad...and now it's just him and his 16-year-old son...oh, and an older boy in college. Across from them is a lovely elderly lady named Eileen Ferris, who lives alone with her darling little dog. And then there's the young family on the other side, the Nadeaus, they have the only young children on this end of the street—twin boys—and she's expecting a baby soon. Across the way from them are the Cables, career couple, no kids... and two very nice middle-aged bachelors, Tommy and Mark, live in that cute little place next to them," she continued, pointing at a white cape with forest green shutters and an actual white picket fence a few houses down.

"What about over there, right across the street from us?" asked Maggie.

Just then, Don noticed his daughter pretending to poke around the flower bed at the side of the garage, and sneaking glances up toward the second story of the house next door.

"See something interesting?" he said, as he made his way toward her.

Blushing, she looked down at a yellow daylily she seemed to find particularly intriguing. "No. I mean, there was somebody looking out the window up there, but now he's gone."

"He?" Don grinned, mischievously. "Would that have happened to be a cute, teenage 'he'?"

She laughed. "Daddy! Cut it out!"

Don looked up at the window in question, and could just about see a pale face framed by an unruly mop of hair, illuminated by the blue glow of a computer monitor. At that exact moment, the boy sneaked a glance back out the window, and their eyes met. Don waved, but the face quickly withdrew into the shadows of the room.

"Hmmm…this neighborhood gets more fascinating by the minute," said Don.

"Daddy! Stop it!" Jenny ran back to the front of the house to her mother's side.

"Hey Don," said Flo. "Want to look around inside the house?"

"Can I start with the garage?"

"Of course!" Flo nodded, and then ducked back into the house. Seconds later, one of the two garage doors rumbled up. Don entered, armed with pen and paper, ready to take notes.

His wife joined him. "It's perfect, honey…and it's easily within our price range."

Don studied the garage rafters and ceiling.

Maggie sighed. "Hon, we've looked at a lot of houses, and this one is far and away the best."

"Maybe…maybe…" he replied softly, approaching the center support beam and hitting it with the flat of his hand. It made a metallic ringing sound.

Flo took a few steps toward Don. "It's priced to sell, and it's in move-in condition. Does the outside suit your needs?" she said, winking at Maggie.

Don nodded. "We do have room to build a second floor here in the garage."

He turned to Maggie and, almost as an afterthought, asked "How's the inside? Did you guys like it?"

His wife smiled, her eyes twinkling. "I think it's perfect, and I love the neighborhood! Let's make an offer."

Chapter 3

Behind the curtain, Muriel was struggling to catch this last bit when a voice right in her ear startled her out of stealth mode.

"What's going on? Somebody looking at the Websters' place?"

Ray, who liked to catch her being a "Nosy Nora," as he put it, had snuck back into the room and was standing right behind her.

"Ah!" Muriel squeaked, "Don't sneak up on me like that! You about gave me a heart attack."

She scowled at her husband, who was dressed for the season in a pair of bright patchwork Bermuda shorts. He swept back his full mop of gray hair, and Muriel supposed a trip to the barber shop was in order. She glanced in the mirror over the bureau. She and Ray still had their original bedroom set—they were smart enough to buy quality—and caught sight of her own short, Clairol-red, permed hair. She thought it unfair that her husband had more hair than she did at this stage of the game.

"Well, if you weren't so busy snooping, you might have noticed me walk into the room," he said. "You seen my gray cap?"

"It's right there hanging up where it's supposed to be, you old goober," Muriel said, feigning annoyance.

"Huh. That's funny. I could've sworn I left it on the newel post downstairs."

"You did. I hung it up, as usual."

"Why'd you do that? I was just gonna put it on again the next time I went out. Now I had to come all the way up here to get it." Muriel had already turned back to her spying post at the window. "So what's up?"

"Looks like Flo the Real Estate Pro finally has a family on the hook. The woman's sold, that's for sure. I don't know about her husband, though. He hasn't even set foot in the place. Just stood there on the lawn for a while, and looked around the whole time she was in the house."

"Probably thinking about how much of a job it's going to be to mow that lawn. Any kids?"

"Just a teenaged girl. Spitting image of her mother."

Ray leaned in to look out the window over his wife's shoulder. Flo and the woman were engaged in a lively conversation which Muriel was straining to hear. The woman appeared to be delighted with what she'd seen, and Flo was going in for the kill. Meanwhile, the girl wandered from her mother's side over to the man—her father, Muriel hoped—although one could never be sure nowadays. As she approached, he began talking to her and pointing to various areas of the lawn and house, hardly pausing long enough to take a breath.

"That Flo looks just like she does on TV," said Ray, stepping back and reaching for the cap hanging on an antique coat tree by the door. "I'm going down to Cottle's to get one of their chocolate donuts. I've been thinking about it ever since I got up. You want anything?"

Momentarily distracted, Muriel said, "Ooh. Get me a cinnamon roll. No, wait, get me a bear claw. And one of those frozen mocha latte things with the whipped cream." Then, turning sideways to look in the mirror again, she patted her midriff and sighed. "No, on second thought, I guess I'll just have a blueberry muffin."

"'Kay. I'll be right back," he promised, chuckling as he headed down the hall toward the stairs.

"Make sure you get the low-fat kind!" Muriel shouted. "And maybe you could wander over there and strike up a conversation with them, find out..." She trailed off as she pushed the curtain aside slightly. The house across the street was quiet again.

Chapter 4

As usual in Maine, summer disappeared in the wink of an eye. Muriel would always feel a pang of sadness as September came along with its thievery, stealing the green from the leaves and the blooms from the gardens. Winter would not be far behind, and winters in Maine could be brutal. She and Ray had never had the money to become snowbirds, like so many of their friends, so they toughed it out. No wonder it was her least favorite season.

By early October, the trees would be a riot of fall color, with pumpkins; cornstalks; and purple, orange, and yellow mums and asters decorating the doorsteps and front porches of Kennebec City.

Franklin Street hadn't really participated in Trick-or-Treating for years now, as there were only a few families with young children. Back in the day, it was *the* go-to neighborhood with all the best candy. Parents would ferry their children from across town just to canvas the neighborhood. Muriel and Ray used to enjoy decorating the outside of their house and seeing all the children in their costumes, but since their own brood had left home, they kept the house dark on October 31st.

This year, 40 Franklin Street was already decked out with cardboard ghosts and jack-o-lanterns, and there were black cats and witches adorning the front door and picture window, even though the family hadn't officially moved in yet. As if in sync, the Nadeaus had already gotten into the act and stuffed some old clothing with leaves, propping the "scarecrow," complete with a worn Red Sox cap on his pumpkin head, on their front porch.

Muriel sat in her recliner by the window early on this Friday morning, stitching an old cloth diaper to a toddler sleeper she had dyed black. She shaped it into a fine pair of bat wings for her great-granddaughter's Trick-or-Treat costume. Hard to believe little Emma was almost three already and talking up a storm.

The loud shriek of a drill pierced the morning and was soon followed by the sounds of hammers pounding, saws whining, and voices shouting commands. Muriel squinted and scowled, setting her mouth in a grim line as she put her project down and took off her reading glasses; she had to use them for crafts, now, too. Her throat constricted as her eyes began to burn and well up with tears.

From his easy chair, Ray lowered his newspaper and looked over at his wife, opening his mouth as if to speak, but thinking better of it. He went back to his paper briefly, then looked up at her again.

"What are you upset about?" he asked, finally.

"Who said I was upset? I'm not upset."

"Yes you are."

"And just how do you know that?" she said, nonchalantly putting her hand to her cheek, hoping he wouldn't notice the wetness.

"Muriel, please. After fifty-five years of marriage, I think I know."

"Fifty-six," she said.

"Fifty-six? Really?"

Muriel said nothing, and stared out the window. Dust mites danced in the streaming golden rays of light. Elmo the tabby (named by little Emma) was lolling on the carpet in the sunshine, spread out to full-length in all his orange-and-white glory, occasionally reaching out a paw to bat at a speck of dust.

"So, what is it?" Ray wasn't giving up.

Muriel picked up her project and heaved a sigh. "I don't know why anyone would buy a perfectly good house and then ruin it."

"You mean the new neighbors?"

Muriel, frustrated, glared at her husband. "Yes, I mean the new neighbors. What do you think I mean? Just look at that mess. They're turning the Wymans' garage into a...monstrosity!"

Ray looked concerned. "Muriel," he said softly, "The Wymans have been gone a long time. The house belongs to these new people now. It's their garage. They can do whatever they want with it."

Now the tears began to fall in earnest. "They should have left it the way it was. It was *fine* the way it was. Why does everybody have to go change everything?"

Ray got up and walked over to her. He perched on the arm of the blue corduroy recliner and stroked her hair. "What's wrong, sugar plum? Why is this getting to you so much? You didn't react like this when the Conways put on the addition a few years ago."

She waved a dismissive hand. "That was over thirty years ago! I was so busy with the children and teaching and you...I hardly noticed."

"Well, I don't see why this is bothering you so much now."

She pushed his arm away. "Oh, never mind," she said. "Just never mind."

Ray returned to his newspaper in silent frustration.

Muriel turned her attention to the scene across the street, where workers were busy creating a new second story over the old garage. The Woodie station wagon pulled up to the curb and Don Cassidy—she'd learned his name from her sources—stepped out onto the sidewalk. He shielded his eyes from the morning sun as he stood and observed the work, exchanging a few words with workers. Muriel reckoned he was looking pretty satisfied, and she couldn't help wondering why the Dickens they needed that room over the garage. What the heck would go in there?

Chapter 5

Scott Anderson was munching on a chocolate-frosted Pop Tart and watching the activity next door through his bedroom window. A senior at Kennebec City Regional High School, he didn't have to be in class until 9:30 on Fridays. He'd been up early anyway, working on a new video game, designing games was his favorite hobby and he hoped to get paid for it someday, when a station wagon caught his eye. He'd been practically counting the days until the new neighbors moved in, ever since he saw the "For Sale" sign come down. He'd had the window open on the sweltering day the family first looked at the house, so he'd heard everything. Their gorgeous daughter was the icing on the cake; he'd crossed his fingers and said a silent prayer that her family would buy the house.

Scott wasn't exactly a ladies' man. He'd never had a girlfriend, unless you counted Sarah Starzynski in the fourth grade. Still, it was nice to dream, although he knew, deep down, a girl like his new neighbor would never go for a guy like him. Pretty girls liked tall guys, and he was only five-foot-nine. Pretty girls liked rugged jock-guys, and no one would ever mistake him for an athlete with his Jell-O physique. Pretty girls liked popular guys, and he would never be that. Then there was the fine, lank brown hair that always seemed to be in his eyes. Pretty girls didn't usually go for that, either.

His buddy Ethan told him the family's name was Cassidy. Ethan's mom was "Flo, Flo, the Real Estate Pro," so he had inside knowledge.

Scott was staring out the window, hoping to see the young beauty come bounding out of the car, when there came a knock at the door. His father opened it without waiting for permission to enter.

He made a big show of stepping over his son's dirty laundry and looking around the room, shaking his head. Scott wondered if he was going to ride him about the empty soda cans, Doritos bags, candy wrappers, or the unmade bed.

Instead, his father let out an angry grunt. "What are you doing? Don't you have to be at school?"

"It's Friday, Dad. I've got late arrival, remember?" Scott replied, swiveling around in his chair.

At first glance, his father looked pretty much the same as always: a tall, good-looking guy in good shape, blond hair graying a bit at the temples. As he came closer, though, the skin around his red-rimmed eyes seemed puffy, and he had apparently developed more wrinkles overnight. Since the loss of Scott's mom to ovarian cancer a year earlier, his dad was a mess.

It was hard on all of them. His parents had been madly in love, and they'd been planning a twenty-fifth anniversary trip to Hawaii when she got sick. As families went these days, he had been lucky to be part of a happy one. His mom was the best.

Now, Scott not only had to deal with the loss of his mom, but in a lot of ways, the loss of his dad, too. It seemed like his father was unable to do anything but plod through each day. That, and drink too much. He sometimes wondered if his dad was just trying to hold it together until graduation day in June, and worried about what would happen once he was at college.

"Oh, yeah. Well, I've got a department meeting at five today, so I'll be home late. Order a pizza or something." He pulled his billfold out of his pocket and handed Scott a twenty-dollar bill.

Scott stuffed it in his pocket. "Okay. But come home after the meeting, okay?" He briefly considered telling his father his rumpled shirt wasn't tucked in all the way, then decided against it.

His dad squinted and his face flushed. "You're not the parent here, you got that?" he said. "If I decide to go out after the meeting, you don't have a say in it."

"Dad, I just..." Scott looked away. "Okay. I got it. Whatever."

A minute later the front door slammed. Looking out the window, Scott saw his father come around the house and head for his car. Mr. Cassidy was standing in his driveway, talking to one of the construction guys, and Scott hoped his dad wasn't going to take the opportunity to complain about the racket. He'd probably have a pounding headache this morning even without the construction sounds. *Please, God, don't let him say anything.*

Mr. Cassidy looked up at Scott's dad with a smile and waved, but the man was busy fumbling in his pocket for his keys. He finally pulled them out, got into his silver Corolla, and backed down the driveway.

"Way to acknowledge the new neighbor, Dad," Scott mumbled. At least he hadn't gotten too close. The last thing he needed was the neighbors figuring out his father was a borderline drunk.

His was distracted by movement from across the way. Mrs. Ellis was standing on the sidewalk, waving at his dad from up the street. Scott remembered her coming to Trick-or-Treat at his house a few years ago with her kid. She'd gained some weight since then. She was wearing a large gray sweater over a pair of black leggings, like she thought that would disguise her figure. Zack was at her side, gaping at the construction work going on next door.

His father did not wave back. He probably didn't even see her. Her smile faded and her shoulders sagged as his dad drove off.

"Awkward," Scott said out loud, and scratched his head. *Oh geez. I wonder if she likes him.*

Chapter 6

"Well, now I feel like a moron," Angie Ellis muttered to herself, absentmindedly gathering her long, brown curls into a ponytail, then letting it fall. She'd been thinking about Sam Anderson on and off for a while now, even though she'd never had the guts to talk to him. She'd read the obituary in the paper and felt so bad for him. Yet something about him intrigued her, and he sure was handsome. She recalled taking Zack to their house one Halloween when Sam had been outside with his wife and sons, just young teens then, and they were terrifying the Trick-or-Treaters with the old fake scarecrow trick. He'd seemed like a good, fun-loving man back then—the kind of guy she'd always hoped to meet. Now his wife had been gone over a year, and she wondered if he could ever be attracted to a wallflower like her. She felt like a school girl with a silly crush, and she chastised herself for feeling so ridiculous: a thirty-four-year-old dental hygienist with a teenaged son.

She was lonely, that was true. The last guy she'd dated, the manager of the Kennebec City Rite Aid, turned out to be a real jerk. Last Valentine's Day, he'd given her a Planet Fitness membership and told her she didn't need chocolate. Later that night he'd told her the card she'd given him was "too romantic," and after he left her house, she never heard from him again. Now she bought her pharmacy items at the CVS across town.

She didn't have time for men, anyway. Taking care of Zack was a full-time job as it was, additionally complicated by the fact she needed to round up more people for their Autism Walk team. The walk was coming up in two weeks and they still needed a few more participants.

"Come on Zack," she said. "We gotta get going or you're gonna be late for school and Mom's gonna be late for work, again."

She tugged on her son's arm to try to get him to keep moving along, but he was too fascinated by the construction activity to move. Angie knew she was once again gonna have some explaining to do when she eventually arrived at work. She was running out of excuses to give to Dr. Brescia.

Chapter 7

The forgotten Halloween costume sat on Muriel's lap. Ray was asleep in his easy chair, the crumpled morning paper at his feet and Elmo curled up on his knee.

The Black Forest German cuckoo clock the kids had given her for Mother's Day many years ago chimed the hour, and the little band came out and played their merry tune. Startled, Muriel glanced up at it, then her eyes wandered to the photos of the children and grand-children looking down at her from the mantel, and her lips turned up in a close-mouthed, bittersweet smile.

It had never been this quiet when the kids were little. Back then, there was always something going on. Toys and crafts littered the house, and the children were constantly laughing, arguing, or playing some sort of noisy game. Then they began school, and there was just enough time to do the housework and prepare dinner before they'd be home again. There was homework to be done (which she invariably helped with), music practice, school events, dance lessons, sports…she and Ray were busy all the time. When the kids were teenagers, their house had been the popular hangout: backyard parties, movie nights and—more often than not—over-night guests on the weekends.

Then, one-by-one, they'd grown up. In the blink of an eye, they had all gone off to college, never returning to live at home. Nancy, their eldest, was a nurse in Allentown. After attending nursing school at U Penn, she settled there and then met her husband, Levi, a welder. They'd never had any children.

Muriel and Ray's second child, Will, was a vice president at New England Insurance, and lived in Hartford with his wife. Their two kids had both moved out west after college. The eldest, Samantha, was a librarian in Roswell. She'd once sent Muriel a Christmas card with a picture of an alien on it, and said she had been abducted by the Land of Enchantment and was never moving back to the cold again. Her brother Jacob was a chef at a fancy restaurant in California, where Muriel had hoped to dine with Ray someday. When he was little, she'd taught Jacob how to bake right here in this house.

Paula was Muriel and Ray's youngest. She and her husband lived in town and owned the hardware store on Main Street, which kept them very busy. She and Ed had one daughter, Karen, who had given Muriel and Ray their first great-grandchild, Emma.

It had been a good life, and Muriel took comfort in the fact they had been good parents. The proof was in the pudding. She'd gotten into the trenches with the right man when she'd married Ray all those years ago. But it had all gone by too fast. Now the house was like a mausoleum; nothing ever moved. As she looked around, she noticed everything was coated with a very fine layer of dust, and there was a cobweb up in the corner above the television set. She would never have allowed that to happen even a year ago, but she just didn't have the heart for housekeeping any more.

The children—and now the grandchildren—had their own lives, and even the ones who lived close by didn't visit as much as she would have liked. At that moment, she would take back every complaint she'd ever had about picking up after the kids, if she could go back in time for one more day of chaos.

Yes, they'd made this life...but how much longer would they have together? She knew she should talk to Ray, but she just couldn't yet. It just wasn't something he could fix. A tear fell from her eye and slid down the wrinkles on her cheek. Where had the years gone?

Just then, the sound of a power drill pierced the air and Muriel was startled out of her reverie. *For crying out loud,* she thought. *Their lunch break must be over. There's never going to be any peace and quiet around here ever again, now those people have bought that house!*

Chapter 8

Two weeks later, Angie was walking Zack home from his after-school program, when he stopped once again, transfixed by a burly bunch of movers shuffling back and forth between a Mayflower moving van and the house at number 40. Mr. Michaud, who had stopped by his mailbox, was also caught up in the activity for a moment. They watched as the men went about their work, carrying furniture, boxes, and crates into the house. The new woman of the house came out and began speaking with one of the movers.

"I wonder what he wanted that new room over the garage for," said Mr. Michaud.

Angie looked at him, surprised that he had spoken to her. "I don't know. It's as much a mystery to me as it is to you."

Ray took a good look at her, "You live up the street, don't you? I've seen you and your boy walking past, but I don't think we've properly met. I'm Ray Michaud." He stuck out his hand, and Angie obliged.

"Yes, we live next to the Nadeaus. We've lived there for nine years. I'm Angie Ellis, and this is Zack. He doesn't shake hands."

Ray looked sheepish. "Nice to meet you two, finally. Nine years, huh?" He shook his head in disbelief.

Angie nodded. "Well, things aren't like they used to be, I guess.

Muriel and I used to know everybody in the neighborhood, but now everybody's so busy..." Ray shrugged. "I guess I'd better get back inside. Don't want the new neighbors to think we're snoopy!" he grinned.

"Snoopy! Ha! I love Snoopy!" Zack said, enthusiastically.

"Okay, Zack, let's get a move on. See you later, Mr. Michaud." Angie caught a glimpse of the curtain moving right behind Ray. She watched him stride youthfully up the driveway.

And don't worry Mr. Michaud...everybody knows it's not you *who's the snoop in the neighborhood.*

She put her arm around her son and cajoled him up the street.

Standing in her customary spot at the picture window, Muriel barely noticed her husband as he walked in. She'd been watching the movers when a maroon Toyota drove by the house. She raised a hand to wave.

"Who's that?" asked Ray. "Do you know that...?"

The question went in one ear and out the other as Muriel whirled around. She'd been stewing over something and had to get it off her chest. "I can't imagine how the man of the house could leave his wife and daughter to do all the cleaning and unpacking. It just isn't right. He was there for one day during the construction and then just disappeared." She turned back toward the window and watched the woman signing some papers on a clipboard.

"He probably decided to stay behind and oversee the movers," said Ray, as he looked over his wife's shoulder in time to see the van back out of the driveway.

"Poor planning, if you ask me..." Muriel trailed off as she saw the Mayflower van drive off and, almost in sync, a familiar orange-and-white truck come rumbling up the street.

"What the Dickens? He brought MORE stuff? Why didn't he let the movers take care of everything?"

"I don't know, darling. Maybe he wanted to take special care of whatever's in there."

"What could possibly be that important? Hmm...maybe he's an antiques dealer. Let's take a gander and see what we can see."

"Oh, come on," said Ray. "Enough snooping for one day. Come to the kitchen and let me skunk you at Rummy."

Muriel reluctantly let the curtain fall back into place and followed her husband into the kitchen. "What were you talking to that woman from up the street about?

Chapter 9

Don very nearly ran into the mailbox while attempting to back the U-Haul into the driveway. "Holy Moly," he said, as he struggled with the steering wheel, a sweat breaking on his brow. "So much for power steering." Finally, he got it straightened out just as Maggie and Jenny came bounding out of the house. The ladies had already been there for several days, painting and cleaning. They'd been staying with Maggie's folks in Portland until the furniture arrived.

When Don finally backed the truck up to the garage doors, he shut off the engine and stepped out onto the driveway, tired and frazzled.

His wife and daughter ran up to him for a group hug. Jenny bounced on her heels and said, "Welcome home, Daddy!"

"Looks like Rudolph is now the golden-nosed reindeer," said Maggie, pointing at his festive tee-shirt. "Did you have mustard for lunch?"

"Yeah. The 'Planet Christmas' group guys in P.A. brought me to Yocco's to get one of their famous hot dogs. I had a couple, actually," he grinned. "Now I know why they're world-famous."

"And I see you picked up a friend along the way," said Maggie, pointing to the snowman in the passenger seat.

Don laughed. "Oh yeah…It's a rare Union Snow Lady. I got it from Rich Motz in Lititz for a song."

"Come in and catch your breath, sweetheart," Maggie said, tugging on her husband's sleeve.

Don really wanted to start organizing his stuff in the new storage room over the garage. "Nah. If it's all the same to you, I'd rather get this unloaded first."

"Oh, come on. It can wait, and you shouldn't do it all by yourself anyway."

"Well, you guys can always help," he said, smiling mischievously.

"We have to get the beds made, and I wanted to unpack some of the kitchen stuff. The truck's not due back until tomorrow afternoon," Maggie said. "You can take the evening off and help us, and then we'll help you in the morning."

"I just really want to get it done tonight. Then tomorrow I can start the setup." Don walked into the garage.

He climbed up the double-wide stairway and unlocked a huge door. "I may have to leave the sleigh in the garage for the time being," he yelled, making his way back down the stairs. "You don't mind parking in the driveway for a few days, do you, hon?"

"Oh, you're so stubborn! Please!" Maggie threw her arms up and slammed them down at her sides. "I absolutely don't want you doing it by yourself. We'll help you tomorrow!"

Don was frustrated. His wife was always so worried about him that she barely let him breathe. He really wanted to do this tonight; it would be fun. So, he ignored her and carried on.

"I want to make sure everything survived the trip alright," he said, more to himself than Maggie—she probably couldn't even hear him.

Jammed inside was the largest collection of outdoor Christmas decorations that had ever made its way to Franklin Street. Plastic and plywood snowmen, elves, angels, Christmas carolers, and other assorted holiday characters threatened to spill out the door. Over a dozen different Santa Claus figures were in there somewhere, along with Mrs. Claus and all the reindeer. Then, there was the life-size Nativity scene that Don had carved himself in his Florida workshop. It featured not only the Holy Family, but kings, shepherds, a camel, a donkey, two sheep, and a cow. The three-walled stable was hinged, and had been neatly folded and packed away safely. There were more than fifty lighted wire-frame decorations, and a half-dozen cases of giant inflatables. Box after box of lights (all neatly labeled), cartons of garland, hydraulic poles, and assorted tools shared space with two miles of extension cord neatly wrapped on reels. The star of the show, a brightly-painted, larger-than-life sleigh that would eventually be adorned with more lights than most Christmas trees, was carefully packed in crate padding at the back of the truck.

Maggie and Jenny came over. Exasperated, he said, "I'm fine. Let me do this, okay?"

Maggie turned on her heel and marched back into the house, muttering under her breath.

Jenny stood by, clasping her hands behind her back. "I guess I could help, if you want, Daddy," she said, sounding like she'd rather have a tooth pulled. Had she been the least bit enthusiastic, he would have gladly accepted her offer.

"Eh, I can handle it, sweetie. Why don't you go and help your mother? She doesn't seem to be in a very good mood," he said with a wink and a smile.

She smiled back, and Don thought it was the prettiest sight he'd seen all day.

"Okay, but if you change your mind or get tired or anything, just give a little whistle!" she said, a reference to a childhood game of theirs based on the Pinocchio movie. She went back into the house.

Don began unloading each decoration and box into the garage and up the stairs, neatly sorting and stacking everything in the newly-constructed storage space. It wasn't very long before he began to sweat, but, determined to get the job done, he worked through his exhaustion. He barely noticed when the street lights came on as full dark descended on Franklin Street.

Chapter 10

Walking up the sidewalk, Scott first noticed that his Dad's car wasn't in the driveway. Then he saw the U-Haul and Mr. Cassidy. He couldn't quite see what was being unloaded without making himself obvious, and he wasn't in the mood for confrontation. Instead, he went in the house, grabbed a bag of Doritos and a can of Mountain Dew, and went up to his room. Determined to get an early start on his mountain of homework, he buried himself in analyzing *The Odyssey*.

A couple of hours later, he heard a loud bang from next door. He looked out the window to see Mr. Cassidy sitting on the van's ramp with his hand clenched to his chest. Scott ran out of the room like lightning.

"Mr. Cassidy! Mr. Cassidy! Are you okay?" he yelled, running across the lawn.

Don looked up, his face red and sweat on his brow. Was this guy having a heart attack, or what?

"Oh, no worries. I'm okay. I'm okay," Don said, panting between words and rubbing his chest.

"You don't *look* okay. Did you fall or something? I was in up in my room and heard a loud noise."

"I just…oh, you know…I just…I just…lost my balance, I guess."

Maggie came running out of the house.

"Don! Don! What happened? What's going on?" She stopped short, looking at her husband, who was obviously in distress.

"Oh no. Do you have your pills? Where are your pills?"

"Okay, okay. I've got them, it's okay. I just had a dizzy spell." Don reached into his pants pocket and came out with a small, amber bottle.

"Let me do that," said his wife, grabbing the bottle. "I knew you shouldn't have tried doing all this tonight." She fumbled for a few seconds with the bottle cap, took out one of the small white tablets, and gave it to her husband. "Put that under your tongue and I'll go get you a drink." She looked up at Scott. "I'm sorry, I don't know your name?"

"I'm Scott. I live next door. I heard the bang," he said, standing awkwardly and gesturing with his hands as he spoke.

"Well, thank you, Scott. Do you mind staying here for a minute while I go get my husband some water?"

"No. I mean, I don't mind," said Scott, shaking his head. "No problem, Mrs. Cassidy." He shoved his hands in his pockets and pretended to look at something interesting on the ground. He didn't know what to say next, so he didn't say anything.

Maggie jogged into the house and returned shortly with a glass of water and her daughter quick on her heels.

"Daddy!" the girl said, running over and throwing her arms around him. "Daddy, you should have let me help you!" she said, tears welling in her eyes. Scott caught his breath—she was so beautiful up close.

Mrs. Cassidy watched as her husband took a long drink. "That's enough work for tonight, Mister. You're coming in the house with me."

Her husband didn't protest. He just sat forlornly, as his color slowly started to come back.

"Hey, Mr. Cassidy," said Scott, sensing an opportunity. "I can finish this up if you want. I'll unload the van for you. Just tell me where you want the stuff."

The girl looked up and seemed to notice him for the first time. "I can do it too, Daddy. I'll help...what's your name again?" she asked, gazing up with her just-too-baby-blue eyes.

Scott, who had been staring at her the whole time, looked down and said, "I'm Scott. I live over there. I heard a bang..." He could feel his cheeks flushing.

"I'm Jenny. Nice to meet you."

He smiled, but before he could say anything, her mom interrupted. "Okay, it's a done deal. Jenny and Scott will finish unloading the van, and you're gonna come in the house with me and lie down on the couch. If you don't start to feel better soon, we're going to the ER."

"Oh, we don't have to do that. I'll be okay."

"Alright!" said Jenny, clapping her hands together and smiling at the teenagers. "Let's git 'er done!"

"Just be careful, okay?" said Mr. Cassidy. "Just put it upstairs for now, and I'll deal with getting everything sorted tomorrow." He rose slowly, his wife grabbing his arm, and said, "Thank you, guys. Thanks a lot." The two adults went through the garage and into the house.

Scott, stared at the contents of the van, which wasn't even half empty.

"Lots of stuff, huh?" said Jenny. "Decorating is kind of my Dad's thing. It's gonna take us all night to get the rest of this stuff unloaded." She paused for a second. "I hope you've got some muscles under that hoodie."

Scott barked a laugh, then silently chastised himself for sounding like a nervous fool.

Chapter 11

"Ray! Raymond! Wake up! You have to see this! Wake up!"

Muriel's husband loved to sleep in on Saturday mornings, but she needed him to get up *now*. Instead, he turned away and pulled the comforter over his head. "For God's sake, Muriel, let an old man get some sleep!"

"Ray, it's seven o'clock. You can take a nap later. You have to see what's going on across the street." It was insanity, that's what it was.

Muriel rose early every day of the week. She was already dressed for Saturday in her L.L. Bean jeans, and a sweatshirt adorned with a kitten playing in a pile of brightly-colored autumn leaves. She'd been lacing up her sneakers when she looked out through the window and saw what was happening.

"What now?" he said, grabbing the covers as Muriel attempted to pull them off.

"That man's a lunatic. It's not even Halloween yet!"

"What? You're talking crazy. Let me see what's going on," Ray said, throwing his skinny, pajama-clad legs over the edge of the bed and angling toward the window. "Well, would you look at that!"

Don Cassidy was just coming out of his garage, carrying a five-foot tall plastic snowman. In the side yard by the garage there were already four other snowmen, each made of molded plastic and distinct from one another, with different accessories such as hats, scarves, pipes, and brooms. They stood in a semi-circle, forming a sort of snowman barbershop quartet.

"Guy's got a snowman convention going on over there!" Ray chuckled. "So that's what he needed all that storage space for."

Muriel turned back to Ray, her face hot. "You think this is funny? This isn't funny! That whole U-Haul must've been filled with this junk. He's planning to light up the whole darned yard!"

Ray got up and headed for the bathroom as his wife continued to build her case.

"We'll never sleep with lights shining in all night long. What about poor Eileen next door?"

"Since when do you give a hoot about Eileen Ferris? All you ever do is complain about her dog barking!"

"Those lights will make him bark all the more!"

Ray stared at her for a moment, shaking his head. Then he closed the bathroom door; he was never going to win this one.

Muriel went on, ignoring her husband. "And the traffic. Oh my Lord, I've seen those ridiculous Christmas displays on TV. They can't even control the traffic from all the people who drive out to see them. We've got to do something about this. Our neighborhood is going to become a circus."

"Relax, sugar plum," Ray yelled from the bathroom. "He hasn't lit up the neighborhood yet. Let's just wait and see just how much of this stuff he has."

"I'm not waiting. He had a whole truck full of it, and this is just the beginning. If he has to start putting it together before we've even gotten through Halloween, you can bet he's planning on putting up a lot more than a few snowmen. I'm calling Roger Girard."

Ray emerged from the bathroom, drying his hands on a towel.

"Oh, don't go bothering Roger about this on a Saturday morning. It's not like he can call a meeting of the Selectmen today. Come on, let's go down to that new IHOP on Kennedy Memorial Drive. I want to try those Elvis pancakes Freddie Fink told me about."

Muriel pursed her lips, thinking it over, and finally gave in. Ray always seemed to know how to distract her, and lately she just didn't have the energy to fight him. Besides, peanut butter and banana pancakes sounded pretty good; she had always loved Elvis.

Chapter 12

Over at 40 Franklin Street, Don Cassidy was just getting started. It was a great morning, and after a good night's sleep by his beautiful wife's side, he was ready for a full day of work on the thing he loved the most. Well, besides his wife and daughter, that is.

Christmas had always been Don's favorite time of year. Since he was a little boy, it had been a time filled with happiness and excitement; somehow a magical glow settled over everything and everyone. That feeling had never left him, as it had so many others. His father, a hard-working man who rarely had time for fun, would always come alive during the Christmas season, making sure the family established yearly traditions, like going out to chop down a fresh tree, arranging for a hayride at a local stable, and, of course, decorating their home inside and out. Don fondly recalled the evenings when his parents would bundle him and his sisters into their station wagon and tour the streets of Punta Gorda, searching for the brightest displays. Although there was rarely any snow in Florida, the people who decorated their houses really brought that Christmas feeling to town. Don's favorites were the animated figures, which had become more popular after he'd seen the first moving Santa Claus in the window of Day's Jewelry Store when he was just six years old.

He'd helped his father string lights around the windows, doors, and shrubbery; together, they'd selected a plastic, light-up Santa to place on the front steps while his mother and sisters decorated the inside of the house to the hilt. Don vividly recalled the front door having a molded Santa standing by a chimney, his sack filled to the brim with toys. This decoration had a flat back so it could be displayed on a wall or door, and had lasted only a couple of years before a hole appeared right in the middle of Santa's beard. Don had searched for years to try to find one like it, to no avail.

His childhood fascination with Christmas lights and decorations had only grown stronger through the years. He'd started saving for a home of his own as soon as he got his first job at the age of fifteen. By the time he'd married Maggie, a girl who loved the season almost as much as he did, they were able to move right into a house. He shared his ideas about building a massive display with his Dad, who'd responded enthusiastically. His Dad was always first on the scene to help with the setup. They worked together like this every year until his death at sixty-one, felled by his first and only massive coronary. Ironically, he'd passed away in the month of December, and Don had continued his display each year in his honor. He'd added a few things each year until he'd had the largest display in Punta Gorda.

The Cassidy's former home had been listed on an online map of "The Brightest Christmas Displays in Florida," and had even won a contest one year on a networking website for decorating enthusiasts. Over the years, he'd befriended countless decorators all over the world through such sites; he found the community full of the nicest, funniest, and most generous people he'd ever met. He'd had a blast meeting a few of them for lunch yesterday.

Don had taken early retirement from his job with the local power company back in Florida after surviving his own heart attack six months earlier at the age of 49—his first. Now, he was planning on taking his Christmas decorating passion to a new level. Moving up here to Maine was just what the doctor ordered. For one thing, he'd finally see his display enhanced by real snow. He thought that might be exciting for Jenny, too. Maybe it would even inspire her to get back into decorating with him, like when she was in elementary school. One of his dearest wishes was that he could pass his passion on to her, just as his father had done with him.

Don was just coming out of the garage with a skein of lights when he noticed a boy of about thirteen standing on the sidewalk. He was wearing a green, down-filled jacket and a red knit stocking cap, even though the morning was fairly warm for the season. His blonde hair stuck out of the edges of the cap like straw.

"Hey there!" Don hollered.

He put down the lights and walked over to where the boy stood, unabashed, staring at him. As he got closer, he could see the open look of dumbfounded joy on the boy's face, not typical of a young man that age.

"Hi! I'm Mr. Cassidy. Who are you?"

The boy took a step back and looked down at his feet. He shook his head from side-to-side, finally speaking without looking up. "My-name-is-Zack-nice-to-meet-you," said the boy, as if he'd rehearsed this line many times. Then, in a softer voice, "I like your snowmen."

"Well, hello, Zack! Nice to meet you!" said Don, extending his hand in greeting. Zack raised his head, but didn't return the gesture. He looked past Don at the group of plastic figures.

"I like your snowmen. Can I…can…can I come…can I come see them?"

Don turned and looked at the group of snowmen. He had yet to lay the complicated system of extension cords and power boxes on his lawn, so it would still be safe to bring the boy over for a closer look. "Sure," he said, gesturing toward the lawn. "Come on over!"

Zack shuffled onto the grass and cautiously made his way toward the snowmen. He was within a few feet of them when he broke into joyous laughter. "Frosty!" he shouted, and began to sing, loudly and happily, waving his hands around. "Frosty the snowman, was jolly happy soul…"

Don stood back, hands in his pockets, and smiled. This was the kind of moment he lived for. He let the boy continue his song, although he apparently didn't know all the words and kept repeating the same few lines over, and over again. Across the street, he noticed the older couple coming out and getting into their car. The man appeared not to notice the commotion, but the woman gave him a stern look that gave Don a tickle of unease. *Well, nice to meet you, too,* he thought.

Inside the garage, the door that led into the kitchen opened, and out stepped Maggie in gray Saturday sweats, and thermos in hand. She looked at Don in amused confusion as she walked over and handed him the beverage. "Well, somebody's happy this morning. Who's this?"

"Honey, this is Zack. He came from out of the blue to enjoy the snowmen this morning. I think this is a good sign."

Zack looked at Maggie and abruptly stopped singing. "I'm sorry. Sorry, sorry, sorry," he said, then turned and pointed. "Look at the snowmen!"

"I know," said Maggie. Then, looking at Don, she added, "Did you decide to do things in a different order this year? Don't the lights come first? And I thought these guys went on the porch?"

"Yeah, usually, but Jenny and that kid…what's his name…Scott… they stored things out of order up there last night, so I had to take these guys out to get to the light bins."

"I'm glad you like them. Did you know that they all have names?"

Zack grasped the red scarf around his neck and fidgeted with the fringe, smiling the whole time.

Maggie pointed to the snowmen one at a time. "That one is Frosty, of course. But this one over here is Alex Delaware, that one is Kay Scarpetta, the one in the green scarf is Harry Bosch, and this one with the red vest is my favorite, Joe Ledger."

Zack kept smiling. "I like them." Then, as though a switch had flipped, he glanced down at the box of lights on the ground a few feet away.

"Christmas lights!" he shouted. Before anyone could stop him, he took two strides and reached into the box, grabbing up a string of multi-colored lights. He looked at them for a second and then began waving them around.

"These are wrong! These are wrong!" he yelled. "Blue, green, orange, red, white, yellow! Blue, green, orange, red, white, yellow!"

"Whoa! Hold on there, buddy!" said Don, reaching out to the boy. Zack pulled away and started to scream.

Just then, a woman came racing across the lawn. "Zack! There you are!" she shouted. "I've been looking all over for you!"

Zack continued to whirl like a dervish, the string of lights carving a dangerous path through the air. "Blue, green, orange, red, white, yellow! Blue, green, orange, red, white, yellow! Blue, green, orange, red, white, yellow!"

"I'm so sorry," she said. "One minute he was with me, and while I was grabbing the paper…" She threw up her hands in frustration. Then, turning to the boy, she said in a calm voice, "Zack, honey. Count to ten. Come on now, count to ten."

Hearing her voice, he stopped suddenly. He looked at her, tears in his eyes.

"Come on, Zack, let's count. One…"

The boy continued to stare at her, breathing heavily. The lights were hanging limp in his hands.

"One…" repeated the woman.

Zack took a ragged breath. "One," he said, then continued along with her, "Two, three, four…"

By the time they got to ten, he had slumped down to the ground, letting go of the lights. The woman sighed, brushed a lock of curly brown hair out of her face, and turned back to Don and Maggie.

"I'm so sorry."

"Oh, it's okay, really," said Maggie, shrugging.

"He was enjoying the snowmen, and then, when he saw the lights, he got all upset," said Don.

The woman reached down and picked up the light string, inspecting it carefully by touching each light. "Ah. I see what the problem is," she said. "Zack gets very concerned when things don't follow a pattern. These lights don't seem to be set in any kind of a pattern. You have two red ones, then a green one, a blue one, and then a single red one, a yellow one, and so on. It doesn't make sense to him." She handed the string of lights to Don.

Don looked down at the string of lights, examining it. He'd never really considered this before. "Huh," said Don. "Whaddaya know?"

"I'll get him out of your hair now. Come on, Zack," she said, gingerly touching his shoulder, "We need to go home now."

The couple looked into each other's eyes. A psychic moment passed between them, the kind that only happens with long-term partners, and Don knew what to do.

"Hold on a sec," he said. "We haven't even really met. I'm Don, and this is my wife, Maggie."

"I'm Angie Ellis," the woman said, shaking Maggie's hand. "Zack and I live just over there, the other side of the Nadeaus."

Don continued, "We just moved in. We have a sixteen-year-old, Jenny. She's still asleep upstairs." He took a breath and then went on. "Is replacing light bulbs something Zack could do? Would it be okay with you if I gave him the job?"

Angie paused for a second, but then said, "Oh no, really, that would be too much trouble. Zack really needs to be monitored… his behavior can be pretty erratic, as you saw. He's on the autism spectrum, in case you hadn't…"

Maggie took a small step forward and spoke softly. "I've taught children with developmental disorders. I have a degree in Special Ed. He'd be…"

Angie went on as though she hadn't heard Maggie, speaking more rapidly. "We really don't socialize much. I have to keep an eye on him constantly. I'm really sorry. You're very nice and all…and uh, welcome to the neighborhood, such as it is, but we'd better be going before he has another meltdown." She gestured for her son to walk away with her. "C'mon, Zackie, let's leave these nice people to their business."

They walked away, the mother careful to distract her son from the scene they were leaving.

"Hmm," sighed Maggie. "Well, we tried."

Just then, the kid from next door came ambling over the lawns. "Hey, there! How are you feeling this morning, Mr. Cassidy?"

Don looked up. "Oh, hey…it's Scott, right? I'm good, I'm good. Thanks for your help last night." He walked over to Scott and clapped him on the back.

"Need any help today? I don't have to be at work until two. I work over at Shaw's, bagging groceries."

"Are you kidding?" said Don. "Sure, I'd like some help."

Ninety minutes later, Muriel took up her usual post. Over breakfast, she had set aside any thoughts of the disaster happening in her neighborhood. Those Elvis pancakes were just as good as she'd hoped, although she may have overdone it a little with the butter and maple syrup. She had been feeling full and happy until they came home. That loud boy from up the street was having a screaming fit in the yard, throwing lights around, and his mother was trying to get him to calm down. Those decorations were *already* causing problems in the neighborhood.

Now that Anderson kid was getting involved in the decorating. Muriel could feel her blood pressure soar as she spent the day going back and forth from her chores to the window. Meanwhile, Ray had gone out into the back yard to check on his bird feeders and clean the birdbath, a job which seemed to be taking an awfully long time.

Chapter 13

Saturday night on Franklin Street was dead as always. Scott sat at his computer, researching an idea he'd had that afternoon while bagging groceries. Suddenly his phone whistled, startling him. It was a text from his older brother, who was down in Boston at college.

Happy Birthday, Dude! Going out with some babes to celebrate tonight?

Scott had completely forgotten it was his birthday. He hadn't looked at a calendar all day, and nobody had wished him Happy Birthday. He smirked and swiftly typed back,

Oh yeah, you know me. Not enough time for all the girls, bro.

He sat and stared at the phone, not knowing whether there would be a reply. Brian was known to pop in with a text and then disappear just as suddenly.

Well, I hope it's happy, man. Later!

Whatever. Scott put down the phone. *Just another day in the life...*

He was lost in research again when he heard the front door bang open and his father come in from wherever he'd been. In spite of himself, Scott swiveled around in his chair and faced his bedroom door, ready to greet his dad in case he came in to wish him a happy birthday. He waited a few minutes. When his father didn't come up,

Scott decided not to go downstairs. "Who cares?" he mumbled to himself, and turned back to his computer screen.

A few minutes later, the sounds of the television came wafting through the heating grate in Scott's bedroom floor. *Oh great. Now he's watching TV, and drinking, no doubt. He doesn't even know it's my birthday.*

He found a website called *Planet Christmas*, and was scrolling through the DIY posts on the message boards, amazed at the wealth of information about creating the best-ever displays. His concentration was broken by the theme song from *The Teenage Mutant Ninja Turtles* blaring up from the TV downstairs. The Turtles had once been his obsession. *What the heck? He's watching my old cartoons?*

Then he heard a little boy's squeals and the distinctive music of a woman's laughter, and realized his dad was watching a video of his fifth birthday party.

He'd forgotten who was at that party, and he couldn't remember the presents he'd received; but he'd never forgotten that Donatello had made a surprise appearance, and that the TMNT theme was blasting from the sound system. Dad was curiously absent during Donatello's appearance, but mom had taken lots of pictures and video. He smiled at the memory.

Don sat in his recliner with a big bowl of popcorn on his lap, happy as a clam. Jenny was getting comfortable on the sofa, as Maggie came in with another bowl for them to share. They were just about to watch Don's favorite movie, *National Lampoon's Christmas Vacation*. It was a tradition to watch it on the evening of the First Decorating Day. Maggie and Jenny had seen it a million times, but still they humored him, and he loved them all the more for it.

"You know, hon, I was thinking that maybe you ought to talk to some of the neighbors," said Maggie, as she placed her bowl on the coffee table and sat down next to her daughter. "You know, introduce yourself and tell them what your plans are."

"You think so? I hadn't really thought about that. Everybody in Punta Gorda was always so supportive of the display," said Don.

"I know, but Maine isn't Punta Gorda. A lot of people put up big Christmas displays down there, but maybe this neighborhood hasn't seen the likes of what you're planning. You ought to at least talk to them about it. You know, just in case."

"Just in case? And what am I supposed to do if somebody doesn't like it?" He stared at his wife, who stared back in silence for what seemed like a whole minute. Jenny didn't say a word.

Finally, Maggie said, "We'll cross that bridge when we come to it."

Don was very uncomfortable with this conversation. Contrary to his ostentatious display, he was usually shy by nature. Sure, if somebody needed help, like the Nadeaus had that time, he'd step up. But mostly he wasn't the sociable type. He liked to let his display do the talking when it came to his love of Christmas. He'd talk to the neighbors, *just in case*, but he couldn't imagine what kind of person would have a problem with it.

It had been a long, busy day, but the new house was starting to feel like home. The movie was starting, and right now he just wanted to relax with his girls.

Angie and Zack Ellis were engaged in a wrestling match. Zack was still showing signs of agitation caused by the day's events: not only the meltdown at the Cassidy house, but an unscheduled visit from Angie's sister, as well. It was fun, but went on a little past his usual bedtime.

Janet was boisterous and lively, and always got Zack riled up—in a positive way. Now, though, he could not calm down enough to go to sleep. Angie tried to swaddle him with blankets, a strategy that usually worked. This time, though, Zack would have no part of it; so she turned to another strategy. She took one of his favorite *Teenage Mutant Ninja Turtle* books, sat in the rocking chair by his bed, and calmly began to read, ignoring his protests.

At last, he sat down on the bed and listened. Within minutes, his breathing was regular again and he was able to settle himself on his pillow. When it appeared he was just about to close his eyes for good, his mother covered him with his heavy blanket and comforter, and kissed him goodnight.

She continued reading until she could hear him snoring softly. Angie liked to call them his "baby bear" snores. She loved the sound— it told her he was peaceful and calm.

She picked up a few toys and dirty clothes scattered around the room and put them in their places before turning out the light. Most nights after Zack was asleep, she tried to spend a few quiet minutes sitting at her mother's antique vanity, brushing her hair. "One hundred strokes a day makes it soft and shiny," her mother always told her. This routine served to calm her after stressful days. Now she stopped before the vanity, part of the huge antique bedroom set she'd inherited when her mom downsized to a condo, and spent a long few minutes just staring at herself in the mirror. What she saw discouraged her. Crow's feet at the corners of her dark-circled eyes, commas at her eyebrows, and the faintest trace of frown lines beginning to carve their way through the skin around her mouth.

She halfheartedly ran the brush through her hair a few times. *Oh girl, your days of being young and pretty have passed you by,* she thought. *As if anyone could ever be interested in you.*

Finally, she went into the kitchen, sat at the table, and logged onto her computer. It had been over six months since her last date with "Mr. Rite Aid," and she was beginning to think she would spend the rest of her life taking care of Zack without ever meeting the right guy.

It was bad enough she was beginning to look her age; she felt much older than her thirty-four years, as well. For the millionth time, she wondered how she could ever have been stupid enough to get pregnant without a wedding ring on her finger; but, as always, her next thought was that she'd probably be divorced from Arthur by now, anyway. He didn't have the gumption to raise a special boy like Zack, as evidenced by the fact he had chosen to stay out of his son's life. A check once a month was it, and thank goodness for that. Without it, she didn't know how she'd manage.

Nope—this was probably going to be her life, and she was okay with that. Still, inside there still burned a tiny spark of hope, so she spent a few minutes looking at the options on *Match.com*. After a while, she realized that every guy she saw reminded her of Mr. Rite Aid in some way, and it all felt hopeless. She was staring at her own profile picture in dismay when her eyelids started to droop. She shut down the computer in disgust and trudged herself off to bed.

Muriel was lying in bed wide awake, trying to read while Ray lay snoring beside her. She'd been staring at page 103 of Jan Karon's latest novel for the last fifteen minutes, mildly perturbed that Ray was able to sleep when she couldn't.

So many thoughts swirled around in her head that she couldn't concentrate on a single one for more than a minute before another intruded. That evening, she'd had some worrying news from a former colleague: a mutual friend suddenly had a stroke. She was also sad because she'd recently learned that their pastor was retiring after thirty years. There were countless other problems, too, none of which she could do a thing about. It was hard to concentrate on just one, but she always came back to the same thing...something she *could* do something about. She had to stop that guy across the street from ruining the neighborhood. He already had lights up all over the bushes, and it wasn't even Halloween yet!

Chapter 14

"**You look fantastic,** Muriel! That's a different shade of red, isn't it?"

"Yes, and thank you! I decided to try that new place in the Concourse. *Salon Sensation*, it's called." Ray had already gone back for seconds on the scrambled eggs, and Muriel was thinking about topping off her omelet and hash browns with a delicious chocolate croissant, when Joy Munden complimented her. She patted her hair self-consciously, flattered that someone had noticed her more vibrant color. Ray hadn't even said a word about it. Her new stylist had suggested it just when she was grasping for something to cheer herself up. She impulsively agreed, and then regretted it when she saw how bright the shade was. Now she wondered if Joy was just humoring her.

"Oh, I've been wanting to check that place out. Looks a little fancier than most of the beauty parlors we grew up with in Kennebec City!"

"I know," Muriel said, laughing. "Remember when Dot Gonyea put up that sign at her place that said Unisex? The whole town practically had a heart attack. I remember Calvin Slater telling me that Lucien down at the Barber Pole was worried about losing business."

Joy sat next to Muriel at a table for six at The Manor restaurant.

On her other side was her husband, Arthur. He had managed the rental department at the hardware store until a decade earlier, when he retired at 65.

Larry and Rachel Charpiat rounded out the little group. They once ran a diner on Main Street, but had closed up shop over a dozen years earlier. Now they were snowbirds, and were getting ready to make their annual post-Christmas journey to Florida in their RV.

The three couples at the table had been friends for years. All their children were friends too; but nowadays, with everybody's kids and grandkids grown up, they only got together for brunch on Sundays after church.

"Didn't we have fun in the seventies?" Joy laughed and patted Muriel on the shoulder. "Oh Muriel, you were always the life of the party. Remember Anne and Paul's housewarming party? They'd bought that big house up on Mayflower Hill when Paul was promoted to management at the mill. Anyway, you were dancing with Ray by the pool and you fell in! We all had a good laugh over that one. The word at the time was that you'd had one too many servings of punch."

Muriel shook her head. "I'm sorry," she said, "I have no idea what you're talking about," trying to look serious. She put her napkin to her mouth and snickered. "That was a beautiful, brand new dress from Sterns, too."

"I remember. You looked like a million bucks. You've never had any problem maintaining that figure, even after three kids."

Rachel started to say something, but suddenly began to cough. As one cough multiplied, her face turned red and Joy began to pound on her back. Rachel shooed her away, cleared her throat loudly, and then took a sip of water, waving her hand in front of her face. "Oh, I must've swallowed the wrong way." She cleared her throat again.

"Anyway, I knew there was something I've been wanting to tell you girls. Guess what? Larry and I have decided to head south right after Thanksgiving this year. Yup. I know we always spend Christmas in Maine, but the Farmer's Almanac is predicting a rough December with lots of snow, so we decided to head down sooner."

"What?" said Joy. "But you'll miss all the parties, and the church Cookie Walk. And our Yankee Swap! What will we do without your reindeer cookies?"

"I know. And I'm sure going to miss all the pretty Christmas trees shining their lights onto the snow, but Larry just doesn't want to chance getting stuck driving through the snow and ice."

"Humph," muttered Muriel. "I wish I was going with you. I sure wouldn't mind missing Christmas in our neighborhood this year."

Everyone looked at her, and Muriel waved her hand as though swatting a gnat. "Oh, this crazy character who bought the house across the street is decorating for Christmas like a danged amusement park. He's already got lights strung up all over the bushes. His house is going to be lit up like the Fourth of July all during the Christmas season. Ray and I won't get a wink of rest with all the commotion it's going to cause."

"Is that so?" asked Joy.

"Ooh, that actually sounds fun," said Rachel. "I'm sorry we're going to miss that."

Muriel was astonished. "Are you kidding? It's going to be a nightmare. And if you don't think so, well, you can just move into our house and we'll take your RV down to Florida." Muriel could tell that her voice was getting louder, but she was losing the ability to control it.

"Oh, come on, dear," said Joy. "It can't be that bad. Where's your Christmas spirit? I'm sure the children in the neighborhood will love it!"

"Yeah," Rachel said. "When did you turn into such a Scrooge?"

Suddenly, Muriel no longer cared about the volume of her voice. "A Scrooge? You've got some nerve, Rachel, calling me names. You try living across from a nut who's got hundreds of lights up already, and has not just one, but five or six snowmen on his front lawn in October. And God knows what else is in that monstrosity of a garage." The mother and children at the next table had stopped eating and chatting and were now staring at her. Muriel felt a pang of embarrassment.

Joy reached out a hand and touched her arm. "Muriel, dear, calm down. We're just having a little fun with you."

"Well, I don't think it's funny!" she said, spontaneously banging her hand down on the table. The sound it made was much louder than she'd intended. The silverware rattled, and now it seemed everyone in the restaurant was looking at her. She was completely humiliated. Just then, Ray returned to the table carrying a full plate of sausage and eggs. His wife stood up, grabbed her coat from the chair, and swung her purse over her arm. "Come on, Raymond, we're leaving. We can settle up our part of the bill at the counter." Ray gave her a pleading look, but she swiftly turned and walked toward the exit without looking back.

"I swear, I'm going to talk to someone at City Hall. I want to know if this is even legal," said Muriel, standing full-on in front of the picture window, hands on hips, not bothering to peek through the curtains anymore.

Ray sat in his recliner, reading the Sunday paper. After brunch, he'd stayed out in the yard for an hour, raking leaves. Then he'd come in for some peace and quiet so he could relax. Muriel wasn't feeling particularly peaceful, though, and right now it was impossible for her to stay quiet. She just couldn't believe what she was seeing across the street.

That Cassidy man must have been out there since the crack of dawn, hanging lights all along the eaves. Muriel hoped that might be the extent of it, yet there he was, rearranging the snowmen on the front porch. That Anderson kid was out there with him now, and Cassidy seemed to be instructing him in how things were to be laid out.

"There's an incredible amount of work involved here, Mr. Cassidy," Scott said. "Did you do this all by yourself when you were in Florida?"

"Oh, no. There were a bunch of us in my neighborhood who used to do it together. We had six or seven houses on our street all lit up. People used to call it Electric Avenue!"

"Still, it takes up so much time…" said Scott.

Don stopped in his tracks and looked seriously at his assistant. "But it's worth every second…think how many people will drive down our street just to see these lights. The memories it will make for children that will last their whole lives. Think how much joy and excitement it will bring to everyone," he said, waving his arms as he spoke.

Scott looked down at the ground. "Well, maybe not everyone," he mumbled. "Some people around here don't get into this type of stuff."

"What do you mean?"

Oh shoot. He doesn't know. Why didn't I keep my big mouth shut?

"Oh, nothing…I just…I think it's way cool. No worries."

"Listen," he said, "If you think anyone's going to have a problem with the lights, you should tell me now so I can go talk to them."

Like *that* would do any good. When Scott was ten, Mrs. Michaud had called the cops because their Halloween display music was too loud. She even called the cops two years ago during his Mom's surprise birthday party in the back yard. There's no way she was going to listen to Don. But instead of saying any of that, Scott just looked at his feet.

"Really. I don't want to cause any problems," said Don. "My whole thing is about making people happy, so if you know of anyone who might not appreciate it, please come on and tell me who it is."

Scott decided that if he told Don now, he might decide not to do the display at all. And then what excuse would he have for hanging out over here? "No, I don't know, really. I was just, uh, thinking aloud."

There was an awkward pause that seemed as though it would last forever; luckily, just then, the front door flew open and out came Jenny. She looked beautiful.

Scott's mind went completely blank.

"Hey, Daddy," she said. "Uh, hi, Scott." Scott nodded as Jenny turned back to her father. "Mom sent me out to get some extra Halloween candy. Rite Aid is having a big sale. Wanna come?"

"No, honey, I can't. I still want to get the diagram for the lawn done before lunch."

Jenny frowned. "Well, how about *you* then? I'll need some muscle to carry all that candy!"

"Yeah, sure!" Scott said, a little too enthusiastically. "If that's okay with you, Mr. Cassidy."

Scott could feel himself beginning to blush again. *What is it about this girl?*

"You bet. It's a nice day for a walk. You two have fun; I'll be here," Don said, gesturing toward the lawn, "doing my thing."

"I'll be back soon, Daddy," said Jenny. She and Scott headed up the street toward the intersection with the brand new Super Rite Aid.

Now that they were finally alone, Scott could feel his heart racing. He'd been thinking about this girl nearly every waking moment since he'd first laid eyes on her, but now he couldn't think of a single thing to say. It didn't help that she just had to look so freaking gorgeous in the fall sunshine. She wasn't saying anything either. What the heck was going on? She had been all Chatty Cathy while they'd been unpacking the decorations the other night, but now, the silence was deafening.

Finally, after what seemed like forever, she spoke up, "So, uh, Scott, umm…what kind of candy do you like?"

Scott barely looked up. "Me? Oh, I like anything, really."

"You're not allergic to peanuts or anything like that, are you?"

"Oh, no." Scott chuckled nervously. "I wish. I could probably lose some weight if I laid off the peanut butter cups." Then, realizing he probably sounded like an idiot, he tried to recover. "I mean, you know, I don't really eat that much candy…"

Jenny interrupted, wagging a finger. "Oh no, you don't! You can't backtrack. You confessed! You're a peanut-butter-cupaholic!"

"Cupaholic?" Scott laughed. With that, their conversation started.

Forty-five minutes later, the pair were heading back up Franklin Street, toting four shopping bags filled with Laffy Taffy, mini Hershey Bars, and pumpkin-shaped Peanut Butter Cups.

"So, your Dad is really into this decorating stuff, huh?"

"Oh, yeah. I saw you helping him from my bedroom window. I'm sorry he's dragged you into this. Don't feel like you have to humor him. It's just his thing, you know? His hobby."

Scott laughed. "No, I think it's cool. It's nice, kind of, to see something fun happening next door. Things have been kind of gloomy here for a while."

They walked in silence for a minute, then suddenly both began talking at the same time.

"Have you noticed that more people have put out Halloween decorations…" blurted Scott.

"So, I've kind of been wondering…" said Jenny.

They both abruptly stopped talking, laughed nervously, and

paused in front of a school bus shelter on the corner. Scott did a little half bow toward Jenny and gestured as if to say, "Go ahead."

Jenny swallowed a smile, and said, "Do you mind if I ask you something?"

Scott shrugged.

"It's just, I've been here for a couple of weeks now, and I haven't seen your parents. Do you live in that house all alone or something?"

"No!" Scott answered, far too quickly and way too loudly. Jenny's eyes widened in surprise. A plastic skeleton hanging from a nearby maple tree made clinking sounds in the breeze.

"I'm sorry," he said, and looked away. *Man, what a dork I am.* "I didn't mean to jump on you or anything. I mean, it's...I live with my dad. I have a brother in college. My mom...she died last year...over a year ago, now."

"Oh," said Jenny. Her expression softened. "Oh, I'm really sorry. I shouldn't have been so nosy. I didn't know..." Her eyes misted and she reached out a hand to touch Scott's arm. "I wouldn't have joked about it if I'd known."

"It's okay, really. No big deal," Scott said. "I mean, I still miss her and everything, but we knew it was coming. She had been sick for a while, so I got to say goodbye to her and everything..." He trailed off.

Jenny frowned. "Still, I'm really sorry. That must be so hard."

Scott bent down to pick up a long stick, and started walking again, twirling it in his fingers.

"I don't really talk about it. In fact, this is the most I've said about it to anybody in a long time."

Jenny opened her mouth to respond, but Scott interrupted.

"Anyway," he said, "about your father's Christmas decorations. I think they're really cool. I like helping him. I hope that's okay with you."

"With me? Why would I mind? Go for it, guy! If you want to become a crazy Christmas dude like my Dad and his friends, I'm all for it," she said with a laugh. "Just don't try to get me involved!"

"Why not?"

"Why not? I just don't see the point. I love my father and all, but every year it's the same thing. He starts putting them out in October and that's all he talks about, then Christmas comes and he and my Mom are out there every night, then it's over in January and they spend the whole month taking them down. It's nuts."

"But if it makes people happy, I think that's a nice thing. And I bet your father would be really happy if you wanted to help him out with it, too."

Jenny shook her head. "I used to like helping him when I was little, but now I just kind of resent it. He spends more time on his Christmas display than he does with me."

"Well, I probably shouldn't say this, but I'd think that over if I were you," Scott said, stopping again. He swung the stick around, using it to scratch at a nearby fence post. Jenny stopped too, and looked at him curiously.

"My mother always tried to get me involved in her hobby—outdoor photography. She wanted me to go with her to outdoorsy locations, she loved to take pictures of birds and animals and trees and stuff. I used to complain all the time because apparently I had better things to do. Believe me, now I'd do anything to have the chance to go with her."

He wiped his eyes, hoping Jenny wouldn't notice his tears. She took a breath and smiled gently. "Okay, I get it. I'm sorry. I'll think about what you said. I really will."

"Okay," he said. He could feel his face flushing. "I'm sorry, I kind of went overboard there."

"No, no, it's okay. Really. Look, there's Dad. Let's see if we can do anything to help out now, okay?"

They picked up the pace and headed for Jenny's house, where Don happily greeted them and put them to work for the next couple of hours, hauling decorations down from the garage loft.

It was after dark when Scott finally returned home. He entered through the back door, took off his hoodie and threw it onto a kitchen chair, and opened the refrigerator to see what he might scrounge up for dinner. At the end of the hall, the living room was dim but for the red ember of his father's cigar and the meager glow from his mother's beloved Tiffany-style table lamp.

He closed the refrigerator and walked down the hall into the living room. His father sat in his easy chair, drink in one hand, cigar in the other. A photo album on his lap, open to a page of snapshots from his first Christmas. The little family was the picture of happiness; Scott in a tiny "Santa Loves Me" red-and-green sleeper, Brian wearing elf pajamas, dad in a Santa hat, and mom, looking beautiful in a jolly red robe. She had been the heart of the family: the center of all happiness, his father's college sweetheart. As he had told them over, and over again, his dream girl. One would never imagine, looking at these pictures, that her time was marked.

Scott's dad looked up at him with bleary eyes.

"Where've you been?" Sam said, obviously trying not to slur.

Scott shrugged. "Next door, helping the new neighbors."

His dad grunted and took a long drink.

"You should see all the Christmas decorations they have. It's insane."

"A bit early for Christmas decorations, don't you think?"

Scott went on: "he's got this thing about getting it all set up for Thanksgiving night. He's really…"

Sam interrupted, "Don't you have homework to do?"

Scott stared at his father for a second. "Yeah…I'll get right on that." He turned and headed for the stairs, then, spontaneously, whirled back around and faced his father again.

"You know, Dad, this isn't what Mom would want," he said. Then he took in a quick breath, swallowed, and his whole body tensed. He hadn't planned to confront his father; it was probably a huge mistake.

His father closed the photo album with a snap and gritted his teeth. "What did you just say to me?"

Scott shuffled his feet. Now he had started, he might as well keep going. "I said, this isn't what Mom would want. She wouldn't want you falling apart like this. She loved you. She loved us. She'd feel awful if she knew what was going on here." His voice broke on the last few words, and tears began to flow down his face.

His father stood up. "This isn't any of your business, do you hear me?" His deep voice rose until he was shouting. "You've got a roof over your head and everything you need. Don't you dare start telling me what Mom would want. I know what Mom would want. I knew her better than anyone…" He choked, then slumped back down into the chair and broke into a wracking sob. "I knew her better than anyone…but I'm not the man she thought I was."

Scott hesitantly stepped toward his father. "Dad…I'm sorry, I shouldn't have said…"

"Leave me alone, Scott. Get up to your room and just leave me alone." He buried his face in his hands.

Feeling helpless, Scott thumped upstairs, his stomach clenched. He knew his family couldn't go on like this, but what was he supposed to do, just bide his time until graduation, then leave his father to drink himself into oblivion?

Scott loved his dad, but he was beginning to dislike him. He missed Mom, too, but you didn't see him taking drugs or drinking and throwing away his life. He knew that's not what his mother would want for him, but he couldn't figure out how to get his dad to understand that it wasn't what she'd want for *him*, either.

Chapter 15

"**Well, Muffin,** that's only twenty-four Trick-or-Treaters this year," said Mrs. Ferris, as the birdsong clock on her kitchen wall warbled. Eight o'clock meant another Halloween in Kennebec City was officially over. She plopped down at the same Chromecraft Formica kitchen table she'd had since 1955. The ceramic candy bowl, circa 1968, was festively decorated with crescent moons and cats, and sat mostly full in the middle of the table. Muffin, a ten-year-old Shih Tzu, sat on the blue-and-white linoleum at her feet.

Eileen Ferris had lived in the tiny two-story home next door to the Michauds since 1950. She moved in with Joe right after their honeymoon, and started helping him in his Lebanese bakery down on Water Street. They'd raised a son here, and even after Joe's death twenty years ago, she'd never wanted to move out. She loved the neighborhood, and she loved this house, even though all the appliances had been in service since the era of olive-colored stoves and refrigerators. She considered herself lucky to still have all her faculties, and she was determined to stay in her little home as long as she possibly could.

"Twenty-four, Muffin. That's the lowest number yet. Back in the sixties, we had so many kids come by that Joe and I used to sit outside on the porch to hand out the candy. There was no sense going inside!" she chuckled, looking down at the bowl. "Too much leftover candy. That's going to wreck my girlish figure," she said, unwrapping a Fun Size Snickers and popping it into her mouth—the dog looked up in the hope of snaffling a bite.

"No chocolate for you, so forget it." She reached into a specially marked canister and pulled out a treat for her doggie.

Mrs. Ferris loved seeing the children in their costumes, and never missed a Halloween at home. She'd hung a plastic skeleton on the maple tree on her front lawn every year for the past six decades. The neighborhood had fewer young children in it now, since the Websters had left town; and the families that used to drive in from the other side of town hadn't come around in years. It didn't help that about half of the houses on Franklin Street were dark, even the Michauds'. She didn't know what had gotten into Muriel Michaud as she'd gotten older. She used to be one of the most fun-loving people on the street, but now she had turned into the proverbial crabby old lady.

"I'm glad I never got crabby, Muffin. Why be crabby when there are so many good things in the world…like you," she said, kissing the pooch on his shiny black nose.

There had been quite a few cars coming and going this evening, but they were all parking in front of the house up the street, where those handsome young men lived. Mrs. Ferris guessed they were having a party, and she wished she'd been invited. It had been a long time since she'd been to a party.

"Well, come on Muffin. I guess it's time to hit the hay," she said, leading the little dog down the hall to the bedroom.

"Gee, we've got a lot of left-over candy," said Jenny, observing the half-full bowl on the kitchen table. "We didn't get anywhere near the number of kids here as we used to get in Punta Gorda."

"No wonder. Most of the houses were dark," Maggie replied.

Don was at the stove, measuring popcorn kernels into a big kettle for the annual post-trick-or-treat viewing of *The Nightmare Before Christmas*. Movies, of course, required popcorn, regardless of how much candy was left over. He was feeling pretty good. He'd gotten a lot of work done on the display, and was on target to light up on Thanksgiving night.

He shook the popcorn pan. "Yeah. I thought that party up the street would be for kids, but I only saw adults going in and out. Those guys did come to the door and give out candy, though, which is more than I can say for our neighbors across the street. There lights were out at Scott's house, too."

"Well, maybe all those people had something else to do," Jenny said. The sound of the popping revved up and filled the room. She filled three tumblers with ice and poured soda pop into each.

"Speaking of the people across the street, that lady doesn't seem very friendly," said Maggie, leaning against the counter and sneaking her hand into the candy bowl for a bag of mini M&Ms. Don was pouring the popcorn into one huge bowl to share with Maggie on the couch, and another smaller bowl for Jenny, who had reserved the recliner earlier. "I said 'hi' to her the other day when she came out to her car, and she didn't even look at me. Plus, I've noticed she seems to look out her window. A lot. Maybe we ought to bring her a pie, or something?"

Jenny rolled her eyes. "Uh, I think that's supposed to work the other way, Mom. Neighbors are supposed to welcome newcomers with baked goods. At least that's what I've read in books. Maybe that's one of those traditions people don't do anymore."

"The proverbial Welcome Wagon. I've never seen it in real life," said Don.

They carried their popcorn bowls into the living room. Maggie said, "You've already talked to her about the display, right?"

He was just opening his mouth to say that he hadn't quite gotten around to it yet, when he spotted Jenny struggling to carry three glasses at once. "Hey, let me take one of those before you spill pop all over the carpet."

"Oh come on, Dad, I've done this a million times!"

As Don tried to take one of the glasses, they all went tumbling down, spilling their sticky contents everywhere.

All three members of the Cassidy family scrambled into the kitchen to fetch paper towels and carpet cleaner. They forgot about the woman across the street for the rest of the evening.

"I don't know why we had to leave so early. We could have stayed and helped tuck Emma in," said Muriel, pulling back the covers on the antique sleigh bed.

They had missed another Halloween on Franklin Street, but at least this year it wasn't just because they didn't want to give out candy. This year they'd been at their granddaughter Karen's house, helping to get little Emma ready. The women stayed at the house greeting trick-or-treaters while the men took Emma out. It had been a fun evening until Emma started having a meltdown. One house too many.

"All that crying was giving me a headache," said Ray, heading into the bathroom. "Better to let her folks deal with it. We'd just be in the way."

"Well, I think I know how to calm a crying child, Raymond. I could have helped," she said, as she climbed into bed and drew the covers up to her shoulders. She could feel her eyes welling with tears.

Ray's electric toothbrush began to buzz. A couple of minutes later he came back in, chuckling.

"You should have seen Emma when she saw somebody dressed up in an Elmo costume. I thought she was gonna die laughing right there on the…Muriel? Are you crying? Muriel? What's going on?"

Ray came over and put his arm around her, but his wife kept on weeping.

"Now listen, my sugar plum, you are beginning to worry me. What is going on with all the tears lately?"

"Nothing. I'm just feeling sentimental. The holidays just make me feel that way."

"Halloween makes you feel sentimental? Since when?"

"Since always. I just never said."

Ray scowled and rubbed his wife's back. "Come on, now. You've got to tell me what's going on. I've never known you to be the type to cry over foolishness. I know something's wrong," he insisted.

"Ray," she said, looking up at her husband. She wondered for the millionth time if he noticed the wrinkles all over her face. She was no longer the girl in her poodle skirt and bobby sox that he'd fallen in love with. Now she was just an old lady, and every single time she looked into his eyes, she felt self-conscious about it.

He kissed her nose, something that had never failed to make her giggle. This time, she couldn't even manage a smile. "Tell me," he whispered.

"Ray, I went to the…" The phone rang, and Muriel pulled her arm out from under the covers and reached for it on the nightstand.

"Oh, come on! You got to be kidding me," said Ray. "Who's calling at this hour? Don't answer it!"

"It's Karen," she said, looking at the caller I.D. "Maybe something's wrong." She put the receiver to her ear.

"Hello, dear. What's up?" she said, trying to sound cheery, wiping her eyes and nose with a tissue from the box on the nightstand.

"Hi, Mémère," said Karen. "There's someone here who would like to speak to you before she goes to bed."

"Oh, isn't that sweet! You put her right on. Hello, Miss Emma!"

"Hi Grand-Mémère," came the high-pitched voice. She loved the sound of that little voice. She could hear Karen whispering in the background.

"What?" said Emma, and now Karen whispered louder, "Tell her you're feeling better."

"I feel better now," said Emma.

"Well, I'm glad you're feeling better. Are you going nighty-night now?"

"Yes," answered the tiny voice.

"Well here's a big kiss for you," she said, smacking her lips together. "Pépère would like to say goodnight, too, okay?" She handed her husband the phone and slid over to the other side of the bed.

Ray happily chattered away. Within a few minutes, Muriel's eyes began to close. Try as she might, she couldn't keep them open.

Chapter 16

At 9:15 on the morning of November third, Muriel and Ray were seated in uncomfortable chairs in the office of Roger Girard, First Selectman of Kennebec City, downtown at City Hall. The building was a brick-and mortar structure that had been in service for as long as Muriel could remember. It smelled old, but she liked it because it was sturdy, dependable, and still useful. No need to replace it with something modern, as so many other towns had done.

Its huge windows didn't do much to keep the cold air out, though. *The heating bill must be sky high.* A bill she and her husband were paying with their hard-earned taxes.

Roger was a tall, heavyset man, bald save for a fringe of brown hair. He was wearing a light blue suit with a dark blue dress shirt and a yellow tie featuring cheeseburgers and ice cream parfaits. He owned a number of fast food franchises in Central Maine, and had been a fixture in city politics for twenty years. Muriel had never spoken to the man, but she knew all about him. If anyone could get something done about those out-of-control Christmas decorations, it was Roger Girard. She couldn't wait to get him on her side.

He had barely welcomed the Michauds into his office, when Muriel began telling him about the man across the street and his

Christmas display. Roger took notes the whole time she spoke.

When she finally paused for a breath, he said, "Now, I understand you're upset, Mrs. Michaud." He looked down at his notes for a second and continued, "but I have to tell you that, as far as I know, there's nothing in the city ordinances that prohibits or limits what the owner of a private residence may or may not put up for Christmas decorations. I'll look into it, but I really don't think anything can be done."

Muriel frowned. This couldn't possibly be true. "Well, there ought to be. You need to do something about that. It's disturbing the peace is what it is, not to mention light pollution or whatever you want to call it."

"Well, now, I don't know about that. Just how bright are these lights? I mean, you make it sound like they can be seen from outer space." He looked at Ray, but he just shrugged.

Muriel rolled her eyes and sighed. "Well, he hasn't actually turned them all on yet."

"He hasn't turned them on? Then why all the fuss?"

Muriel sat up straight. She couldn't believe what she was hearing. "It doesn't take a moron to see what these lights are going to do. He's got a million of them out there. Along with snowmen and angels and more. An entire U-Haul full of Christmas decorations. We don't want that kind of attention on our neighborhood...the people, the traffic on the street. It's going to be a carnival. Don't you need a permit to hold a carnival?"

"Look, if Franklin Street was, say, part of a housing development with a home-owners' association, you could limit or regulate a variety of things. But the city doesn't have any such regulations, I don't believe." He managed a weak smile as Muriel sat, grim-faced, gripping her pocketbook. Ray sat stoically by, having barely said two words since walking through the door.

"Look, the way I see it, Mrs. Michaud, it sounds like a nice thing for the community. People will enjoy it. Have you talked with your neighbor to see how late he's planning on having these lights on?"

This took the cake. She leaned forward in her chair and, as though she were talking to a child, said, "No, I haven't talked with him. He's obviously off his rocker. I'm not going to approach a man like that. God knows what would happen! And besides, if anything, it's he who should approach us. We've been living here the longest, after all."

Roger just looked at her, nodding his head as though he understood. Maybe he was finally getting it, so Muriel went on. "Just think of the congestion—you'll need police out there, patrolling and directing traffic."

"If the traffic gets heavy, we can work something out. It will only be for the Christmas season, after all. I'm sure we can spare some traffic cops to provide a service to the community."

Feeling desperate now, Muriel pulled out her last salvo. "Maybe there's a law against pollution."

Roger shook his head. "I'm not sure having a Christmas display really constitutes pollution, Mrs. Michaud."

Muriel could feel her anger rise, and noticed Ray creeping over in his chair, farther away from her. This was getting ridiculous. Why couldn't this man see to reason? This was not at all what she had expected from this meeting, and she felt completely disrespected. "Littering! The crowds will leave trash all over the street. And think of the riffraff that might use the crowd as an excuse to break into people's houses," she said, a crescendo in her voice, "there must be some kind of law you can enforce!"

"I've already told you I don't recall there being pertinent laws about this on the books. I will look into it, but other than that, I don't know what I can do for you," he said, shifting in his rollaway chair.

Muriel slammed her hands down on the armrests of her chair and raised her voice. "How can I make it any clearer? Crowds of people. The noise, the trash, and all of the hubbub. We have a nice, quiet street, and we don't need scads of people driving back and forth, gawking at us, or those infernal lights shining through our windows at all hours of the night. Never mind that it's an inconvenience...it's a gall-darned fire hazard. Don't you see? If there's nothing preventing it now then you must *make* a law against it!"

Roger put his hands up in a defensive gesture. "Look, Mrs., uh, Mrs. Michaud, here's a thought—the next Selectmen's Meeting is in a few weeks, the Thursday before Thanksgiving. If you can muster up some support for shutting down the display, we might be able to do something. Why don't you circulate a petition amongst Kennebec City citizens? This change would also affect any other possible displays throughout the City. Get at least a hundred valid signatures, bring it to my office within a week or two, and I'll get it on the agenda for that meeting. Maybe you can convince the Selectmen that there should be an ordinance," he said. He raised his eyebrows at Ray, as if to encourage a response. Ray stayed silent. Muriel couldn't believe he wasn't backing her up.

Muriel nodded. "Okay. I'll do it. But in the meantime, I want some research done on your end. Find out if there's any law we can get this guy on. I want this travesty shut down!"

"I'll do my best, Mrs. Michaud," said Roger, rising from his chair and towering over her. "Now, if you'll excuse me, I have a meeting in about ten minutes that I need to prepare for."

Muriel paused. She wanted to say more, but she glanced at her husband and he shook his head. She held fast to the arms of her chair for a few seconds, then abruptly stood up. Ray scrambled to his feet.

"Thanks for taking the time to see us," Ray said, offering his hand.

Roger grabbed his hand and shook. "Oh, no problem. That's what I'm here for!" he said, guiding them to the door. Suddenly, he sounded cheerful again, as though he'd done them a big favor. "I'll see what I can find out and be in touch with you folks. In the meantime, get started on that petition. And remember, the town's pre-Thanksgiving sales are starting tomorrow!"

"Never mind about the sales. You see what you can do about those decorations, all right? I have your word?" she asked, looking him straight in the eyes.

"Oh, you bet. You have my word, Mrs. Michaud," Roger assured her, quickly closing the door.

Disappointed by the lack of an immediate solution, and miffed at Ray, Muriel held her tongue on the way to the car.

"Thanksgiving sales, my foot," she finally said, as they buckled their seat belts and drove off.

Muriel sat stiffly in the passenger seat, still gripping her pocketbook.

Finally, Ray spoke up. "Something is definitely getting to you. I mean, besides the Christmas lights. Is…is something else going on? Because I get the feeling there's more to this than meets the eye. You've been so upset…"

Muriel interrupted, and even she was surprised by how loud her voice sounded in the car. "*No! Nothing else is wrong!* Why does there have to be something else? Isn't this *enough*?" On the word "enough," she burst into tears and began digging through her bag for a tissue.

"Okay, okay, I'm sorry, hon," said Ray. "It's okay, it's okay. Stop crying now."

Muriel carried on sobbing as they turned up Franklin Street and pulled into their driveway. Mercifully, there was no activity in house across the street.

"Hey sugar plum," Ray said, as they headed into the house, "I'm getting the urge to skunk you again at Rummy. You wanna take me on?" He headed for the kitchen drawer where they kept the playing cards.

This was Ray's usual way of trying to distract his wife when something was wrong, but today, she didn't have the heart for it. "No," she said. "I'm feeling a little tired. I'm just going to go upstairs and take a nap." Her husband sat down at the kitchen table and dealt himself a hand of Solitaire, and Muriel hung up her coat and started up the stairs. "You should rest up, too," she said. "Because first thing tomorrow morning, we're going to every house in the neighborhood to start collecting signatures."

Chapter 17

Don Cassidy climbed the Michauds' front steps two at a time, rang the doorbell, and waited, a big smile on his face. His gray woolen cap was pulled down snugly over his head, and he was wearing his work gear. The door opened and the old man Don had seen puttering around stood there, a wide-eyed look of surprise on his face.

"Hi neighbor! Thought it was about time I came over and introduced myself. I'm Don Cassidy. I bought the house across the way there."

The man didn't say a word at first, but smiled a cautious smile as he shook hands with his new neighbor.

Don continued. "Guess you've seen my little project going on across the street. I thought the considerate thing to do would be to come over and talk with you about it so there are no surprises."

He paused, but the old guy remained mute, nodding and staring.

"Uh, is your wife around? Could I maybe come in and talk to you both for a few minutes?"

Mention of his wife seemed to snap the fellow out of his momentary confusion. "No!" he said. "Uh…she's napping upstairs. She hasn't been feeling well. I really don't want to wake her up, if that's okay with you."

"Okay then," said Don. "Can you and I talk for a few minutes?"

The man snuck a quick glance up the stairs, stepped out onto the stoop, and quietly closed the door behind him. "Sorry," he said. "I was caught off guard there for a minute. What was it you wanted to talk about?"

"Well, as I said, my name's Don and I'm your new neighbor."

"Oh yeah, yes," said the man. "I'm Ray Michaud. My wife's name is Muriel. We've lived here most of our lives. Pretty quiet neighborhood, you know. We pretty much keep to ourselves here."

Don nodded. "I noticed that. I just wanted to talk to you about what I'm doing over there, putting up my Christmas display and all. I like to be considerate of my neighbors."

"Yes, well, the wife and I were wondering about that. Just how much of a display do you plan to create over there? Looks pretty… extensive…I guess you'd say." Ray's laugh was giddy.

"Yes, sir, it is. I'm proud to say I had one of the biggest displays in Florida before we moved. I'm hoping to do the same thing up here. Bring a lot of joy to the neighborhood. Make memories for the kids. You know, cheer things up on Franklin Street."

"Oh now, I'm not sure we need cheering up, you know. Things have been just fine here for a while now," said Ray.

This wasn't promising, but Don forced a smile. "I understand. But I think once you see how happy it makes people, you'll change your mind. There's nothing like the looks on the faces of the children when they watch the lights and all the animated characters."

Ray looked across the street. "Looks like you've got over a thousand lights up there now. That's going to shine pretty bright through our windows, I imagine."

"There will be forty-seven thousand lights in all, Mr. Michaud," Don said, and the old man grimaced visibly. "But don't worry. I'll only be lighting them up early in the evening. They'll be turned off by nine o'clock each night."

"But what about the traffic? Don't these displays bring a lot of people in from all over ten-acre lot?"

Don smiled. "Sometimes that can be an issue, but we'll be out here directing traffic every night, and we'll make sure people aren't blocking your driveway, or anything. Really, Mr. Michaud, it will only be from six to nine every night. And we'll be raising money and food for the Kennebec City Food Pantry…We'll have a donation box over there. It's all for a really good cause." Don was talking too fast, suddenly. This man was making him nervous.

Ray stared at the newcomer with his wide blue eyes for what seemed like an eternity. Finally, he spoke. "Look, you seem like a nice young fella, and I'm sure your heart's in the right place. I don't really have a problem with your display, but my wife, well, she's another story. She's all up in a dither over it, and I can't talk her out of it."

Don felt his smile collapse. "Oh?"

"Yes, and I'm sorry, she doesn't like it at all. We've even been to the Head Selectman to see if anything could be done about it."

Don's stomach lurched. This was more serious than he'd expected. In fact, he hadn't even considered that anyone here was going to try to stop him from putting up his display.

Ray went on. "Look. Roger Girard—that's the guy we talked to— he said he didn't think anything could be done about it. But I'll be honest, I don't think Muriel's gonna give up. This is really upsetting her. I'm sure you understand."

Don suddenly felt too warm in his winter garb. This was beginning to make him angry. These people went straight to the Board of Selectmen before talking to him about their concerns?

"No, Mr. Michaud, I don't understand. I don't understand why anyone would have a problem with a joyful celebration of the Christmas season. As far as I know, we aren't violating any laws. I'd be glad to talk with your wife about it, explain to her what we are doing here."

Ray laughed, a short, sharp yap. "Ha! You don't know my wife, son. Once she gets a bee in her bonnet, you'll be hard pressed to talk her out of it."

"Well, look. I don't want to be contentious, but I just don't know what to do here. I have my rights as a homeowner, and as long as I'm not violating any laws…"

Ray looked stern now. "I see. Well, I guess you're in for a fight, then. I'll try to talk to her, but so far she hasn't wanted to hear any of it. She doesn't want those lights shining in our house at any time, she doesn't want to deal with extra traffic on the street, and that's it. I'm sorry, son. I don't think I can talk her out of this."

Don could feel his face getting redder.

"Why don't you just take the year off from your display? Get to know the neighborhood a little better, and then maybe you'll see that this isn't the right thing to do here," suggested Ray.

Don was normally a mild-mannered man, but he couldn't understand this couple's determination to thwart what he saw as a wonderful thing for the community. When he opened his mouth to speak, his voice came out sounding more rigid than he had intended. "Frankly, Mr. Michaud, I've been getting to know this neighborhood. Doesn't seem like the people around here have very much joy in their lives; I think this is just the neighborhood that needs my display. I'm going to move forward with it until someone official tells me to stop. You have a nice day, now."

He turned on his heel and left, marching heavily across the street, more determined than ever to create his most dazzling display to date. He'd already crisscrossed the roof and festooned the bushes around the house with color-changing lights. The electrician was scheduled to come that afternoon to install a couple more boxes, and he'd inspected all his extension cords and laid out the grid over the weekend. The rest of the day would be spent placing as many of his blow molds into their assigned spots as he could. Hopefully, he would be able to corral Scott and Jenny when they got home from school, and talk them into setting up the stable for the Nativity figures. Every bit of the project was laid out on his timeline. As long as there were no unexpected delays, he might just be ready to light up on Thanksgiving night. He was sure to win his neighbors over, once they saw the joy it brought.

Chapter 18

The crisp beauty of Maine in October swiftly passed into the cold gray of November, almost as if a switch had flipped at Halloween. Winter was in the air, and radio stations were starting to take predictions about when the first substantial snowfall would occur. The leaves that had been so colorful just a couple of weeks earlier were now brown, dry, and falling by the score. It was the first Saturday of the month, and folks were outside in their down jackets and lined flannel shirts, raking. A brisk wind was blowing leaves around their path, as Muriel and Ray made their way from house-to-house on Franklin Street.

Muriel—bundled up in her everyday coat and woolens, petition and clipboard in hand—trudged through the mounds of dead leaves, her husband struggling to keep up with her. She was glad of his company, but she hoped he wouldn't slow her progress down. "Come on, you old coot," she said. "We've got a lot of ground to cover today."

"Gosh, sugar plum," Ray said. "I haven't seen you so determined in years. To be honest, I'm a little worried. Used to be you'd get all hepped up over volunteering at the winter coat drive or putting together care packages for soldiers during the holidays. But this is a whole 'nother can of beans."

"Well, I don't know why you're so surprised. I should think you'd feel the same way I do about this whole mess. I'd like to see *you* get a little more 'hepped up' about it, frankly."

Ray had nothing to say.

So far, most of the neighbors they'd visited had either not been home, or declined to sign the petition. By the time they knocked on Eileen Ferris' door, Muriel was feeling quite frustrated.

The little old lady seemed amazed to see them. "Muriel Michaud!" she exclaimed. "You haven't knocked on my door in a dog's age. What brings you here?"

The truth was that they had been good friends once upon a time. In fact, Eileen's daughters used to babysit the Michaud children, but they'd grown apart as their children grew up and moved away. After that, they didn't have much to say to each other except for occasional comments about the weather. Then Muriel called the police on the Fourth of July last year, because Eileen's dog was barking non-stop at the fireworks display over the municipal airport. The dog behaved that way *every* Fourth of July, but for some reason, the noise had driven Muriel crazy that year. She hadn't spoken a word to Eileen since.

Seeing the older woman reminded her of where her life was headed, and the thought of turning into a shriveled-up raisin with no one but a dog to talk to made her feel sick inside.

"Well, you know, life has been so busy, and the kids always need us for one thing or another..." The lying came easy. She could never tell Eileen the truth.

Muriel cleared her throat. "But anyway, we're here because Raymond and I have put together a petition to stop that man across the street from going forward with his Christmas display."

"Oh, yes! I've been watching him. Can't wait to see what he's going to bring out of that garage next!"

Muriel ignored Eileen and went on. "We think it's going to cause a great disturbance in the neighborhood, and we're asking the Selectmen to put a stop to it."

Eileen looked downright mystified. "Why would you want to stop him?" she asked. "I think it'll be pretty to have those lights twinkling in the snow. I can't wait to see it all lit up."

"But, don't you understand what a nightmare it's going to be, with all the traffic and so forth?" Muriel was beyond frustrated now; she was truly aggravated. What was wrong with the people in this neighborhood? Why couldn't they see her point of view?

I'm surrounded by idiots.

"To be honest, I hadn't really thought about that, but you know what? I think it will be exciting. Maybe it will bring some of the old fun back to the neighborhood." Eileen's eyes twinkled. Muffin, who had scurried out onto the porch and was winding his way between Muriel and Ray's legs, let out a short yip, as if by way of agreement.

Muriel nearly lost her balance and had to grab her husband's arm as the dog continued to scoot about.

Just then, a loud buzzing sound came from across the street, and everyone turned to see what was going on. The dog pranced over to the edge of the porch and began yapping in earnest.

Don Cassidy was out on his lawn using some sort of contraption stuck into the grass. "Oh Lord, what's he doing now? What is that thing, Raymond?"

"Post-hole digger. You use it when you want to put up a fence. Or a flag pole. Maybe he's putting up a flag pole. Can't imagine he'd put up a fence in the middle of the lawn."

Muriel turned back to Eileen. "There. You see what I mean? Breaking the silence of a perfectly nice Saturday morning."

"What are you talking about, Muriel? That's not any louder than a lawn mower."

"Oh, never mind," Muriel huffed in frustration. She made her way back toward the porch steps, Muffin yapping after her. Ray lingered at the door.

"I'm sorry for bothering you, Eileen," he said.

"Oh, it's no bother at all," Eileen said, her voice creaky, but jolly. "You come by any time. Muffin and I love company!"

Ray caught up with his wife on the walkway, but she continued to march, staring straight ahead as she said, "Why did you apologize to that old biddy? She obviously doesn't even know what day it is, she's so ancient. I don't know why we even bothered."

"Oh, come on now..."

"Let's go over and see Sam Anderson," she said. "I'm sure he doesn't want any of this lunacy ruining his peace and quiet."

"Are you sure? The Andersons used to love making a big deal about the holidays."

"Yes, I'm sure. Things have changed. His life is quieter now. He's done with all that silliness now that he's a widower."

Muriel was about five feet from the sidewalk in front of the Andersons' house when she was startled by the sound of a roughly-running engine from up the street. She looked up to see a red pickup truck, most definitely going over the speed limit, barreling down the pavement toward her. Surprised, she stood frozen in her tracks, expecting the driver to slow down and stop. Her husband grabbed her arm and pulled her away; the truck went zooming by.

"Good Lord! That guy almost hit you!" Ray was panting. He pulled his handkerchief out of his back pocket and wiped his brow.

Muriel's was clutching her chest and she was gasping, trying to catch her breath. "Who...who was that? I've never seen that truck before."

"Guy didn't even slow down. I have no idea who that was. I didn't even get a look at the driver. Ought to know better than to drive like that in this neighborhood."

They stood on the sidewalk for a moment, collecting themselves, when Ray suggested, "You want to call it a day, hon?"

His wife was appalled. "Absolutely not. I'm fine now. I say we keep on with our mission," and with that, she marched up the walkway to the Andersons'.

The porch was badly in need of repair, the gray paint chipped and completely worn away in some spots. Muriel rang the bell and they waited. After a minute or so she rang it again, then opened the screen door and used the scuffed brass knocker.

"All right, all right already! I'm coming!" came a deep voice from inside. It was not a happy voice. Muriel glanced at Ray just as the door whisked open. Sam Anderson, looking disheveled stood there, glaring. "Oh, it's you. What can I possibly do for you?" he said, combing his fingers through his wild hair and pushing it straight back from his forehead. He needed a haircut and a shave, and his voice sounded as though his throat was filled with wet gravel. There were puffy bags under his red-rimmed eyes.

Muriel, alarmed at his appearance, gulped, then gathered her wits together. "Hello, Mr. Anderson," she smiled. "My husband Raymond and I are here to ask for your help with something."

Sam stared at her, expressionless. "Yes? What is it? I'm very busy."

She kept smiling. She knew she had to get through to this man, despite their past differences. He'd see to reason. "This won't take much of your time. I suppose you've noticed the rigmarole going on next door?" She waved her free hand toward the Cassidy house.

Sam didn't even cast a glance in that direction. "Yeah, I've noticed. So, what about it?"

"Well, obviously, it's going to create a nuisance here in our neighborhood, and my husband and I are circulating a petition to try to get it shut down." She thrust the clipboard toward him. "We're hoping you'll agree and sign it."

Sam squinted and rubbed the salt-and-pepper stubble on his chin with one hand, making a sandpapery sound. He looked down at the petition, then slowly drew his bloodshot gaze up toward his neighbor's eyes. He broke into a rather sinister looking grin. "You've got to be kidding me, lady. You're a real piece of work, you know that?" He let out a short, spiteful laugh.

Muriel pulled the clipboard back against her chest. This reaction startled her, and she was feeling a little scared, now. "Why? Whatever are you talking about?"

Ray was quick to protectively put his arm around his wife. "Muriel, let's go. Let's leave this man alone."

A growing flush of red made its way up from Sam's collar and his hands clenched into fists. His voice grew louder through his gritted teeth. "Do you honestly think I've forgotten how you called the police on us when we were celebrating my wife's birthday? She cried for hours afterwards. She just wanted a little happiness on her special day, a little fun…and it was taken away from her in an embarrassing scene. All because of you, you nosey…"

"Hey now, that's enough," said Ray, raising a hand in a "stop" motion. But Sam didn't stop. Now Muriel was truly frightened, frozen to the spot.

"What's wrong with you, anyway?" Sam went on. "Can't stand the thought of people having fun? Well, don't you worry, lady. Nobody's having fun over here anymore."

Ray held his wife tighter and steered her away from the door. "We're leaving. Okay? That's enough. I'm sorry we bothered you." He hurried Muriel down the steps. She had begun to weep.

"You know what? I might just go over there and help that guy put his lights up just to spite you!" Sam yelled, slamming the door shut.

Once the couple was safely back on the sidewalk, Ray stopped and hugged Muriel tight. "Okay now, sugar plum. It's okay." He patted her back several times. "Now, now. Let's give this up for today and go home."

Muriel quickly pulled her head away from his shoulder and looked into his eyes. She felt her resolve strengthen. She'd lived long enough and seen enough that she wasn't going to let herself be intimidated by that brute. "No. No, no, no. I am not giving up that easily!" She pulled a crumpled tissue out of her purse and dabbed at her eyes. "Let's keep going. There are lots of houses we haven't been to yet."

"Really?" said Ray. "Aren't you tired?"

"Yes, really. I'm not tired, and I'm not letting that man stop me. He's just angry and mean, and he can't see to reason. Imagine, bringing up his dead wife like that. What kind of man would do that?"

Several of the folks farther up the street hadn't even known about the house on the end being decorated, and some even said they'd look forward to seeing it lit up. Although they did manage to convince a handful of people to sign the petition, Muriel's mood grew darker each time she failed to convince a neighbor of its menace to the community.

On the way back down the street, Muriel noticed a Toyota Camry that hadn't been in Mark's driveway there when they'd walked by the first time, and felt a thrill of hope. She marched up to the front door and banged the shiny, scratch-free knocker several times. A colorful autumn wreath hung from a wire above it.

"These folks are sensible. I know they'll see my side of things."

"What? How do you even know these folks? I've never seen you talking to anyone over here. I'm not even sure who lives here," Ray said.

Just then, the door opened and a trim, handsome man of about thirty smiled at Muriel and Ray. He was clean-shaven and wore wire-rimmed spectacles.

"Muriel, honey! What are you doing here? I never see you out and about in the neighborhood! And this must be your handsome hubby!" The man stuck out his hand. "Hi, I'm Mark. And you must be Ray! How nice to meet you!"

Ray took his hand. "Yup. Nice to meet you, too." He seemed puzzled.

"Come on in, come on in," said Mark, opening the door wide and gesturing for them to enter. "I was just getting to my Saturday chores, so it's not exactly spic and span in here, but you're welcome to visit."

"Oh, no, that's okay," said Muriel. "We can't stay. We just wanted to talk to you about that madness going on across the street from us." She pointed toward the Cassidy home.

"Well, come on in. I can't stand here with the door open all day. I wasn't raised in a barn, as my dear old Dad would say."

The Michauds cautiously stepped over the threshold and into an impeccably-kept living room with sunny yellow walls, white woodwork, and a comfy-looking light blue sofa with matching loveseat. A glass-topped coffee table held a bouquet of fresh flowers in a white porcelain vase. Several pricey looking paintings hung on the walls, and a stately antique grandfather clock stood in a vestibule over by the staircase.

"Can I get you folks some tea? I've just made some Magic Cookie Bars as well. They're so good they ought to be outlawed."

Mark took a lingering look across the street before closing the front door. He shook his head and said, "Isn't it just so gaudy? I can't *imagine* what it's going to look like when it's all lit up. Woo-hoo! The circus has come to town!" He spread his arms wide to emphasize the craziness and laughed.

"You can say that again," said Muriel. "You've got to help us stop it." She offered him the clipboard. "We've started a petition."

"A petition? Oh, how quaint! You're just like the villain in a movie, Muriel! Shutting down the festive Christmas display. You bad girl!"

He furrowed his brow and shook a finger in her direction.

Muriel clenched her lips together in a grim line. "Now, look here. That's enough fun. This is serious business. This spectacle is going to cause a lot of trouble for us here on Franklin Street, and we don't need it."

"Oh, don't get your panties in a twist, darling. I hear you. Pass that thing over here and I'll sign it for you." He grabbed the clipboard and examined the petition. "Hmm, doesn't look like you've convinced too many people."

"Well, we haven't been at it very long," said Ray.

"And we're going all over the neighborhood, don't you worry. There are enough sensible people around here who will see eye-to-eye with me. I'm taking this petition to the next Selectmen's meeting and we're going to shut him down."

Mark took the pen, scribbled his name and address, and handed the petition back to Ray. "Well, good luck! Are you sure I can't get you some tea and a goodie?"

She ignored the offer and stood on her tiptoes, attempting to look past Mark into the back rooms of the house. "Is…is, uh, your roommate home? Do you think he'd like to sign it?"

Ray put his hand on Muriel's arm. "Hon," he whispered. "We ought to get going."

Mark shook his head. "Oh no, sweetie, Tommy's not here. He's out shopping. But I'll run it by him when he gets home. If he's interested, I'm sure he'll take a jog up to your house. That okay?"

"That's just fine," said Ray. "We've taken up enough of your time. We still have quite a few streets to cover."

Mark smiled. "Okay, then. I guess I'll just have to eat them all myself." He patted his flat tummy. "By the way, Muriel, you are looking quite chipper today. You haven't seemed like yourself at all the last few times we've bumped into one another. I was worried about you. But I guess having a mission is just the thing to pump a little life into you, huh? Why, I swear you've even got a rosy glow!" He pretended to give her cheeks an affectionate pinch.

Muriel smiled, giggling girlishly, and drew away. "Oh, now, you stop that, silly. You're making an old lady blush."

Mark led the couple to the front door. "Old is just a state of mind, sweetheart. You take care of yourself, now. Don't go getting all worked up over this stuff."

"Okay," said Muriel, "But you make sure to ask your roommate to come up and sign the petition when he gets home. We need all the support we can get on this."

"Thank you, thanks for your time," said Ray, reaching out to shake Mark's hand. "Nice to meet you."

Mark started to close the door. "Oh, same here. Don't be a stranger, now, Ray!" he said, as the door clicked shut.

"Now, how the heck do you know that guy?" Ray said. "I've never even seen him and he lives just a few houses up from us."

"Well, if you took care of the bills, you'd know him. He works down at Kennebec Valley Bank and Trust. Every time I see him, he acts like we're old pals. You know, he's one of those friendly types." She shrugged her shoulders and laughed.

Ray stopped suddenly. "Wait a second," he said. "Is he the one giving you all this gossip about the neighbors?"

This was awkward. The cat was shooting out of the bag. "What are you talking about?"

"You know darned well what I'm talking about. You keep gossip-ing about the neighbors, and when I ask how you know that stuff, you say you have your *sources*. Is that guy your *sources*?"

Muriel let out a quick, sharp laugh and continued to walk. She enjoyed her little, gossipy relationship with Mark, but she knew her husband wouldn't approve, so she would deny, deny, deny. "Don't be ridiculous. I hardly know him. Now, let's get going. We have a lot of work to do today."

She strutted up the street with a renewed vigor in her step. Mark's fun personality always made her feel that way.

The pair gathered only twenty-one signatures that day, but Muriel was undeterred. The next day at coffee hour, right after the ten o'clock service at St. Francis, she managed to cajole another nineteen signatures from people who owed her a favor from one time or another.

On Sunday evening, she had a long phone conversation with Paula and explained the whole situation. She convinced her daughter to bring the petition to the hardware store and talk her employees into signing it. By Wednesday, every one of the thirty-two employees of Kennebec City Hardware had signed it—even the stock boy who lived in Winslow, the next town over. He used his aunt and uncle's Kennebec City address.

Next, the petition went to Karen, who said, "Only for you, Mémère." Karen promised to take it to her Mothers' Group when they met for a Wednesday playdate, and to her book club at the library that evening.

Muriel went to pick up the petition from Karen late Thursday morning, making sure to time her visit just right so she'd catch Philip. He usually came home for lunch from his job at Larochelle & Gilroy, Certified Public Accountants. He took the petition back to work with him; he always *was* such a good grandson-in-law.

First thing Saturday morning, Muriel was at Kennebec City Savings and Loan to deposit Ray's social security check. She made sure to get into the teller line for her friend Mark.

"You've been a busy bee, Miss Muriel," he said, his gleaming smile nearly blinding her as she stepped up to the desk. "Your petition seems to be going all over town!"

She smiled. "And how do you know about that?"

"Well," said Mark, leaning in, "I just happen to play racquetball after work on Friday evenings with Jimmy Gilroy...you know, of Larochelle & Gilroy—where your granddaughter's husband works?"

"Mm hmm?"

"And he told me that Philip talked all the partners into signing your petition, even though Heather Larochelle said she doubted anything would come of it. She actually asked if you were some kind of Scrooge."

"Well," Muriel huffed, "that's rude!"

Mark waved his hand in a "no worries" gesture, and went on talking at a clip. "Philip moved on to the office staff, where he wrangled more signatures. And then, after dinner, he and your grand-daughter walked around their neighborhood with their kid and asked their friends to sign. They called it "The Petition to Keep Grand-Mémère Happy! Most people signed it, but some of them said they were going to put up some lights this year because they felt sorry for your neighbor." Mark looked at Muriel for a beat, his eyes wide. "I'm telling you, girl, you've really started something in this town. I love it!"

She put a hand up to her cheek, flabbergasted. "I'm not the one that started anything! That man across the street is the one who started the trouble!"

Mark smiled. "Well, apparently he didn't know what he was getting into when he ticked off Muriel Michaud!"

Darned right, thought Muriel. News travelled fast in Kennebec City, and she didn't care how she got the signatures, as long as she got them. Deep down though, she felt a pang of sadness after hearing this story, and she wasn't quite sure why.

One week after starting out, Muriel had exactly one-hundred-and-one signatures on her petition. She and Ray took Karen, Philip, and Emma out for lunch and ice cream at Friendly's to celebrate, reveling in the company of their family as they celebrated their victory. She just knew things were going to turn out okay.

The conversation was lively. They talked about Emma's preschool accomplishments and told her a story about the first Thanksgiving. Muriel made a colorful turkey by tracing Emma's hand with the restaurant's crayons. "Do you think it's too early to take her down to Plimoth Plantation, Mémère?" Karen asked.

"Oh, you have a little while left before she understands about that. Maybe once she starts school. We took your mom and your Aunt and Uncle down there when they were in elementary school, and they loved it."

"Well, I hope the two of you will go with us when she's old enough. That would be fun!"

Muriel smiled. "God willing, dear, God willing."

The cheeseburger baskets and fish fries were scarfed up. Just as the sundaes arrived, Emma turned her big eyes to Muriel and said, completely out of the blue, "Grand-Mémère? Why don't you like Christmas?"

Chapter 19

Saturday afternoon was the designated time for mega-tree construction at 40 Franklin Street, and Don was overseeing the project put together by Andy Nadeau and Scott Anderson. Mega-trees were majestic wire-frame trees festooned with twinkling lights that were essential elements of most over-the-top Christmas displays. Don had loved those trees ever since he'd seen a video of a house with four of them flashing at once. Don's mega-tree was 25-feet tall and towered over all other elements of the display—except for Santa up on the roof, of course.

He had already created the base with PVC pipe and concrete the week earlier, and this morning, Andy and Scott had made good progress with the rest of the construction. They were threading the light strands through the top piece when Scott said, "So, Mr. Cassidy, I was doing some research online about how we could, you know that thing we talked about? How we could synchronize your lights to music. It would be so cool."

"Scott, I told you, maybe next year. This year, it's all I can do just to get everything up and running," said Don. "And I certainly don't need to do anything more to aggravate Mrs. Humbug over there." He felt a knot begin to clench in his stomach.

"You must know about the petition, huh?"

"Oh, don't get me started about that, I'm having a good day. Yeah, I heard about it."

Andy chimed in. "She actually asked me to sign it. Like she hasn't seen me over here helping."

Andy's gaze suddenly darted to the side, and Don noticed the blonde kid from up the street standing on the sidewalk, talking to himself. He looked around but didn't see the mom anywhere in sight. *Uh-oh.*

"Hi Zack! Whatcha up to?" Andy said. "This is cool, huh?" He rose from his crouch and walked over to where Zack stood, stopping about a yard away. "What's that, buddy?"

"Blue, green, orange, red, white, yellow," said Zack. He fiddled with his scarf and rocked from side-to-side as he spoke.

Don was relieved that at least the kid wasn't screaming this time. "He's been here before," he said quietly. "I've asked him if he wants to help, but his Mom put the kibosh on that."

"Blue, green, orange, red, white, yellow," Zack repeated, a little louder this time. The red scarf was flapping like a flag in a strong wind.

Don approached the boy slowly. He didn't want another meltdown like last time. "I know," he said. "You told me a couple of weeks ago." What nobody knew was that Don had already spent a boatload of extra time resetting the lights he'd already strung up so that they were in Zack's preferred pattern. The sequence was burned into his brain, and he just couldn't set them up without fixing them after the boy's outburst. He hadn't yet done the remaining lights, though. "Does your Mom know you're here?"

"She says it's okay for me to watch. She says don't bug you. Bug— not like squishy bugs—not *bother* you." Zack blinked several times and looked down at the sidewalk. Then he mumbled something that sounded like, "I could fix your lights."

"If you want to help, you wouldn't be bugging us, at all. The more the merrier! Especially at Christmas!"

Andy jumped in. "Tell you what. Let's take a walk down to your house and I'll talk to your Mom. Maybe she'll say it's okay if I tell her that I'm here. Sound good?"

Before Zack could respond, the Michauds' Dodge came up the street and turned into their driveway. "Well, speak of the devil," Don said.

After lunch, Muriel and Ray ran a couple of errands and then headed home. She was feeling relieved, but she wouldn't say she was happy. Listening to some of her neighbors' reactions had niggled the back of her brain and made her wonder—just a little—if she was in the wrong about the display. And Emma's question at lunch, *that* had completely thrown her. Of course a child couldn't possibly understand such things. On the one hand, her good sense prevailed and she knew that she was in the right. After all, no matter what anyone else thought, this display was going to cause nothing but problems; if she was the only one who could see that, then she had to be the voice of reason. She had to follow through on what she had started. No, that wasn't right. She had to follow through on what that *man* across the street had started. This was all his fault, not hers. On the other hand, she didn't want Emma thinking she was a mean old Grinch. She didn't fancy the community thinking that, either.

Such were her mixed emotions as Ray drove toward home. When her cell phone rang, she almost didn't answer it because she was feeling so troubled, but when she pulled it out of her purse and saw that it was Paula, she accepted the call.

"Hello, Paula! We just had a lovely lunch with Karen, and Philip, and Emma…"

"That's good, Mom. Did Karen tell you about the trip?"

"Trip? What trip? She didn't say anything about a trip."

"Ugh. She was supposed to tell you. Philip's family has invited us to Italy with them for the holidays."

Muriel was stunned. *Italy! Our dream trip! How wonderful!* She and Ray had always dreamed of visiting Rome. The Coliseum, the Trevi Fountain, things she'd only read about or seen in movies. This would solve all her problems. She might not even have to be here to experience the chaos in the neighborhood during Christmas week. "Invited us?" she said. "Oh my goodness, this is such short notice, and I'm not even sure our passports are in order."

"Mom…"

"I don't even know if I can find your father's. Let's see, the last time I saw it…"

Ray made the turn onto Franklin Street.

"Mom, listen to me."

"It takes a while to renew a passport and let's see, when was that last trip to Montreal? I'm not sure if it was five years ago, or…"

"Mom! Please listen! This trip is for Philip's family. Karen and Emma…and they've also invited us, because, you know, we're the other grandparents. Ed and I are paying for our own plane tickets… but…I'm sorry, Mom…you and Dad aren't invited. They don't really know you." She went on, but Muriel didn't hear the rest.

Her concentration was kidnapped by the action going on at number 40. Paula's words became meaningless sounds. "Oh, my word!" Muriel shouted into the phone.

"Mom? I knew this might upset you, and I…"

"I'm sorry, Paula. I have to hang up now," said Muriel, and she clicked off the phone and threw it into her purse.

Emma's question at lunch had been bad enough, and this short conversation with her daughter had upset her even more, but when she saw what was going on across the street, her stress bubbled up into a volcano of bile in her stomach. She began to shake. "What are they doing?" she asked Ray, her voice rising. "Every day there are more and more people out there!"

Ray pulled the car into the driveway and put his hand on his wife's arm. "Calm down, sugar plum," he said. "It doesn't matter what they're doing. You have your petition. You're going to take care of it."

Muriel whipped her head around and glared at her husband. Hot tears flowed from her eyes and she knew that the mascara she'd put on for the lunch date must be running. "He's turning the whole neighborhood against us, that's what he's doing. Almost none of them agree with me as it is, and if I go through with the petition I'm going to look like an evil old woman, just like Mark said. I'm going to be known as the witch who ruined Christmas. Even our great-granddaughter thinks so!"

"No, no, no…don't be silly."

"Silly? You think I'm being silly? Now you're turning against me, too? Well, I've had it with this stuff!" Her mood had reached fever pitch. She'd never felt such intense anger in her life; she knew now what it meant to "see red." All her good judgment had long since left her, and she felt electric-shock impulses driving her to *do* something. 'Nervous breakdowns' were what they called such things when she was younger. A complete loss of control and faculties. She knew what was going on, but she was powerless to stop her actions. She wrenched the car door open and stepped out onto the driveway, waving the manila envelope containing the petition.

"How about this, Mr. Christmas-man? We're going to shut you down," she yelled.

"Muriel! Stop it!" Ray said, as he stumbled out of the car. He took his wife's arm, attempting to guide her toward the door.

She shook her arm out of Ray's gentle grip and continued to glare across the street. "He's got at least ten Santas out there. Ten! Why does he need so *many?*"

"I don't know, hon. I don't know. Let's go in the house, now."

Muriel pretended she hadn't heard him. She continued in a voice loud enough to be heard across the street. "Well, ten Santas, fifteen snowmen, nine million lights…it doesn't matter because all of it is going right back into that hideous new storage area. I'm dropping this petition off with Roger Girard first thing Monday morning. We'll be at the Selectmen's meeting next week, and then you are done, Mister Christmas-man. Then everyone in the neighborhood can have a peaceful Christmas, the way it should be." She actually began to sing, "It's the most wonderful time of the year," as she twirled around and sashayed up the steps and into the house.

Chapter 20

Zack pushed open the side door of his house and burst into the kitchen, Andy right behind him. "Ma! Ma? Maaa-MA!" he yelled. "Say it's okay, Ma!"

Angie was sitting with her laptop at the kitchen table, working on her bills. She stood and raised her hands in a "calm down" motion. "Zack, Zack, quiet down. I'm right here. I can hear you," she said quietly. Then it hit her that he was wearing his winter coat, hat, and scarf, and she spoke a bit more sternly. "What the heck is going on? You've been outside? I thought you were watching your cartoons in your room. You know you're not supposed to go out without telling me." She shot a puzzled look at Andy. "Hi, Andy. What's this all about?"

Zack began to speak so rapidly that he was barely understandable. Andy said, "Why don't you let me handle this, kiddo? Like we talked about?" Zack closed his mouth and stood completely still, save for his fingers fiddling with the fringe of his scarf.

"Ange, I've been helping the guy on the other side of us, Don Cassidy, put up his Christmas display and it seems Zack is interested in helping, too. He came over and stood on the sidewalk to watch. I've never seen him act so interested in anything, so I told him I'd come over and ask if it's okay, as long as I'm over there to supervise."

"Oh, I see," she laughed. "Just two big kids aiding and abetting each other, are you now?" She had always appreciated the interest Andy Nadeau had shown her son. Thank God for the Nadeaus. They were the only friends she had in the neighborhood.

She turned serious as she looked at her son. "Well, first of all, Zack, I'm not very happy about you going out of the house without telling me. It's not okay. What do you have to say about that?"

Zack looked at the floor, and mumbled, "I'm sorry."

"Excuse me? I can't hear you when you look down at the floor. Would you raise your head, please, if you have something to say?"

Zack quickly said, "I'm sorry."

"That's better. Don't do it again." Then, looking up at Andy, she said, "Zack has been over there before, and he had a little meltdown. I'm not so sure this is a good idea, Andy. And besides, do you think it's safe? That guy's got all kinds of wires and things all over the lawn."

"Angie, I swear, I'll watch over him. I've been with him enough to know what to do. He really wants to help. It'd be good for him, don't you think?"

"Yeah. Good for me," said Zack. "Good. For. Me!"

Angie sat there for a minute, considering. "I don't know." Finally she said, "He really needs supervision. Do you promise you'll keep a close eye on him and come get me if anything goes wrong?"

Andy held up three fingers and pronounced, "Scout's honor, Ma'am."

"Okay then," Angie said. "But you need to bring him back by six-thirty for dinner. And you be careful, Zack. Do everything exactly the way you're told, okay?" She smiled and looked him straight in the eye. "I'm glad you're going to help."

"Yesss!" Zack said. "Let's go." With that he wheeled around and was out the door, Andy on his heels.

Chapter 21

The Saturday lunch meeting at work had been pointless; Sam
Anderson could barely contribute because he was so distracted. All
week, he'd been thinking about the episode with that battle-axe from
across the street. God only knew how he'd kept from reaching out
and wringing her scrawny neck. He couldn't believe that, after calling
the police on his family's celebrations—twice—she had the audacity
to ask his help in putting the damper on someone else's fun. But
there was more to it than that.

Deep down, something else had been eating away at him since
she came to his door, and this afternoon he finally figured out what
it was. Thinking about the times she'd called the cops reminded him
how much Stephanie had loved celebrations. Big and small, from
birthdays to the kids losing a tooth, she was always up for making
an ordinary day monumental. She had loved Christmas most of all.
So much, in fact, that when their older son had finally reached an age
when he questioned Santa, she looked at him seriously and said, "Bri,
do you want to live in a world where there's no Santa Claus?" Brian
had immediately answered, "No." "Okay then," she'd replied. "'Nuff
said." And that was the end of that.

They'd never told either of their boys Santa wasn't real; to Stephanie's mind, just because you never saw him, didn't mean he didn't exist. She was all about the magic. Living it, and making it real for everyone else. God, how he missed her. During this week, it had been slowly dawning on him, though, that he'd done nothing to keep her memory alive for himself and his boys. His recent conversation with Scott came back to him with a gut-punch; a sort of delayed reaction. Now, he was starting to see the light. He'd been foolishly wallowing in his misery. He was giving no thought to all the promises he'd made to his wife about family traditions, nor doing his best to keep them going without her.

As soon as he got home, he went upstairs to see if Scott was in his room and, not finding him there, checked his phone to see if there was a text. Nothing. He went back downstairs to look around, in case Scott had left a good old-fashioned note. On his way down, he happened to glance through the side window on the landing, and saw Scott over at the neighbor's house, helping with the Christmas display. Sam froze there at the window, watching his son smiling and talking to the blonde kid from up the street. He hadn't seen Scott smile like that in ages, and it appeared that he was genuinely happy to see the kid. *God, he looks just like his Mom*, Sam thought. *And look at him. He's the one keeping Stephanie's traditions alive.*

Sam watched for a few more minutes until he was distracted by the Michauds pulling into their driveway. He looked over that way and saw Muriel get out of the car, waving a manila envelope around and shouting something. Poor Ray was trying to hold her back, but she was yelling at him, too. The commotion was so loud, Sam could hear it through the closed window. Then, to his astonishment, she whirled around and began to sing as she headed into the house.

Good God. It must be the petition. She must have somehow gotten the signatures she needed, and now she was actually gloating.

Sam didn't usually believe in signs, but if there ever was one, this was it. He could almost hear Stephanie—not whispering—but practically shouting in his ear to get his butt over there and help that guy put up his Christmas decorations. He wasn't really doing it to spite the old lady—although he wouldn't mind if it burned her butt—he was doing it for his boy, and for their future. He hurried to the hall closet and grabbed his parka and gloves, then threw open the kitchen door and headed out and across the driveway.

Scott couldn't believe what he was hearing. Mrs. Michaud was singing. Loud and clear, in a voice that sounded like five cats caught in a rain barrel, she was singing "The Most Wonderful Time of the Year," and she was doing a kind of little dance in her driveway. She looked like she was losing her mind. *This is like something out of one of those soap operas Mom used to love.* He looked at Mr. Cassidy, whose face was as red as the sleigh he was decorating. He appeared frozen, and Scott had the momentary image of him standing out there all winter with his—what did he call those things? Oh yeah, his blow molds. Just standing out there with his rosy cheeks, decorating the lawn like old Santa and his elves.

As if all that wasn't surreal enough, behind Mr. Cassidy, he could now see his father striding across the lawn. Scott's jaw, already hanging open, nearly dropped to the ground. He sprang into action, scrambled past Mr. Cassidy, and ran up to his father to see what was going on. If his dad was wasted he had to stop him before he made a fool of himself and embarrassed him, too. He caught him just at the edge of the lawn, out of earshot of Mr. Cassidy, and stood in his way. "Dad, what are you doing? What do you need?"

Sam put an arm around his son's shoulder. "It's okay, Scotty. I know what you're thinking, but don't worry, I haven't had a drop. I've just decided I wanted to help, that's all. I saw you over here, and

I thought maybe I'd come over and lend a hand, too." He looked at Scott with eyes that were clear and bright. There was no smell of alcohol on his breath.

Scott couldn't believe it. His father was sober. "Really? You want to help?" It seemed too good to be true.

His father smiled. There were a lot more wrinkles around his eyes than there used to be, Scott thought, and dark circles under them, too. His voice was gentle, though; a tone Scott hadn't heard in a long time. "Yes, Scotty, I really do. I think it's what your mother would want. I know I've been a jerk this past year and I've let you down; I'm so sorry. I've had a really hard time dealing with Mom's death and I guess…well, I guess I *haven't* really been dealing with it. But I think your Mom is sending me a sign that it's time to do something good for a change. Maybe spread a little cheer. Please let me help. I think it's what she would have done, don't you?"

At first Scott couldn't say a thing; he was so blown away that he was at a loss for words. He couldn't believe that this was the real thing. All he could manage was a mumbled, "Yeah." An image of his mom putting up her little lighted Christmas village popped into his head and the words came tumbling out of him. "Yeah, Mom would have loved this."

His dad seemed sincere, and at least wanted to try. Whether he could follow through or not remained to be seen, but for now there was only one thing to do. "Come on, and I'll show you what we've been doing." He took his father's arm and led him over to the sleigh, where Don was standing. Scott looked across the street to see that Mr. and Mrs. Michaud had gone into the house, but Mr. Cassidy was still frozen in place. "Mr. Cassidy? Mr. Cassidy, I want you to meet my dad."

Mr. Cassidy did a double-take, as if coming out of a trance. "Oh, hey. How are you?" he asked, halfheartedly. The color had receded from his cheeks and he was now a sickly shade of white.

"I'm good, I'm good," said Sam, reaching out to shake his neighbor's hand. "Looks like you've already met our resident wicked witch." He raised his eyebrows and nodded toward the house across the street.

"Mr. Cassidy, are you okay? You don't look so hot," said Scott.

Before Don could say a word, Andy and Zack came bounding around the corner. "Hey guys," said Andy. "Zack's Mom said he could help." He noticed Scott's dad, and for just a second he seemed confused, as if he was wondering who this was. Then recognition seemed to blossom.

"Hey. What's up?"

"I'm here to help. Sign me up. What can I do?"

"I can help I can help I can help!" said Zack. "I can help with the lights. Make a pattern!" He bopped up and down on his heels.

Don took a deep breath. "O-kay," he said, and seemed to gather himself together. He turned to Zack and smiled broadly. "Well, as you can see, young man, I'm getting ready to string some lights around the sleigh." He pointed to some strands of lights that were stretched out on the lawn. How about you check and make sure all of them go in a pattern? I'll get the box of spares from the garage, and you can change any ones that need to be changed, alright?"

"Alright!" Zack exclaimed, and clapped his mittened hands together several times, a thousand-watt smile on his face.

Chapter 22

Muriel was still singing to herself as she hung her coat in the hall closet. "It's the most wonderful time…"

Ray leaned against the doorway and waited for her to close the closet door. "What has gotten into you? We need to talk."

"Talk about what?"

"I think you know what. Come on, sit down." He gestured toward the sofa. "I want to know what's going on with you. That woman out there in the yard…that little show you just put on…that's not you. I'm beginning to get seriously worried by your behavior, and I don't want you to avoid the subject anymore."

Muriel mustered up her most defiant look. She tried to gather her resolve again, but she couldn't do it. Instead, she burst into tears. "I don't want to talk. I can't explain why I did that. I'm just so overwhelmed and no one understands, not even you." She sat down in an armchair and continued to sob. She felt like she was never going to stop.

After a while, Ray asked, "Should I call the doctor?"

This suggestion alarmed her. She didn't want anyone else involved. She knew she'd gone over the edge, and had to try to fix this with Ray as soon as possible. She wiped the tears away and took a few deep breaths. "No, no," she said urgently. "I'm fine. I'm okay now. I'm really okay. Please don't call anybody."

Her husband shook his head. "You are not okay. What I just saw out there, well, if I didn't know you better..."

Muriel interrupted, "Well, there's nothing to worry about. I was feeling a little down for a while, but everything is fine. Really, now I've got that out of my system, I'm alright."

Ray sighed. "Come on," he said, softly, patting the sofa cushion next to him. "Come over here and sit with me for a few minutes."

She walked over briskly and sat down, grasping the envelope in her lap. "Okay," she said, in a shaky voice. "I'm sitting down. Are you happy now?"

He pried the envelope out of her hands and wrapped her in a tight hug.

"Look. This has gotten out of hand. I know you're upset about the display, but your behavior lately...well, it doesn't seem like my Muriel. I'm worried, that's all. Have you been feeling ill? Maybe you need to talk to Dr. Dalton."

Muriel sat silently for half a minute, looking down at their clasped hands. Ray didn't push it, but she knew he was not going to let this go. Finally, she decided to confess. "I've already talked with Dr. Dalton. I saw her a couple of months ago because I hadn't been feeling well. We had a long talk, and she gave me a prescription."

Ray pulled back in surprise, still holding his wife's hand. "What? You didn't tell me. She gave you medicine? What for? What's wrong? Why didn't you tell me?"

"I didn't want to tell you. There's nothing really wrong with me. I ripped up the prescription and threw it away. It's just foolishness. I'm fine."

"Well, now I'm *really* worried," Ray said, staring at her with wide eyes. "Muriel, tell me what on earth is going on!"

Chapter 23

The twinkle in Zack's eyes was one of the most beautiful sights Don had ever seen. So much so that they pushed aside thoughts of Muriel Michaud, even though she sashayed up through the back of his mind.

The afternoon flew by; everyone working on their tasks and enjoying each other's company. Sam and Scott went down to the hardware store and bought two dozen more packages of replacement lights. Esmerelda made an appearance with the twins, bringing over a store-bought banana bread and small paper plates. The twins played their part, bringing the plates around to the guys, and happily getting schooled in the jobs each was doing.

It seemed that hardly any time at all had passed before the sun was sinking down behind the trees. Don stood back in the middle of the street and admired his transformed house; Maggie and Jenny came driving up in the Woodie, back from the pre-Thanksgiving sales in town. Of course he wouldn't be switching the lights on yet, but it was still a glorious sight.

The band of merry snowmen was gathered on the porch between two life-sized nutcrackers he'd picked up at Christmas Expo in Gatlinburg a few years back. Zack and Andy had wound lights through the posts and railings of the porch, every single light taking its proper place in the pattern. The festive Victorian carolers were singing away, the woman decked out in her finest blue gown and the gentleman wearing a glossy top hat, standing by their lamp-post near the front door. Not far away stood the life-sized sleigh, festooned with lights, waiting for Santa to arrive.

Jesus and His family were in their stable, placed a respectful distance from the sleigh on the front lawn. They were flanked by the Three Kings, a camel, two shepherds, a cow, three sheep, and a donkey. Ten glorious angels were arranged on poles behind the stable; a row of four on the bottom, then three more, two, and then the most elaborate angel on the top. To the left of the stable were ten choir boys, their mouths opened in a hymn of praise. To the right stood the Little Drummer Boy, frozen as he offered his rhythmic gift to the Baby Jesus.

There was still the driveway, where pairs of four-foot toy soldiers would guard the entrance from either side. Lining the driveway behind them, and branching up the walkway to the front porch, would be a border of bright candy canes. They would lead to the steps of the porch, where Don planned to put a Teddy Bear, a Gingerbread couple, and one of his favorite Santa Claus blow molds— the one with the list of good girls and boys.

That was only one of the Santa Claus figures—others would be placed all around the house, as well. There was one placed amongst the elves and their gaily wrapped presents at the very front of the lawn, soon to be joined by five brightly-lit spiral trees. And then there were the inflatables to be placed on the lawn on either side of the house. In spite of all the progress they'd made today, Don still had his work cut out for him. There were only twelve days until Thanksgiving and he still had to get Santa and the reindeer up on the roof.

"It's going to be amazing," whispered Maggie, who'd snuck up beside him. "But what's even more amazing is how you got all these people to help you!" She took Don's hand. Just as she did so, Don noticed Jenny was standing over by the mega-tree with Scott, who was introducing her to his dad. Flo the Real Estate Pro had told them about Mrs. Anderson's death. He had seemed like a man drowning in grief. Now here he was, with his son, looking happy. Maggie turned her head to see what he was watching. She smiled. "You're a miracle worker."

"Not really," said Don. "I wish Jenny still wanted to work on it with me. I was hoping she might get interested again, especially with Scott helping. Although, now that I think of it, I guess he isn't really her type. She doesn't really go for the nerds, does she?"

Maggie laughed and shook her head. "Regardless of him being a nerd—and that's a little harsh—I can't believe you thought she'd want to work on the display because there's a boy involved. Honey, you don't know your daughter. She's not going to do anything she's not interested in, boy or no boy."

"Well, then maybe she'd want to work on it just to be with her dear old dad."

Maggie smiled and put an arm around her husband's shoulders, giving him a light squeeze. "Don't worry, I'm sure she'll help me decorate the inside. That's her contribution." She looked around at the helpers. "Let's all celebrate the day's hard work by going out for pizza!" she shouted.

Everyone cheered. Scott and Sam went home to wash up, promising to meet them at Sergeant Pepperoni's on Upper Main Street. "I'm gonna bring Zack home and see if I can talk his Mom into coming with him. I think Angie needs to be a part of this," said Andy.

"Great," said Don. "As I always say, the more the merrier!" *Wish I could talk Mr. and Mrs. Michaud into joining the gang,* he thought. *Now that would be a real miracle.*

"*Mama!*" yelled Zack, despite of the fact that Angie was right there slapping burger patties together when he and Andy walked through the kitchen door. The two guys brought twin blasts of cold air and happiness into her kitchen. Zack smiled the toothy grin that always made her day, and lowered his voice a bit. "Oh, hi, Mama," he said. His fingers were doing their dance of joy.

"Hi Ange," said Andy.

"Well, look at you two, all rosy-cheeked. Did you have fun?"

"Yes I had fun," Zack said. "Now we go for pizza! You have to come!" His arms hung by his side, but his fingers were still wiggling.

"Yeah, we're all going for pizza and we thought maybe you'd like to join us," Andy said. "You guys can come with us in the van."

"Pizza? But I've just started making dinner...we're having cheeseburgers, your favorite."

"I know, but come on, Mama. Everybody's going to Sergeant Pepperoni's!" said Zack, and did a little hop in his Larry Mouse boots. "We can have cheeseburgers tomorrow!"

"Who is going? Just us and Esmerelda and the boys?"

Andy stuck his hands in his pockets and leaned against the wall. "Esme's gonna stay home. I'm taking the boys so she can have a little quiet time with Luisa."

Then Zack drew a deep breath and spoke enthusiastically, "It's them and Mr. Cassidy and Mrs. Cassidy and Jenny and Scott and his dad. Everybody who was putting up the decorations."

"I don't know. I've already started..." she said, gesturing toward the burger fixings on the counter. Then she stopped as what her son said dawned on her. "Wait a minute. Did you say Scott and his dad? You mean Mr. Anderson?"

"*Yes*. He came over and helped. He helped put up the tree. He helped Scott. They're meeting us for *pizza*," said Zack.

"Well, then, we'd better get going. I can't pass up pizza!" said Angie, and she went down the hall to get her coat and bag, smiling to herself. There was even a bit of a spring in her step.

Chapter 24

Muriel absolutely refused to talk to Ray about what was bothering her, or give him any further details about her visits to the doctor. Instead, she fled into the kitchen and began organizing the cupboards that she'd already organized a few days earlier. Meanwhile, her husband settled in the living room to watch a football game. After a while, Muriel brought him a bowl of cheese crackers and a glass of ginger ale to enjoy with his sports. Then she sat down and read some more of her book, although she had to read the same two pages about five times before she could concentrate on what was happening in the story. Around four, she started putting together a shepherd's pie for supper.

Over the meal, she asked about the game, even though she'd never cared for football. Basketball was much more interesting; although in her opinion, the Celtics had never regained their luster since the days of Larry Bird. Ray didn't say much in response, and Muriel was starting to feel guilty about not opening up to him. Finally, after she cleared the dishes, she made herself a cup of tea and sat back down at the table, where he was still sitting in silence, staring off into space.

"Look, I know I went a little overboard earlier, but I've just been feeling anxious about this Christmas light foolishness. I'm better now. I'd just like to go upstairs and turn in, okay? I'm very tired and I want to read for a while. This new Jan Karon book has really grabbed me."

Just then, the cuckoo clock called out seven o'clock. The little band of musicians picked up their instruments and played their festive tune. Ray patted his wife's hand. "All right, sugar plum. I wish you'd tell me what the doctor said, but I'm not going to push it anymore."

Muriel rose and adjusted her skirt, looking down at him. "Thank you. I'm alright. You'll see. Once we get this all straightened out at the meeting next week, everything will be back to normal." She went upstairs and readied herself for bed. Ray had not turned in by the time she fell asleep.

Upon arriving at the pizza place with Zack and the Nadeaus, Angie looked for the Franklin Street group and found them nearly right away. It was easy to spot Sam Anderson; he stood out like a pinup in a magazine. "Get a grip," she mumbled to herself, "You're thinking like a schoolgirl, don't you start acting like one!"

In any case, it was Mr. and Mrs. Cassidy she really wanted to talk to first, and she managed to get through the crowd and over to them before everyone sat down.

"Hello," she said, "Mr. and Mrs. Cassidy, I don't know if you remember me, but I'm Angie, Zack's mom. I just wanted to apologize to you for my behavior at your house a couple of weeks ago. You know, when Zack had his meltdown over the lights? You were so kind to him, and I was just rude. I'm sorry."

Mrs. Cassidy looked surprised, but then she reached out and put her hand on Angie's shoulder. "First, you don't need to apologize. It was a stressful situation for you, and we completely understood.

And second, please call us by our first names. I'm Maggie, and this is Don."

Don nodded his head. "Yeah, no apology necessary. We love Zack, and we're happy you're letting him help out. You know, Maggie has a Masters in Special Education, and she's really great with kids."

This sounded vaguely familiar to Angie, as though perhaps they'd said this to her on the day they first met, but she was so frazzled that day, it had all gone in one ear and out the other. She was embarrassed.

Maggie invited Angie to sit next to her, and the three of them took their places at the long table. "We moved here too late in the year for me to get a full-time teaching position, so for now, I'm just subbing," Maggie said. "The good news is, that means I'm available if you ever need care for Zack, after school or on snow days. Do you have a full-time job? In addition to caring for Zack, I mean."

"Oh yes, I couldn't make it without it. I'm a dental hygienist." From there, the conversation led to Zack and his unique personality and needs; Maggie knew all the jargon and was familiar with the skills training Angie had studied, as well as the calming techniques she had recently been trying out with her son.

It felt great to meet someone who understood what their life was like. She felt like a new friendship was being forged right then and there. The million-dollar bonus was that Maggie was willing and capable of helping with Zack if she ever needed it.

"Okay if I sit here? Oh, hello! I don't believe we've officially met," said Sam Anderson, as he sat down next to Maggie.

It was after ten when Angie finally had Zack settled in bed and she had a chance to sit down and think about the evening. She was so happy to have discovered Maggie Cassidy that she hadn't even noticed at first when Sam Anderson approached the table. She'd looked over, and suddenly he was there. He introduced himself to her as though he'd never seen her, and he was so pleasant, talking with everyone and even laughing a little, like a changed man. Angie hadn't seen him this animated since...well, since before his wife passed away. It was as though he'd somehow turned a corner. She was heartened that he showed an interest in Zack and even asked for some flyers for the Autism Walk to post at the University. She'd been delighted to see a sparkle in his green eyes.

Now, performing her nightly hair-brushing ritual in front of the vanity, she looked up and noticed a sparkle in her own eyes, too. "There's something I don't see every day," she said to herself. Then she smiled even wider.

Chapter 25

After a night of fitful sleep, Don Cassidy awoke on Thursday morning with an acidy ache in his stomach. The past five days had gone by in a flash as he worked furiously to try to get most of the display up before the Selectmen's meeting.

Tonight, Muriel Michaud would be presenting her case for shutting down his display. Maggie and Jenny were planning to attend, but there was no way he would set foot through that door. It wasn't that he was weak; he just couldn't bear the thought of having to explain himself to a bunch of strangers. Besides, he still had to get Santa Claus and the reindeer up on the roof, something he'd never done in Florida. That's all that was left to accomplish, and then he would be all set—a week ahead of schedule.

Andy Nadeau had promised to help him after supper. It would be dark by then, but Don had three spotlights, and with the streetlamps, there would be plenty of light. He'd spend today attaching Santa and the reindeer to the pallets that they would hoist up to the roof with the cherry picker. He'd had some trouble figuring out how to position the blow molds on a peaked roof, but his friend Larry from North Carolina had told him how to attach "legs" to the pallets that would hold them steady. To keep the whole thing from blowing off during a Maine snowstorm, Andy and Don would haul fifty-pound sandbags up, and use bungee cords to attach Santa's sleigh to the chimney. The little boy in him got excited just thinking about what it would look like up there. He couldn't wait to hear the "oohs" and "aahs" as children came to see his house.

Don went to the bedroom window and lifted the blinds. The sky was overcast; it didn't seem cold enough to snow, and he sure hoped it wasn't going to rain. Maggie had gotten a call to sub at the high school, and she and Jenny had already left for the day. He dressed in brown corduroy pants and a red *Planet Christmas* sweatshirt, and went downstairs to pick up the newspaper on the porch. As he bent down to pick up the *Kennebec City Journal*, he saw the headline just under the fold on the front page:

SELECTMEN WILL DECIDE FATE OF
EXTREME CHRISTMAS DISPLAY
By Deborah Noack

He went inside, poured a cup of coffee from the pot Maggie had made that morning, and took it to the dining room. Frowning, he sat at the table and read the article:

> *Kennebec City Selectmen will have more on their minds tonight than the usual business of running the city. Listed on the agenda is a petition, circulated by long-time residents Raymond and Muriel Michaud of Franklin Street, which asks the city to put a stop to an outdoor Christmas display being erected at the home of their neighbor, Donald Cassidy. The Michauds claim the display will cause traffic problems, disturb the peace, and be a general threat to the well-being of the neighborhood. They*

were able to get over one-hundred Kennebec City
citizens to sign a petition agreeing with them.

"It's unnecessary, and a disturbance to the peace
of the community," said Mrs. Michaud. "We love
Christmas as much as everyone else, but we don't
feel the need to go crazy over it."

When asked to comment, Chairman Roger Girard
said only that Cassidy is not violating any current
laws or ordinances, but that the Selectmen would
open the floor to comment from the community at
tonight's meeting, which begins at 6:30 p.m. at the
Kennebec City Town Hall.

Donald Cassidy, the homeowner putting up the
decorations, declined to comment, but a reporter
visiting the home, at 40 Franklin Street, did find
a more extensive display of Christmas decorations
and lights than has previously been seen in this city.

One neighbor who was happy to comment on
the display was 92-year-old Eileen Ferris of 37
Franklin Street. "I think it's wonderful," she said. "It
will bring joy and happiness to everyone who sees it,
and I, for one, cannot wait to see it all lit up."

Mrs. Ferris said she would be attending tonight's
meeting.

Don set the paper down on the table and picked up the coffee
mug. "Here's to you, Mrs. Ferris. I hope you do get to see it all lit
up." He took a long drink of the warm brew, and felt the acid in his
stomach bubble.

The house was too quiet. He needed something to do to get
his mind off what the evening might bring, so he booted up his

laptop and decided to spend some time on one of the DIY Christmas forums. There was a thread there with advice on how to handle contrary neighbors, but he doubted anyone out there had ever seen the likes of Muriel Michaud. It had been just his luck to buy a house across the street from the Grinch's mother.

Chapter 26

The bell for fourth period lunch had just rung, and Scott was heading toward the cafeteria when he saw Jenny Cassidy coming down the hall. She was talking with Chuck Andrews, one of the football players, and was just about glowing as she walked. Scott quickly looked down, operating on the theory that if he didn't look at her, then she wouldn't see him, either. He was dressed in a flannel shirt, open over a Ramones tee shirt, and jeans he'd owned since middle school—now a little snug around the waist. The whole outfit was wrinkled and looked like he'd taken it out of the dirty laundry hamper, probably because he had done that very thing this morning. *Chuck Andrews,* he thought. *Of course. She's already going for the jocks.*

As luck would have it, the flow of students through the cafeteria doors put Jenny and Scott just about side-by-side entering the busy room.

"Hey, Scott," she said. "I was starting to wonder if we went to the same school. I hardly ever see you!"

Scott felt himself flush. "Uh, have you been looking for me? 'Cause I'm always here. In fact, I got the perfect attendance medal all through elementary and middle school."

Jenny laughed, reached out and put a hand on his arm. "Chill,

Scott. I was just giving you a hard time. How are you?"

"I'm okay. Do you have lunch now?"

"Yeah, I do, but I'm, uh…" She looked around, but Chuck Andrews had disappeared into the cafeteria. Her shoulders slumped.

Scott felt his face get even hotter. "Oh, okay, um, never mind…"

Suddenly he felt a heavy hand on his back and he lurched forward, stumbling into Jenny and dropping his books. "What the heck?" he said, as the sound of cackling laughter echoed through the room. Rocky Stratton, a big creep who was always in trouble, was behind him laughing, and looking around as though he expected a round of applause. He was about six-foot-three and huge, with a green Mohawk and two stud piercings under his bottom lip. Two of his equally idiotic-looking minions were with him.

In a heartbeat, Jenny sidestepped around Scott and went directly over to Rocky, turning her head up directly under his pimply face. Scott, who had bent down to pick up his books, was suddenly face-to-face with the kitten cartoon on her backpack, and he fleetingly thought of his old cat Dinah, who'd died when he was in fifth grade. *Crazy, the things that come into a person's head when you least expect it,* he thought.

"What's your problem, jerk?" Jenny said.

Rocky's face expressed mock surprise. "Whoa, call off the dogs! I didn't do nothin'," he said, holding up his hands defensively.

"You pushed Scott. You need to apologize," Jenny said.

"Or what? You gonna head butt me? Hah!" said Rocky, looking at his pals. "Your porky boyfriend ought to watch out. He was standing in my way."

Scott stood up next to Jenny. "Don't talk to him, Jenny, he's an idiot. I'm just gonna go," he said, shaking his head. His hair fell into his face as he bent over again to pick up a book he'd missed.

Jenny put her hand on his arm again. "No, Scott, don't go. This butthead needs to apologize."

Rocky's head snapped back in surprise. He smirked. "Oh, let him go. Let him run away like a baby and let his mama fight his battles," he said in a sing-song voice.

"For your information, idiot, his mother is dead." She paused and let that sink in. Rocky's mouth opened and he started to say something, but it came out as a grunt.

"What's your problem, anyway?" Jenny said. Her voice was as loud as the cafeteria was quiet.

Then Rocky suddenly snapped his fingers and pointed at her. "Hey, wait a minute. I know you. You're that new girl...the one with the crazy father."

Jenny's mouth fell open. It was a look Scott had seen on many of his female classmates. "My father? What's my father got to do with this?"

A small crowd had begun to gather, pushing Scott to the sidelines. At the mention of Jenny's father, Scott pushed his way back through just in time to hear Rocky yell, "He's the moron who's putting up his Christmas decorations already, right? The whole town's signed a petition against him."

"Shut *up*!" Jenny flew at him, both hands pushing against his chest. Scott stepped in and pulled her away.

"C'mon Jenny. Don't waste your time. He's a moron and everybody knows it."

"Come on people, break it up, break it up," the nasal voice of Mr. Bedell, the Assistant Principal, rang out over the murmur of the crowd as they parted for him to step through. "Everything okay here, Mr. Stratton? Ms. ...uh, Ms. ..."

"Cassidy. I'm Jennifer Cassidy."

"Everything's just fine here, Mr. Bedell," Rocky interrupted, the smile of an angel on his face now. "Peachy keen. Just gettin' to know the new girl."

"Well, that's mighty nice of you, Mr. Stratton. Let's keep our enthusiasm down a little now, shall we?"

"Yeah, and get a life," Jenny said, still looking at Rocky.

Mr. Bedell ignored the remark. Rocky bristled, but then backed down and walked away with his buddies. He mumbled something only they could hear, and they all burst out laughing.

"Okay people, party's over. Everyone settle down and eat now, period four lunch is almost out of time," said Mr. Bedell, and Jenny and Scott walked over to get in line together.

"I can't believe it," Said Jenny, picking up a tray.

"What? You didn't have jerks like that in Florida?"

"Yes. But they didn't dare mess with me. That moron—what's his name?

"Rocky Stratton," said Scott, as they moved through the line.

"I can't believe he would say something like that about my father. How does he even know anything about us?" She pointed at some greasy-looking pizza and the lunch lady slid a slice onto her tray.

"This is a small town, Jen. Everyone knows everything about everybody."

Jenny stopped short and looked at Scott, holding up the line of kids behind her. "Well, I'm not letting them do this to my father. One of the reasons we moved up here, and why I had to leave all my friends in Florida, was so my dad could have his display someplace where there was snow. I didn't really want to do it, but after his heart attack, Mom and I agreed he should have his dream come true. I can't believe the people in this town. They're ganging up on him!"

She was looking directly into his eyes. It felt as though there was no one else around, even though they were surrounded by people. He considered his words carefully before he spoke. "So, your Dad did have a heart attack? I wondered about that the first night I met you guys. I'm sorry."

The lunch lady glared at them. "Keep the line moving, kids. Take your discussion to the table."

Scott moved on and Jenny followed.

"I'm going to that stupid meeting tonight and I'm going to speak up for my dad," she said. "My mom is going, too." She found a table with a couple of empty spots at the end and they sat down across from each other. "Would you..." she looked down and twisted her napkin around. "Would you come with us?"

Scott, who had been fumbling with his pint carton of chocolate milk, nearly dropped it. "Me? You want me to come with *you?*"

Jenny stared. "Yes. I do. It would really mean a lot to me. I mean, you've been helping him with everything and I thought you might want to, you know, *defend* him, I guess. Will you do it? Will you come with us?"

"Absolutely," Scott said, earning a smile from Jenny.

As the period was almost over, they ate their lunches in a hurry; Jenny finished first. "Thanks for everything. I'll see you tonight." She headed back to the counter, dumped the trash and left her tray, then walked back up to Scott as he got up from the table. She stepped closer to him and whispered in his ear. "I don't think you're over-weight at all."

Then she twirled around and walked quickly away. Suddenly, he felt like he could do no wrong.

Chapter 27

The morning was dragging on, and, try as he might, Don couldn't focus on anything, what with all the negative thoughts swirling around in his head. He felt so stupid for uprooting his family for a hobby. Yes, Maggie's family was here in Maine and she'd wanted to be closer to them, but he knew the real reason his wife and daughter had sacrificed so much was to make him happy. On top of all that, he felt even stupider for buying a house without meeting all the neighbors first. They were going to shut down his display tonight, he just knew it, and there was absolutely nothing he could do about it.

He pushed away from the table and walked into the bedroom to lie down. This kind of stress was exactly the kind of thing the doctor did *not* order. He knew he had to calm down, think positive thoughts, try to find peace.

He closed his eyes.

Lord, thank You so much for all the blessings You have given me. Thank You for Maggie and Jenny, and thank You for the roof over our heads. Thank You again for saving my life. Oh God, please help me in this situation. I know it's just a Christmas display, but I was hoping to bring some happiness to people around here, to lift up their hearts during Your blessed season of joy. I'm just a man and I can't change the world, but I'd like to continue what my father started and bring smiles to people's faces. If it is Your will, Lord, please soften this woman's heart, and this community's heart, so that I may bring glory to Your name through my display. I ask this in the name of Your Son, Jesus. Amen.

Before he even realized what was happening, Don was snoring away, softly.

"Hi, Mrs. Marshall! Come on in," said Angie, motioning for her next patient to come down the hall. Mrs. Marshall, an attractive, older woman with perfectly coifed silver hair, was there for her six-month cleaning. The practice was busy today and Angie had been working non-stop all morning. Still, she greeted Mrs. Marshall with a smile. "You look lovely today. Did you just come from the hairdresser?"

"Oh yes, my weekly wash and set. Esme at Hair After does a good job," said Mrs. Marshall, folding the newspaper she had been reading and placing it on the table. "I was just reading this story in the paper about the meeting tonight and that horrible Christmas display they're putting up over on Franklin Street. Did you see the article?"

"No, I didn't," said Angie, tying a plastic bib around Mrs. Marshall's neck. She felt a prickle climb up her spine. "What did it say?"

"Well, it said that Muriel Michaud…she goes to my church, she's the town busybody and everybody knows it…anyway, this fella moved in across the street from her and is putting up a giant Christmas display with something like a million lights, and Muriel is trying to shut him down. She circulated a petition and everything."

Angie, curious, took an extra few minutes arranging her instruments. "Is that so? I haven't heard anything about that." Mrs. Marshall didn't know that Angie lived on Franklin Street, and Angie didn't see any reason to tell her. But Angie hadn't heard anything about a petition. She had no idea that nosy so-and-so was causing a stink about Don Cassidy's display.

"It's true. Old Muriel is all worked up about it. A petition, mind you! She actually dragged her poor husband door-to-door one Saturday to try to talk people into signing it. I heard she couldn't get enough of her neighbors to agree with her, you know, so she ended up bullying her kids into helping her. Her daughter and son-in-law own the hardware store, you know, so all their employees had to sign it or lose their jobs!"

Now it made sense. Angie and Zack usually weren't home on Saturday mornings because that's when they went to Special Olympics practice. They must've been gone when the Michauds had come around. "Wow. That sounds pretty extreme."

"Oh, she's worried that the lights and everything are going to cause problems, you know, disrupt the peaceful neighborhood, and she's probably right on that score. It'll be interesting to see what the Selectmen have to say about it."

"I guess so. I wonder if a lot of people will turn up for that meeting. Did you say it was tonight?"

"Tonight at seven. That's what it said in the paper."

"Well, I guess we'll see." She sat down on the stool next to her and said, "Open up, Mrs. Marshall." Then she got to work.

At five-thirty, Don had put on his down jacket, hat, and gloves, tied up his work boots, and gone outside to putter around as he waited for Andy. Maggie and Jenny had come home from school, eaten a quick dinner with him, and then gone off early to City Hall so they could get good seats at the meeting. The cherry picker was parked in the driveway, waiting to haul good ol' Santa and his team of reindeer up to the top of the roof. Don decided to turn on some of the bigger inflatables to help set the mood, although it was against his personal code to turn on the lights before Thanksgiving Eve, when he would run his first test.

The prayer and the nap had done him good, and when the ladies came home, they'd found him outside, nailing the Santa into his sleigh and each of the reindeer to their pallets. He was feeling positive, even when he saw Ray and Muriel Michaud come out of their house, get in their car and drive off. There was no song and dance this time, but Don knew they were headed for the meeting. This could all be over in a matter of hours, but nothing was going to stop him from getting Santa and his team up on that roof for all the world to see before he was shut down.

Andy sauntered over around six and they set to work.

Chapter 28

As she approached City Hall, Angie saw television and newspaper vans from all over the state. She guessed that a Grinch-like story during the holiday season was big news. With all the commotion, she was glad she'd found a sitter for Zack.

The chambers were packed wall-to-wall with people, and many others were spilling out into the hallway. In addition to the usual concerned citizens, there were various people carrying signs like "LIGHTS OUT" and "NO SCROOGES ALLOWED" (with a big red circle with a line through it over the word "Scrooge") and people on both sides of the matter carried signs that said, "KEEP CHRIST IN CHRISTMAS." It seemed people couldn't agree whether an over-the-top Christmas display was honoring Christ's birthday or commercializing it.

A few people came in costume. There was at least one Santa, several elves, and a life-sized Grinch carrying a sign that said, "GO AHEAD, PUT UP THE LIGHTS. I'LL JUST STEAL 'EM!" Angie laughed to herself and only half-jokingly hoped Don had security cameras.

As she made her way through the crowd, she saw one of her patients. "Hey Angie! Can you believe this?" the man said. "I've been to a lot of Selectmen's meetings but I've never seen a crowd like this."

Then the man was absorbed by the mass of people.

Angie spotted Maggie and Jenny seated in the front row, with Scott sitting beside Jenny. "Hey Angie, I saved a seat for you," said Maggie, patting the seat to her left. The Michauds sat in the same row, across the aisle, and neither party made eye contact with the other.

Though the room was full of people, Angie hardly recognized anyone. She could imagine how Maggie and Jenny must be feeling. Being new in town definitely put the family at a disadvantage tonight. As she craned her neck to look at the crowd, she noticed a little elderly lady using a cane and walking slowly down the aisle. She recognized her as the woman who lived across from the Andersons. Her vintage faux-fur coat had seen better days and she sported a white knit cap with a pom-pom on her gray head. The woman stopped beside Angie. "Hello there, dear," she said. "Could I sit in this row with you folks?"

Angie rose. "Oh, absolutely. Ma'am. You're Mrs. Ferris, aren't you? We'd love to have you sit with us," she said. Everyone moved down a seat to accommodate her.

"You may call me Eileen," said Mrs. Ferris. "Though I suppose most anyone who knows me now just calls me Mrs. Ferris. I'm so embarrassed we've never met. I've seen you and your boy walk by my house on several occasions." She removed her hat and white knit gloves, placing them carefully in her huge leather handbag.

Mrs. Ferris stuck out her hand, and Angie took it in hers. It felt cold, like a featherless little bird. "I'm Angela Ellis, and I'm very pleased to meet you. Right here are Maggie and Jenny Cassidy, and of course you must know Scott Anderson, since he lives right across from you."

Mrs. Ferris took her seat and said, "Oh yes, I used to be friendly with his mother. She was quite a firecracker, that one. A bright spot in what has slowly become a dull neighborhood. Although, I must say, I've been seeing more of *everyone* ever since that gentleman began putting up his Christmas lights. Seems the neighborhood has suddenly come alive again because of him. You're his wife, aren't you?" She smiled at Maggie as she unbuttoned her coat, leaving it on.

"Yes, I am. I'm Maggie. I'm very glad to meet you. That's just what Don hopes to accomplish with his display. Bring people together, bring them happiness."

"And he'll get to do it, if I have anything to say about it," said Mrs. Ferris, reaching into her handbag and coming up with a roll of Peppermint Lifesavers. She offered it around to her seatmates. "Care to have one?"

Don enjoyed the handling the cherry picker, sending Andy up to the roof: first with Santa in his sleigh, and then four more times with each pair of reindeer, and one last time with Rudolph. Andy also brought several sandbags and bungee cords with him on each trip. Once at the top, he went about the task of moving each piece to the roof, placing it carefully and setting the sandbags down. When everything was up on the roof, Don climbed up the extension ladder and began the process of attaching the sleigh to the chimney.

Andy was crouched down by the chimney and Don was gingerly making his way around it with the cords when the twins suddenly came screaming across the lawn.

The din in the meeting room was tremendous. Some people sang Christmas carols; others loudly shouted their opinions. Angie was half expecting someone to scratch their fingernails across a chalkboard when at last Roger Girard rose and stood at the podium.

"Attention ladies and gentlemen." He cleared his throat. "Excuse me, but it's seven o'clock, time to begin the meeting." The room began to quiet. "Now, uh, we have a lot of Old Business to discuss before we get to the matter of the Michauds' petition, and I hope you'll all participate or spectate respectfully as we go over the business of the city."

Angie was surprised that the crowd actually shut up.

"Would everyone please rise for The Pledge of Allegiance?" asked Roger.

"Daaaaaaaaddy! Daaaaaaaaddy!" The twins stopped next to the ladder and Ricky started to climb up.

"What are you doing?" yelled Andy. "Stop that right now! Don't climb up here!"

Both children were hollering at once and all the words tumbled and jumbled over one other. What came out loud and clear was this: "The baby is coming! Mommy said to come get you! The water is broken and the baby wants to come out!"

"Oh my god," said Andy. He looked at Don. "I have to go. I have to go right now. I'm so sorry. Come on down the ladder and we'll get it finished tomorrow, okay? You shouldn't stay up here alone."

Don was a bit flustered by this sudden change in plans, but he felt confident he could take it from there. "Oh, nah, it's okay. I just need to check everything one last time and then I'll be down. I'll be fine. You go ahead now, and good luck with everything."

"You sure?" Andy asked, but scrambled down the ladder without waiting for an answer. He yelled back, "I'm so sorry!" and then vanished into the house, leaving Don somewhat bewildered, standing between the chimney and Santa.

Esmerelda is in labor. Good grief. If this happened in a movie, no one would buy it. But since I'm up here, I might as well finish the job. He knew deep down that he should probably not be up here by himself, but the work was almost done. He'd be okay. If they shut down his display tonight, he'd at least have Santa up on the roof; and even if he couldn't light it up, it would still bring smiles to the children passing by.

He secured the bungee cords and moved over to begin checking the sandbags.

Angie was bored by the first part of the meeting. The same old business was discussed: whether or not the town should fund repairs to one of the elementary schools (with the same old arguments between parents of school-aged children and seniors who didn't think their taxes should support schools now that *their* children were all grown up), a town-wide recycling plan, and a couple of other issues that had been going in and out of town business for years. She found herself surreptitiously scanning the crowd for Sam Anderson, but didn't have any luck finding him. Then she realized that he'd probably come and sit with his son even if he did show up. Finally, Roger Girard said, "That concludes Old Business. Now we'll move on to New Business. First on our agenda, we'll take up Mr. and Mrs. Michaud's petition, since I suspect that's why most of you are here." He picked up the manila folder and took out a bundle of papers. "We've had our Secretary check the names on this petition. Lisa, would you like to report on that?"

Lisa Berube, a petite, efficient woman, nodded and adjusted her glasses. "Yes, of course. Well, we went over every name on the list and checked addresses to make sure all the signatures were valid citizens of Kennebec City. Our examination revealed that three of the signatures were invalid; not citizens of Kennebec City. So that left ninety-eight valid signatures on the petition."

"What? That's not right!" blurted Muriel, standing up, her voice rising over the murmuring crowd.

Roger Girard raised his hands in a calming motion. "Now, now, no worries, Mrs. Michaud. We accepted the petition nonetheless, otherwise we wouldn't be here discussing it tonight. Everyone just settle down."

Muriel sat back stiffly in her chair, and Roger continued. "This petition requests that the Selectmen pass an ordinance that will limit the size and scope of any residential Christmas displays in Kennebec City. Before considering whether to develop such an ordinance, the Selectmen request public input. We will now open the floor for public comment on this matter so that community members may speak to this request. We ask that you confine your comments to two minutes, and if someone has already said what you were planning to say, that you refrain from repetition. When you approach the microphone please state your name and your address before beginning. The floor is open."

Muriel rose from her seat and made her way to the microphone. She looked much older than Angie thought she would be. She'd assumed Muriel was in her early seventies, but the woman who stood in front of the crowd looked more like eighty. Maybe this whole thing was taking a toll on her. From her skirt pocket, the old woman took a crumpled piece of lined paper scribbled with notes and opened it up. She looked at it for a second or two, then cleared her throat and began to speak in a voice too loud for the microphone. "My name is Muriel Michaud." The sound boomed through the room and, startled, she stepped back.

Roger Girard leaned forward in his chair. "It's okay, Mrs. Michaud. You can just speak in your regular voice and everyone will hear you just fine."

Muriel nodded and took a tentative step back toward the mic. She looked at the paper again and then began to speak in a more regular voice. "I...my husband and I, that is, live at 39 Franklin Street in Kennebec City. We created this petition in response to the outrageous Christmas display currently being installed at the home across the street from our house, at 40 Franklin Street, for the record." She cleared her throat and glanced at Lisa Berube. "Anyhow, the display is huge and unreasonable...the likes of which we've never seen in Kennebec City, having lived our entire lives here."

She glared at Roger Girard. "We feel that our point of view should count for something, being long-time residents. But we came to see Mr. Girard and he was not sympathetic to our complaints."

Roger started to say something, but Muriel continued. "He insisted that we start this petition, so we did. We went to a lot of trouble to get these signatures, and now, here we are."

She turned toward the assembled audience and her gaze swept the room, then settled on Maggie, with venom in her eyes.

"We value the peace and quiet of our neighborhood, which was just perfect until these...these out-of-staters moved in and started putting out their Christmas decorations in September. In September, for goodness sakes! They didn't bother to ask anyone or find out how their neighbors felt about this madness, they just went ahead and did it," Muriel said. She turned again toward the Selectmen's table. "Now, I...uh, we... don't mind a few lights around a door frame, but this man has hundreds, maybe even thousands of lights all over his house. He's got snowmen and Santa Clauses by the dozen and I don't know how many of those giant blow up things. It's just chaos, I tell you. My husband and I have seen these kinds of things on television and they just destroy neighborhoods. The traffic, the litter, the noise and the lights and music on until all hours of the night. I can just imagine..."

Lisa Berube spoke up. "Excuse me, Mrs. Michaud, but your two minutes are up."

Muriel blinked but did not stop talking. In fact, her voice grew a bit louder. "I can just imagine the circus that the Christmas season will bring…"

Lisa spoke up again. "Mrs. Michaud, I'm sorry but your time is up."

"I have more to say," said Muriel, raising her voice. "And I demand to be heard."

Angie's hands clenched her purse. This was turning into a showdown. A murmur ran through the crowd as Lisa tried again. "Please, Mrs. Michaud…"

Muriel turned a deep red, and Angie wondered if she might have a stroke right there on the spot. She whipped around and faced Lisa. "Don't silence me, you impertinent young woman. People need to know what's going on!"

The words rang throughout the room. The crowd immediately hushed and all eyes were on Muriel. Roger Girard leaned forward in his chair again and opened his mouth to speak, but before he had the chance, Ray got up—his back hunched as though he didn't want the crowd to see him—and approached his wife. In a gentle voice he said, "Muriel, come and sit down now. You made your point and other people need to have their turn to speak." He reached for her arm. She resisted for a few seconds and stood glaring at Roger Girard, but then followed his wife back to their seats.

Don had just set down the fourth sandbag on the pallet holding Santa and the sleigh when he had to stop and take a breather, sweating despite the cold weather.

When did fifty pounds become so heavy? He took off his hat and tossed it down to the ground below, followed by his gloves. That's when he felt the first snowflakes on his hands. He looked up at the snow, then smiled and scooched down to the pallet holding Rudolph.

Eileen Ferris began to rise from her chair and Angie stood to give her a hand. She offered to walk her to the microphone, but Mrs. Ferris waved her off and approached the microphone slowly, clutching her handbag. She spoke in a soft but firm voice. *What a contrast to Muriel Michaud,* thought Angie.

"My name is Eileen Ferris and I live at 37 Franklin Street. My house is also across from the Christmas display Muriel mentioned. I, personally, think it's a wonderful thing for our neighborhood."

Mrs. Ferris was suddenly drowned out by a fury of voices, both disagreeing and agreeing with her opening statement. Roger pounded his gavel. "Ladies and gentlemen, please quiet down and let the lady speak!" He pounded twice more before the voices died down.

"Anyway, as I was saying, I'm in support of Mr. Cassidy's display, and I don't think any ordinance is needed. In fact, I wish more people in the town would show the kind of spirit he is showing. I've lived here for ninety-two years, my whole life, and Kennebec City used to be a wonderful community for children and families. But this town has been depressed since the last mill shut down thirty years ago, and people here could use something to lift their spirits. We used to have a Nativity scene in front of the City Hall and we don't even have that any more. I'm sure no one would mind if we had that and some symbols of other holidays as well, like a Star of David. We don't even have lights or Christmas carols downtown like we used to when my children were little. This city has forgotten the holidays."

The noise of the crowd rose again, even louder this time, and once again Roger slammed his gavel down on the desk. "Enough!" he shouted. "Please show your respect to Mrs. Ferris."

The old woman hardly seemed flustered by the din. She waited until the noise died down and then continued speaking. "Anyhow, I think that as long as Mr. Cassidy, and anyone else with these kinds of decorations for that matter, shuts everything down at a reasonable hour and manages the traffic, then he should be allowed to have his display. And I'll go out and direct the traffic myself, if I have to. Just get me an orange vest and a flashlight and I'll be on the corner in a jiffy." She smiled and turned away from the microphone, walking slowly back to her seat as several people cheered and applauded.

"Thank you so much, Mrs. Ferris," said Maggie, as Eileen sat down.

"Mrs. Ferris, you rocked the house!" Jenny smiled and gave two thumbs up, as did Scott.

No kidding, thought Angie. *She should run for office.*

While she was speaking, two men and one woman had lined up behind Mrs. Ferris. Now, as the first man stepped up to the microphone, three more people got into the line.

Don moved fairly quickly across the roof. Andy had placed the sandbags well, so Don didn't have to lift many more. He only had to adjust a few. He'd just hefted the bag on the last pallet—the one anchoring Donner and Blitzen—when he felt a sudden, searing pain in his left arm. He dropped the bag and sat down hard on the roof, legs splayed, unable to catch his breath. "Oh no," he whispered. "This cannot be happening now. I need to calm down, that's all. I just need to calm down." He put his head back and felt the cold snow fall on his face.

"...and I just don't think we need this kind of disruption in our neighborhood. In any neighborhood in Kennebec City, in fact," said Nick Cable. The owner of number 43 Franklin Street continued, "I can see a few lights and a few decorations, the normal stuff, but this is just too much. I think an ordinance to limit the number of lights and decorations one homeowner can display is called for, and definitely specify the hours that such a display may be lit. Thank you," he said, and turned away.

The woman behind him stepped up to the microphone.

Chapter 29

When Sam Anderson first pulled into his driveway, he didn't notice anything out of the ordinary. Then, as he closed his car door, he looked over and saw that some of the big blow-up decorations at Don Cassidy's house were inflated, but no other decorations were lit except for a couple of spotlights. No one seemed to be around. There was a cherry picker sitting idle in the driveway.

Maybe Don decided to go to that infernal meeting after all. If I were him you wouldn't catch me there for all the tea in China.

He stood looking around for a few seconds, then noticed that the giant snow globe with the reindeer carousel inside looked lopsided, as though something large had fallen on it. He took a few steps forward to get a better look.

Angie sat back in her chair and caught a quick glance at the clock on the wall in the back of the room. Eight-fifteen. The line didn't seem to be getting any smaller, and worse than that, there was no clear agreement from the people on whether an ordinance was even needed. Eileen Ferris had surprised her by speaking so eloquently. In fact, Angie had no idea that downtown Kennebec City had ever been decorated for the holidays. Of course, many of the stores that probably once featured festive window displays were shuttered, and she was sure there was no money in the city budget to string lights on every pole across Main Street.

"...and on behalf of the Kennebec City Knights of Columbus, we would like to throw our support behind Mr. Cassidy and offer our services directing traffic nightly, should he need us." A chorus of cheers rose from the crowd as "Mitch" Mitchell turned and walked back to his seat.

An attractive blonde woman in her mid-thirties stepped up to address the Selectmen. Angie didn't recognize her.

"My name is Hazel Teanutt and I live at 57 Elm Street here in Kennebec City. I'm a media specialist at Kennebec Valley Regional High School." She patted her hair and fussed with her silk scarf. "I'm here to say that I agree with the Michauds. I don't celebrate Christmas, and I don't want anyone's so-called religious beliefs shoved down my throat just because I happen to be driving down the street. I think such displays should be totally banned."

"That's ridiculous!" someone shouted.

"She doesn't speak for me or my family!" shouted a woman from the back. The crowd's arguing intensified.

Hazel Teanutt raised her voice to be heard over the rising chatter. "This country was built on the tenet of religious freedom, which also includes freedom from religion. I sincerely believe the world will be better off..."

At this, the crowd became so loud that Roger Girard was forced to pound his gavel several times. No one paid heed. "Attention! Attention, please, ladies and gentlemen," he said into the microphone, to no avail.

Suddenly the door burst open and in rushed Officer Darren Baker of the Kennebec City Police Department. He walked straight up to the Selectmen's table and leaned over to speak to Roger. The commotion in the room came to an abrupt halt. Hazel Teanutt pursed her lips, looking annoyed. Angie got the feeling that things were suddenly taking a bad turn, and she held her breath as Roger said something which wasn't quite audible to the crowd, gesturing toward Maggie. The officer walked toward her.

"Mrs. Cassidy?" he said. The crowd began to hush.

"Yes? Yes, I'm Margaret Cassidy. What's...?"

"Can we step outside the room, Ma'am? I need to speak with you privately."

Jenny stood up quickly. "What's going on? Is something wrong with my Dad? Tell us. What's going on?"

Maggie got up quickly and took her daughter by the elbow. "Come on, sweetheart. Let's just follow the officer and find out what he wants." It all happened so fast that Angie didn't have a chance to ask her if she wanted her to go along for moral support. Instead, Angie, Scott, and Mrs. Ferris exchanged looks, as Officer Baker led Maggie and Jenny back down the aisle, through the doorway, and into the hallway. The big oak doors closed behind them.

Roger leaned into the microphone. "Uh, ladies and gentlemen, I've just received some news, and in the light of this information I believe we should table this subject for the night and perhaps, uh, perhaps take it up again at the next meeting in December."

The crowd erupted. The news people perked up. Everyone wanted to know what was going on.

"Without giving too much detail, I can tell you that Mr. Cassidy had an accident tonight and is currently at Kennebec Valley Hospital. I'm guessing he probably won't be able to continue with his display this year, but until we know more, we're tabling the discussion. Now let's move on to other business."

A murmur of surprise and disbelief rose from the crowd as people began to move toward the door.

Muriel turned to Ray. She was flummoxed by the sudden commotion, and worried that her carefully planned strategy for shutting down the monstrous display was being undermined. "What's going on? What's happening? I don't understand why they have to stop the meeting. We don't even know what happened to him," she said.

"Well, it must be pretty serious or I don't think Roger would have tabled the matter," said Ray, patting Muriel's hand. "I guess we can head home now." He rose from his chair.

"Wait! Wait, Raymond!" She stood up and spoke in a loud voice, "I demand to know what's happening. My husband and I worked hard to bring this matter before the Selectmen. We won't have it brushed aside like this." The commotion around them abruptly came to a halt, and everyone seemed to be staring at her.

Roger Girard rose from his seat, walked around the long table, and made his way over to Muriel. Ray stood up as well.

Roger spoke in a low voice. "Mr. and Mrs. Michaud, Donald Cassidy seems to have suffered a quite serious accident. I sincerely don't think his display is going to pose a problem on Franklin Street this year. Now, why don't you just go home and…"

Muriel felt her heart begin to pound. She suddenly felt dizzy, and she could not believe this man was speaking to her this way after all her hard work to bring this matter to the public's attention. "Don't patronize me, Roger Girard!" said Muriel. "I was paying taxes before you were even a twinkle in your father's eye. Now I demand that we continue with this matter. It may be over for this year, but what about next year?"

At this, Ray spoke up, surprising Muriel into silence. "For God's sake, Muriel, will you listen to yourself? The man is injured. We have no idea how bad, and here you are talking about next year? They're going to take it up again before Christmas. Good Lord, I can't even believe I'm hearing this. Now close your mouth and let's go home."

Ray turned and made his way toward the back door, moving so swiftly and with such vigor that Muriel could hardly keep up with him. The sea of people parted to let them through, and Muriel was embarrassed to see her neighbors staring at her as she passed by. She was waylaid by a young child who was blocking the aisle, and it was then she heard that woman from up the street—the one Ray had been talking to the other day—turn to the Anderson kid and say, "Oh my god. We have to go to the hospital and see if Don is alright. See if there's anything we can do to help Maggie and Jenny."

Oh sure. Worry about them. Who cares how I feel?

Chapter 30

As Muriel climbed into bed, she heard the sound of a familiar television game show theme coming from the living room. Other than that, the house had never felt so quiet. Ray hadn't said a word to her all the way home. For all she knew, he was planning to sleep downstairs. They hadn't had a disagreement like this since the kids were teens, and the more she thought about it, and the meeting, the queasier she felt.

Her children—Paula hadn't even shown up at the meeting—were busy with their own lives and didn't seem to care much about hers. Now her husband didn't want anything to do with her. Her throat felt constricted, and sudden, hot tears came pouring out of her eyes. She began to sob, and the sobs turned into pain-filled wails, breaking the silence. She didn't even try to hide it from her husband this time. Elmo, who had been sprawled at her feet, jumped up quickly and ran out the door in search of a more peaceful corner of the house.

Just as Muriel had hoped, her loud crying brought Ray up the stairs. He stood in the doorway for a second, looking at her, and then came over and sat down on the bed beside her. He took a few tissues out of the crocheted tissue box holder and tried to dry her eyes. She let him. Then he plumped up his pillows against the headboard and stretched out beside her. He patted his chest, an old signal that meant he wanted her to slide over and put her head there. As she did, he wrapped his arms around her just as they'd done in the old days, when it was cuddling time. Her sobbing gradually decreased until she was sniffling quietly.

Moonlight filtered through the bedroom drapes, casting silver shimmers across the walls. Muriel rose up on one arm to look at her husband, and saw that his eyes were shining with reflected light. "Ray," she said, "I really need to talk to you."

He nodded. "Then talk to me, Muriel. You know I'm always on your side, sugar plum." He lifted his head off the pillow and leaned down toward her, kissing her softly on the lips. "I love you. Tell me what's going on."

Muriel lay her head back down on his chest. She was silent for a minute, trying to compose her scattered thoughts, and then everything just spilled out. "Ray, I've been feeling bad for a long time. I think it started even before Thanksgiving last year, when the Anderson woman died. We've seen a lot of people come and go in our lifetime, but that one just hit me hard. She was so young, and I felt so remorseful, knowing I had called the police on them those times. I wanted to take it back. I just…I just felt so awful when she died."

"Oh Muriel, you can't do anything about that now…"

Muriel interrupted him. Now she had started, she couldn't seem to stop. "In January, it started to get really bad. After New Year's I had a hard time putting the Christmas things away. Remember? You went over to Freddie Fink's to watch football, and I took down the tree all by myself."

"But you never want to come and watch football with me," Ray said.

She shook her head. "That's not the point." She paused, took another tissue from the box and dried her eyes. Ray said nothing, listening patiently.

"As I took down the tree, I just kept feeling sadder and sadder, until finally I had this growing feeling of dread, like it might be our last Christmas. At our age, who can tell? And these thoughts kept swirling around in my head. Every ornament, every decoration we've collected over the years on our travels… they all made me cry. I saw our whole life together pass before my eyes, but instead of making me happy, it just made me feel scared. Like our time together might be coming to an end. Like we won't be collecting any new Christmas ornaments." At these last words her throat constricted and she began to sob again. Ray gently rubbed her back. After a minute or two, she had collected herself enough to begin speaking again.

"I thought I'd feel better once the job was done, but the whole month of January I felt down. Winter never seemed so long before, but this year just dragged on by. It seemed like spring would never arrive."

Ray interrupted. "I remember one day coming in and finding you staring out the window at the bird feeder. Usually you look content when you're doing that, and you tell me about all the birds that have been visiting; but that time you were really quiet. I thought something might be wrong, but I didn't say anything. Should I have said something, Muriel?"

"No," she said. "I really thought it was just the winter blues. But then spring finally arrived, and I didn't feel any better. In fact, I felt even worse, because I knew I should be feeling better, but I didn't."

Ray stroked her hair. "So it wasn't just the winter."

Muriel shifted a little, shook her head "no" and nestled up against her husband again. Ray pulled the covers up over her shoulders—that always made her feel secure. She could hear his heartbeat, the heartbeat she'd been listening to for so many years. "In June, I went to see Dr. Dalton for my physical, and she asked how I was doing. I don't know why, but I found myself telling her how I had been feeling. I didn't want to...I was afraid she'd think I was just an old fool...but it all came out like a dam bursting."

Ray opened his mouth to speak, but Muriel kept going, "I told her...I told her that I was just unhappy all the time, and she asked me some questions, and before I knew it I was crying and telling her that I feel old, so old. I can't stand to look in the mirror any more. I hate to see what has happened to my face and my body."

Ray tilted his head. "I love your beautiful face and your body," he said, leaning down to kiss her again. She turned away.

"Oh, don't be ridiculous. Sometimes I don't even want you to look at me because I'm so embarrassed about my wrinkles." She twisted and bunched the tissue with her fingers. "Every time I look in the mirror I'm reminded that the best times of my life are far behind me, and now all there is to look forward to is trouble. Our health can't hold out forever. One of these days one of us is going to get sick, and then the other one will have to be the caretaker, and, well, you know..." She coughed several times, and then continued. "Our children are all grown up. Even our grandchildren are grown up. What's left for us? I'm afraid of dying. I think about it all the time. The way things went for my mother, I'm lucky I've lived this long," she blurted, and then the tears came again in a torrent.

Ray patted her back. "Muriel, Muriel. No one is dying here. Why didn't you talk to me about this? I would have been happy to listen, and try to cheer you up. I had no idea you were feeling this way."

Muriel pulled away and rested her head in her hand. "I didn't want you to know. I was afraid I would just make you feel bad, too."

"Well, I wish you'd given me a chance. But that's neither here nor there. What did Dr. Dalton say?"

Elmo padded back into the room and stopped by the side of the bed, his tail flicking up as it did when he expected attention. Muriel reached over and patted the bed, a signal for the cat to jump up.

After a few minutes' purring and kneading, he finally settled in a small space between the couple.

"She said these feelings were normal for someone my age, but that it wasn't normal to be obsessing over them. She said I was clinically depressed, and recommended I see a therapist in Augusta; someone who specializes in 'geriatric mental health.'" Muriel sniffed.

"Did you go?"

"Yes, I went. I went twice a month from July to September, and it didn't do any good."

Ray looked puzzled. "When...?"

"I told you I was going shopping with Paula, and one time I told you I was going to the movies with the girls. I made up a lot of excuses, and you didn't question any of them."

Ray looked hurt, but Muriel went on. "Anyway, she wanted me to take some kind of anti-depressant, and I didn't want to. I don't need that. I've lived all these years and managed just fine. Why should I take medication now? I ripped up the prescription and threw it away, and never went back."

Ray remained silent as this last sentence hung in the air. Finally, after what seemed like an hour, he said, "I can't believe you've been seeing a therapist and I knew nothing about it. I feel like a fool."

There was another long silence. Then Ray took a deep breath and said, "Well, sweetheart, I think it's like anything else. If you had diabetes, or some other illness, you'd take the medication, wouldn't you? I don't see how this is any different."

Muriel shook her head. "I don't need to go on drugs. Seeing her wasn't helping, anyway."

As if on cue, Elmo reached out a paw, and she gave his head a scratch. "Sweet Elmo, I don't know what I'd do without you," she whispered. "I'd given up on the therapist, and was just muddling along, and then this man moves in across the street and starts all this decorating business, and it was just the straw that broke the camel's back, I guess."

"But why does it bother you so much? What does his display have to do with anything you've been feeling?"

Muriel pounded down on the mattress. "Don't you see? How he could just move here and start all this? Like he owns the neighborhood. Why should he get to do that? This used to be our neighborhood. We had friends here, but now no one here cares about me... uh, us anymore. No one would care if I died. I wouldn't be missed." She burst into wracking sobs as she sat up, rose from the bed and started pacing back-and-forth, speaking through her tears. "It should have been me instead of that poor young mother. She had so much to live for...and I...I don't have any reason to be around anymore. Nobody needs me anymore."

Ray dashed over and grabbed his wife in a tight embrace where she stood. He held her close for a long time, whispering in her ear and stroking her hair. "Sweetheart, sweetheart, don't say things like that. Take a deep breath. I need you. I've always needed you and I always will." He whispered tender words of love until she stopped crying. Muriel always felt safe with his strong arms around her, and she wondered why it had taken so long for her to express her concerns. Of course he would understand. Ray had always understood—and he'd always known just what to say. She pulled her head away without breaking the embrace, and looked at him. When she spoke, her voice was soft and ragged.

"Don't you see, Ray? I don't even want Christmas to come this year, and here he is, throwing it in our faces. All that happiness out there, while in here, it's just quiet and lonely."

Muriel stopped speaking. She suddenly realized that was it. That was the real reason Don Cassidy's display had bothered her so much. It reminded her of how fun and joyful Christmas was, once, when the family still had their annual traditions: the Advent calendar, "Baking Sunday," making Christmas cards, leaving cookies for Santa and carrots for the reindeer, gathering the kids 'round the tree on Christmas Eve to open just one gift (it was always new matching pajamas). All these things that she had loved so much were gone from her life forever. She felt her chest tighten and more sobs build in her throat. Christmas just hasn't been the same since the kids all left, and this year I'm dreading it more than ever."

"You've been getting more and more upset every day," Ray said.

"Oh, you don't even know the half of it," said Muriel, swallowing the sobs.

"What do you mean?"

She took a deep breath. "I meant to tell you this before, but other things kept happening. Anyway, when Paula called on Saturday… remember? While we were on our way home from lunch?"

Ray nodded.

"Well, she told me that Philip's parents are taking them all to Italy for the holidays. To Italy! Karen, and Philip, and Emma, and Paula and Ed are going, too."

"Really? Wow. How come nobody told me? You've known this since Saturday?"

"Oh, I was going to tell you, but then I saw what was going on across the street and I just got so upset, and with all of that hoopla and such…"

She paused, recalling the scene she'd made in the driveway, which now made her feel foolish.

"Well, I guess Karen and Philip were supposed to tell us at lunch, but they must have decided not to for some reason. I don't know."

"That's gonna be one expensive trip. Are Philip's parents footing the bill for the whole thing?"

"Yes. Well, Paula and Ed are paying their own air fare, but they're all staying together. And we're not invited."

Ray scratched his head. "That makes sense. We hardly know Philip's parents. I can't imagine they'd even think of inviting us."

"But it's not fair!" her voice rose again, and tears filled her eyes. "For all we know, this could very well be our last Christmas, and we're going to spend it alone."

Ray sat up and handed over another tissue. "Hold on just a minute. This is not going to be our last Christmas! And besides, you shouldn't look at like they're doing something to us. They have a chance to go on a wonderful trip. I think they should go. When are they leaving?"

Muriel dabbed at her eyes. "The third week of December. They're going to be gone for two weeks, until after New Year's."

"Then let's plan on having a nice time with everybody until then. We'll have everyone here for Thanksgiving, right? We'll have a wonderful time, and when the time comes for them to go, we'll see them off with smiles on our faces. And then you and I can make this the best Christmas ever, just like we did in the old days."

"Oh pooh," said Muriel. "The old days are a long time ago. We're the ones who are old now."

"I have an idea," Ray said. "Let's get away ourselves. But let's not wait. Let's get away tomorrow. We don't have a ton of money, but we can at least take a little trip. Let's go to the White Mountains for a few days: we can go antiquing, go out to eat, spend some 'quality time' together." He chuckled. "We haven't been there since the kids were little and we went to Storyland."

"Storyland! Oh, that seems like another lifetime ago. Paula was just a baby the last time we went there. Remember how scared she was of the Big Bad Wolf? But then she saw the real piglets they had in the yard, and she laughed and laughed. I loved the sound of our kids laughing when they were babies, so jolly and full of life." She sighed. "I'd give anything to turn back the clock and be back there again. Where did all the time go?" She felt her facial muscles involuntarily scrunch up, and the tears began to flow again.

"Oh Lord, I just can't seem to say the right thing, can I?" said Ray. "Look, we can't turn back the clock. You know that, but we can make new memories, and we can have fun together like we did before we had kids. Look at me—don't you think I want that? I don't want to sit around here and wait to die. I want to enjoy life while I'm still on the right side of the ground. Come on, Muriel. Let's go on a little getaway, just the two of us."

She considered his proposal. "What about Elmo?"

"I'm sure Paula will be happy to come over and look in on Elmo and feed him. Come on, sugar plum, it will be fun. I really want to do it. Can we? Please?" He took her hands in his, and looked at her with those Paul Newman eyes she'd never been able to resist. He sounded like a little boy. "We can get a new Christmas ornament!"

Muriel couldn't help but smile. "Oh, okay," she said. "I guess that would be fun. It would be good to put all this crazy stuff behind us, since I guess it's not going to be an issue any more."

"But there's one more thing you have to do for me."

"What's that?"

"We're going to send Mr. Cassidy some flowers and a get-well card. And I don't want to hear one word about it. And, oh, well, might as well make it two things. When we get back, I want you to call Dr. Dalton; and, if it's okay with you, I'd like to join you when you go to talk with her. I intend to be by your side every step of the way through this, my sugar plum."

Chapter 31

The emergency waiting room was filled with people in various states of distress, but Angie immediately spotted Sam Anderson, who was dozing in one of the garish orange, hard-backed chairs. She silently pointed him out to Scott, and whispered, "What's your dad doing here?"

"Heck if I know," he replied, and shrugged.

"Let's let him sleep until we find out what's going on," said Angie. As she approached the nurse at the reception desk she leaned in to Scott and whispered, "Just follow my lead."

"Excuse me, I'm here to inquire about a patient who had an accident earlier this evening. Could you tell me if Donald Cassidy has been brought in here?" She made sure to use her most polite tone of voice, even though she already knew the answer.

"Are you family?"

Angie didn't hesitate, but spoke right up, as she'd anticipated this question on the drive over. "Yes. I'm his sister."

"And what about you?" the nurse asked, looking at Scott.

"Um..." Scott said, but before he could finish, Angie interrupted. "He's my son, and my brother is his only uncle. I'm a single mom, you know, and they have a special relationship..." Angie trailed off, hoping she'd said just enough to be convincing.

The nurse punched some buttons on her computer keyboard and then looked at the screen for a few seconds. Without looking up she said, "It looks like he's still in an exam room. I can take you down there, but you must be very quiet, and I don't advise staying long."

The nurse ushered them through the double doors and down the hall, past a dozen or so curtained rooms, until they came to one at the end. She drew the curtain aside and said, "Your sister-in-law is here," and she stepped away to let Angie and Scott enter.

The light in the room was harsh. Maggie sat by a gurney holding her husband's hand. Jenny sat by her mother's side. Don, wired up with various monitors, appeared to be sleeping. His leg was in a splint, and his color was bad.

Angie slid into the room with Scott behind her and spoke softly. "Hi, I hope you don't mind...I told them I was Don's sister, and that Scott was my son..."

She was interrupted by Jenny, who popped up out of her chair and threw her arms around Scott so abruptly that she almost knocked him off his feet. "I'm so glad you're here," she said. "I mean, thank you for coming," she mumbled in embarrassment. Scott turned beet red and didn't say a word.

Hmm, that was interesting, thought Angie. *I wonder if he realizes that she likes him. Angie suddenly felt a stab of empathy for Jenny. These Anderson men!*

"We thought you guys might need some moral support," Angie smiled. "If you'd rather have this be family time, that's okay too. We'll go out to the waiting room with Sam."

Maggie looked up with a tear-stained face and reached a hand out to Angie. "Thank you so much for coming."

"Of course. "Angie paused and looked at Don. "So, how's he doing?"

"He's had another heart attack, worse than his first. But thanks to Sam, the first responders got there in time," Maggie said.

"My dad?" said Scott.

Maggie nodded. "Yeah. He was coming home from work, and he thought something looked amiss with our decorations. He went and investigated and found Don where he'd fallen off the roof. He called 9-1-1 and stayed with him while they waited for the ambulance."

"Oh, okay, that's why he's out in the waiting room." Angie's mind wandered for just a second to the vision of Sam sleeping, but then it dawned on her. "Oh, my gosh. Don actually fell off the roof?"

"Yes," said Maggie, then Jenny interrupted.

"And you're never going to believe this," she said, speaking fast and looking back and forth between Angie and Scott. "But the doctor said one of his Christmas decorations may have saved his life. He fell on top of one of his inflatables. The giant one with the carousel inside. It broke his fall. He still broke his ankle, but it could have been a lot worse."

Angie smiled and shook her head. "Well, isn't that something. So, what's going on now?"

"We're just waiting for him to be prepped for an emergency angioplasty," said Maggie. "They're going to put a tube in his artery to unblock it, and then put in a stent to keep it open. After that they're going to repair his ankle while he's still under."

Jenny, who had been brightly telling the story of Don's fall just seconds earlier, was now looking at her father again; she suddenly began to sob. Angie knew that emotions could run rampant at a time like this, so she reached out and put a reassuring hand on the girl's shoulder.

"Oh, Mom," said Jenny, "We shouldn't have let him do the display this year. This never would have happened if we'd stopped him. Who cares about that stupid display anyway? All it does is take him away from us."

Now the truth was out, and Angie understood why Jenny had not been outdoors helping her father all these weeks. She resented the time he took out of their lives to do so. She kept her mouth shut, as this was a family matter.

Maggie took Jenny's hands in hers. "Jenny, listen to me. We couldn't have stopped him even if we'd tried. Your father loves this Christmas decorating thing. It's his passion, it makes him happy, and since he can't work, it's really all the joy he has in life. Besides you and me, of course." She smiled. "And I understand how you feel about it taking him away from us. I struggle with that, too. But for now, don't worry about what we should or shouldn't have done. Your father should have had the sense to get down off the roof when Andy left.

"But there is absolutely nothing to be gained by placing blame. What's done is done. Our job now is to make Daddy comfortable and show him how much we love him. Agreed?

Jenny met her mother's gaze and nodded slowly. She sounded exhausted. Agreed."

Just then a handsome older man in mint-green scrubs came into the room. His ID announced that he was Ben Haskell. He was accompanied by a female nurse who slipped into the room behind him.

"Hi, folks. I'm Ben. I'm here to take Mr. Cassidy down to the operating room," he said. "Oh, okay," said Maggie, and she kissed her husband's forehead and gave his hand a squeeze. Ben rolled him through the door and off down the hall.

Up stepped the female nurse, a kindly looking woman of about sixty, extending a hand. "I'm Jeannette. You're all family?"

Angie wasn't sure what to do, so she just nodded along while Maggie and Jenny responded, "Yes."

"Would you like to go to the surgical waiting room?" asked Jeannette.

Angie turned to Maggie and asked, "Do you want us to stay?"

Maggie looked frazzled, and Angie really didn't think she ought to be waiting here with just her daughter. One thing she knew about herself, she was good in a crisis. God knows she'd had enough of them over the years with Zack. If she stayed, it would mean she'd have to call Zack's sitter and see if she could hang at the house a while longer. Her heart told her that staying with Maggie and Jenny was the right thing to do, even though she barely knew them.

"Yes, yes, that would be good, if you could…for a little while? You don't mind?"

"No, of course not. I just need to make a phone call. Scott, let's go out in the waiting room and tell your Dad what's going on. He can go home and I'll give you a lift back later if you want to stay."

Jenny reached for Scott's hand. "Oh, please stay. It would really mean a lot to me." Angie took note. Something was definitely brewing here.

Scott nodded. "Okay," he said. "Sure." He was turning red again. This time the shade was more pomegranate than beet. Angie stifled a giggle.

"Good. Let's go tell your Dad, and you two go on ahead and we'll find you in a few minutes." She started to turn and then added, "Is there anyone I can call for you?"

"Oh, no thank you," Maggie replied. "I'll call my parents in the morning. No sense in waking them up now, they'd just be up all night worrying."

"Okay then, we'll catch up with you in a few," said Angie, and she and Scott made their way back to the waiting room.

Sam was still dozing when they found him, and Scott bent over and shook his shoulder gently. "Dad, dad, wake up."

Sam opened his eyes, and looked around for a second as though he didn't know where he was. Then he sat up quickly. "Oh. Oh shoot. I didn't mean to fall asleep." He shook his head as though to clear the cobwebs and looked at Scott, and then at Angie, blinking. "What are you guys doing here?" His hair was tousled and he had a bit of five o'clock shadow. Angie couldn't help but think he looked kind of sexy.

Scott sat down beside his father. "The police came to the Selectmen's Meeting and took Mrs. Cassidy and Jenny out to tell them about the accident. We heard about what happened and came straight here."

"We thought Maggie and Jenny could use some support. We didn't even know you were the one who found him," Angie said.

Sam brushed a hand through his hair and yawned, covering his mouth with his other hand. "Oh, yeah, well, I got home and noticed that something seemed wrong over there. I just did what anybody would do."

Angie looked straight into his eyes. "He's really lucky you were there, Sam," she told him. "You probably saved his life."

Once everybody was settled into the surgical waiting room, Angie made tea them tea from the cart. The room was pleasant and calm, decorated in shades of blue and green.

Maggie's teacup rattled on her saucer, as she put it down on the table at her side. She said, "Oh my, I've been so distracted I forgot about Sam. He's not still waiting out there, is he?"

"No, no, don't worry about that. I updated him on what was going on, and he decided to go home and get some sleep, once I assured him I'd get Scott home safely." Angie didn't add that she wished he'd stayed, but she knew it wouldn't be possible to pretend he was family too. There was only so much fibbing she could handle.

For a moment, they just sat, holding their steaming cups. Angie was trying hard to think of something brilliant to say, but everything that came into her head sounded trite. Then Maggie started talking.

"Don was my first and only love. We met in college, University of Miami. He was a junior and I was a sophomore. I had a work study job as a library aide. He'd come looking for books about electronics. Then, one day, as I was helping him find them, he told me about his family Christmas display. There was a twinkle in his eyes—a joy in his voice as he talked about the lights and decorations. I couldn't help it. I fell in love with him on the spot."

Jenny put her arm around her mom. It was clear to Angie that Maggie really needed to talk, and she was glad she'd made the decision to stay. *It doesn't matter what I say,* she thought. *What matters is what she needs to say.*

"Our first date was a horse and buggy ride at Charmingfare Farm. They used to put lights and decorations on a bunch of buildings and take people on Winter Wonderland rides. There wasn't any snow, but I didn't care. I was hooked."

She took a sip of her tea and smiled.

"He graduated before I did, moved back to Punta Gorda, and got a job working for the power company. As soon as I graduated, we got married—in Portland, where I'm from—and honeymooned in Bar Harbor. Don loved looking in the Christmas shops on Main Street there, but I just wanted to enjoy the scenery. We made our home back in Florida, and after about two years we started trying to begin our family, but God had other plans. I didn't get pregnant with Jenny until I was thirty, and what a joy that was! She was definitely worth waiting for. Meanwhile, every year, our display got bigger and bigger. Then Don had his heart attack and the company offered him early retirement with benefits. It was a good package so he took it and we made the big move up here.

"You know, in Florida, everybody loved Don's Christmas display. Jenny and I always got into the spirit by decorating the inside of the house. We were going to do that here, too."

Jenny piped up. "You should see our lighted Christmas village. I've never seen a bigger one. We add something new to it every year, don't we, Mom?"

Angie was touched. She imagined doing the Christmas village with her mother was Jenny's way of bonding with both parents. She seemed like a good kid, and clearly Scott thought she was something special. He couldn't be more obvious if he tried, and he was trying so hard not to be obvious. Right now, though, he was just sitting in the chair like a lump. Angie suddenly realized that Scott had been through his own terrible medical crisis with a parent not that long ago, so this had to be doubly hard for him, which made it even sweeter that he was hanging in here for Jenny.

"We sure do," said Maggie. She looked down at her tea for a moment. "The thing is, we never had one problem in Florida. Not one. I never imagined we'd move up here right across the street from somebody so unpleasant. Maybe we ought to think about moving back."

Scott suddenly blurted out, "No, no, you can't move back." Then he caught himself. Angie, sensing his embarrassment, took the reins.

"Oh, please don't think about going back," she said. "You've already done so much for this neighborhood. You have no idea. Everybody was staying in their own little cocoon before you got us all together, and I'm certain I'm not the only one who was feeling lonely. You guys have brought us all together. It's kind of a miracle, really."

Maggie, looking worn, nodded and said, "Well, let's see if the miracle extends to my husband. We can't decide anything until we see how he comes out of this. *If* he comes out of this." With that, tears began streaming down her face again.

Chapter 32

Bright and early Friday morning, Muriel, already dressed for the trip, went out on the front stoop with Elmo and picked up the paper. Right there on the front page was a picture of her with Ray at the Selectmen's Meeting. She quickly scanned the article about the meeting for news of Don Cassidy's condition.

There it was, in a sidebar to the main article on the second page.

KENNEBEC CITY DECORATOR
IN SERIOUS CONDITION
By Deborah Noack

As local citizens were debating the pros and cons of his home Christmas display last night at a Selectmen's Meeting, Franklin Street resident Don Cassidy apparently suffered a serious heart attack and fell from his roof, where he had been working on the display. Next door neighbor Sam Anderson found Cassidy, unconscious, and immediately called emergency services.

Good Lord, Muriel thought. *I didn't think he was actually going to have a real heart attack. Well, I hope he's alright. He'll need to rest now— no more of this decorating nonsense.*

Muriel folded the paper, worked hard at turning her frown into a smile, and walked back through the front door. She went upstairs and threw some things into a duffle bag while Ray was busy in the bathroom. "Come on, Ray," she said, knocking. "You said you wanted to hit the road early. I already packed for you. You just need to grab the toothbrushes."

She was in the kitchen reading the newspaper article about the meeting when Ray came bounding down the stairs in his cap and grabbed his jacket out of the coat closet. "I'm ready to hit the road. But first we're gonna do what you promised me we'd do. We've got a phone call to make. Look up the number for Kennebec City Florists for me, would you, sugar plum?"

As she reached for the phone book, Muriel tossed the paper into the magazine basket. She would read the rest of article when they got back, but for the sake of her sanity and because she had promised Ray, she was going to put all thoughts of the Christmas display debacle out of her head for now.

The last bell of the day had rung, and Scott Anderson was on the way to his locker when he saw Jenny by the water fountain, talking to two girls from the drama club. He didn't really know Jocelyn Kelleher and Christina Duford, but he knew their crowd, and they weren't usually friendly toward him. He had already decided to keep walking when he heard Jenny call his name.

"Hey, Scott!"

He pretended he hadn't heard her. She called again, "Scott, c'mere!"

Christina and Jocelyn turned to face him. There was no way he could ignore them now.

"Hi!" he said, awkwardly. He raised his hand in a weak salute and nearly collided with two guys coming the other way. He was so much clumsier around Jenny than he ever was at home. "I didn't expect to see you here today. How's your Dad doing?"

"He's okay," said Jenny. "He's gonna be in the hospital for a few days. I figured I might as well come to school."

Her eyes were puffy and she wasn't wearing any make-up. It didn't matter. She was still the prettiest girl in school. "The doctor says he's going to be all right. He came through his surgery with flying colors. Thank goodness your dad found him." She smiled and sniffed, then looked straight into his eyes. "Anyway, I just wanted to, you know, thank you for coming to the hospital last night."

Scott laughed nervously. "Oh, I guess that was kind of dumb. There wasn't really anything I could do there. We would have stayed later but, you know, Mrs. Ellis had to get home to Zack…" He broke the gaze, looked down and trailed off.

"It's okay. It was so nice of you to be there, even just for a while. It meant a lot to me. So, thank you." She kissed him on the cheek. Scott's face grew hot, and out of the corner of his eye he saw Jocelyn and Christina looking at each other.

"Well, I guess I'll see you later then," said Jenny, hoisting up her backpack.

He took a step back to get out of the way. "Uh, okay. Sure," he said quietly, as Jenny and her friends began walking down the hall. He watched them for a few seconds, his mind a total blank, when suddenly a thought from the previous night's midnight hour came into his head and he took a stumbling step toward them. "Hey! Hey, wait a minute, Jenny! Hold up there for a sec!"

The three girls stopped and looked back at him. *They look like Charlie's Angels,* thought Scott, and stood stunned for a moment. Suddenly he was there on the couch with his mom, watching that old show on DVD. She had loved it, and when he was little he'd thought her just as pretty as the Angels.

He snapped out of his momentary stupor. "I thought of something. Last night I thought of something I'd like to do for your father."

"Well I gotta go or I'm gonna miss the bus," said Jocelyn. "See you later, Jenny."

"Yeah, text me later," added Christina, and the two girls took off, leaving Scott alone with Jenny.

After explaining his plan, Jenny said goodbye to her two friends, and Scott accompanied her to her locker, talking a mile a minute.

They went outside to wait for the bus together.

"Boy, this is the most I've heard you talk since I met you. Who knew you could get so excited about something?" said Jenny, as the bus driver swung the door open and the group began to board. Jenny and Scott sat together, and he told her more about his idea.

The flurries from the previous night had turned into a freezing drizzle, creating an inch of slush on all the roads and sidewalks and making the walk home from the bus treacherous.

"Want to come to my house and I'll show you what I found?" asked Scott.

"Sure, why not?" Jenny replied. They held their jackets close against the cold, eager to get into the warmth of the house.

They went around to the side to enter through the kitchen door. Once inside, they removed their winter gear, hung it up on the pegs in the mud room and placed their boots on the mat, before going into the cluttered kitchen. Jenny took a swipe at the crumbs around the toaster, then noticed at the coffee rings on the counter and the dust on the top of the microwave. Scott was suddenly embarrassed; he hadn't realized how untidy the place was. He hadn't invited any friends over in a long time; he never knew when his father might be drinking so it was safer just to make their home off-limits to the few friends he did have. Things did seem to be changing, but Scott couldn't help but feel a little skeptical. Maybe he could encourage his father by brightening things up around the house a bit, do some spring cleaning, even though it was winter. For now he just said, "Yeah, I know. Mr. Clean would have a field day in here."

"I like all this stuff. I've never seen so many lighthouses!" She looked around at the lighthouse-themed curtains, cookie jar and canisters, and the lighthouse sun catchers on the kitchen windows. Scott's mom had left her touches all over the place, even if they were covered in a layer of greasy dust and fingerprints.

"Yeah, my mom was really into them. She and my dad even got engaged at sunset at Portland Head Light."

"Really? Oh that's so romantic!"

"Yeah," said Scott. "She really wanted to have a house by the ocean one day. That was her plan for when my brother and I grew up, that she and Dad would move to the coast. Obviously…well, you know." He realized he was turning this opportunity into a downer, and he looked around nervously, his gaze landing on an open bag of snacks. "Want some Doritos?" He grabbed the bag and held it out to her.

"Sure," said Jenny. "Got a bowl?"

"Uh, yeah, but what do we need a bowl for?"

"Because we're civilized, dummy," she said, taking it upon herself to open up some cabinets and search for one. She brought out a large red bowl with a lighthouse design. "Got anything to drink?"

"Oh yes, m'lady. We hath a selection of Mountain Dew and Dr. Pepper. Which would you prefer?"

"Ew. I guess I'll just have water."

"Sorry, we don't have any of that," said Scott, and they both broke out laughing. Her laugh sounded like the wind chimes his mom had loved so much, and his heart started to beat a little faster. He was so excited to have her here in his house, and she seemed to be happy to be with him. This was crazy.

He set his laptop up on the kitchen table. "You gotta see these," he said. "You're gonna be amazed by what people are doing with their displays."

They were seated at the kitchen table, "oohing" and "ahhing" over some videos when they heard Sam's car pull into the driveway. Scott's stomach automatically clenched. Would Dad really be sober?

Jenny was still looking at one particularly amazing video. "This seems like it would take a lot of work, though," she said.

He turned his attention back to her. "Not really. We could do this. We could make your dad's display kind of, uh, go with the music just like these decorators did. Will you help me? It would be a great surprise for your Dad, even if we just had it up when he comes home, just for that one night so we don't tick off Mrs. Michaud."

By the time he'd finished talking, Jenny had a funny look on her face. She looked kind of sad. "You know, you're more in tune with my Dad right now than I am." She sighed. "Sure, I'd love to help. This would really cheer him up." She smiled, even though she still looked like she was going to cry. Scott didn't know if he would ever understand girls and their emotions.

Sam came through the outer door, disturbing these thoughts. Scott looked up and took a chance on faith.

"Hey, Dad. Come here. We've got to show you something."

Sam took off his coat and boots and walked into the kitchen. He seemed sober. "Hi Scott, how was…oh hey. You've got company," he said, closing the entryway door. "You're Don's daughter. Jenny, right? Sorry about the mess."

All of Scott's muscles relaxed as he realized his dad was sober. He hadn't even realized he was tensed up. "Dad," said Scott. "Look at this." Sam looked at the monitor over his son's shoulder for a few seconds and broke into a smile.

"This is fantastic," he said. "Where is this? Has Don seen it?"

"I've showed these to him, but he says it takes too much time. But there's a guy down in Augusta who's selling the hardware to make this happen, and he's even already got some sequences he'll share with me," said Scott. Sam shook his head in confusion.

"Sequences," Scott explained. "Those are the computer programs that make the lights dance. It takes a lot of time to create them, but this guy already has a bunch of songs sequenced so it really wouldn't take any time at all for us to set it up. Just gotta set up the hardware and plug in the lights. There's this one song—*The House on Christmas Street*—that talks about all the stuff decorating the house, like the bunch of snowmen, and even Santa on the roof. It's perfect for Mr. Cassidy's display. Anyway, I've been studying up about it online. I know just what to do, and I want to set this up to surprise Mr. Cassidy when he comes home. What do you think, Dad? Jenny said she'll help me. Will you help, too?" Scott looked at his father eagerly. He knew he was talking really fast, but he was so excited.

Sam looked straight into his son's eyes, and a funny look came over him. Scott thought for a second that he might start crying. "There's so much of Mom in you, son." He ruffled his hair. Then he looked at the monitor again. "Well, I don't know. I guess, technically, there's no ordinance because nothing was decided last night. So there's nothing to stop us from finishing up the display."

"Nothing except Mrs. Michaud," said Scott. "The minute she sees one light go on you know she'll be on the phone to the cops."

"Well, maybe if we just light it up for one night. Just so Daddy can see it," said Jenny. "Maybe she won't mind if it's just one night? We could talk to her."

Just then, the doorbell rang "You expecting anybody?" Sam said.

"I don't have a clue," said Scott, getting up. Suddenly there came a flurry of pounding on the back door. Scott darted around the kitchen table, nearly tripping over a chair, and opened the door. Zack Ellis stood there in the mud room, hands pounding the air as though the door were still closed. His mother stood close behind, asking him calmly to stop. It took them a second to realize that Scott was standing in the doorway, looking bemused. "Hello," he said.

Zack pushed past Scott and entered the kitchen, slush on his boots making wet tracks on the stained linoleum. His mom grabbed his elbow to keep him from stepping in any farther, but he shook her off. "Hi Jenny," he said, waving enthusiastically. Then he clasped his hands behind his back and stood rocking from side-to-side, looking around the room.

"Hey Zack! How are you?" said Jenny. Zack smiled, his eyes darting from corner to corner.

"Hey, Angie. Come on in and join the party," said Sam.

Angie slipped off her ankle boots and stepped into the kitchen. "Zack, come back here. You're making a mess. Come here and take off your boots."

"It's okay," Sam said. "He's not causing any harm."

"Well, I hope this isn't a bad time. We were walking home from Zack's afterschool care and we were talking about what happened to Don. Zack had an idea and wanted to share it with Scott. Before I knew it, he was over here ringing your doorbell. To tell you the truth, I'm surprised he even knows this is your house!" Her cheeks were rosy from the cold air outside. She pulled down her hood and her hair fell out in a tangle of curls onto her shoulder. Scott had never realized how pretty she was.

Zack's hands flew out from behind his back and began fluttering under his chin. "I have an idea, a good idea," he said, smiling broadly.

"Well, hang on a sec," said Sam. "Let's get your coats off and I'll put on a pot of coffee." "Would you like some cocoa or something, Zack?"

"No, no," said Zack. Then he looked up at his mom. "No, thank you please," he added.

"Want some Doritos?" Jenny held out the bowl and Zack immediately stuck his mittened hand into it, causing the chips to fly out and scatter across the table and floor. Jenny laughed.

"Whoa. Sorry, sorry, sorry!" said Zack, pulling off his mittens and bending down to collect some of the bits. His hat fell off onto the floor, leaving his blonde hair sticking out in all directions.

"Oh, don't worry about it," Scott said, as he got the dustpan out from under the sink and swept up the mess. "You definitely don't want to eat these now, though. The three-second rule doesn't apply around here."

"He's a little excited," said Angie, helping Zack off with his coat and stuffing the hat and mittens in his coat sleeves. Sam took the coat on his arm, then reached out, helped her off with her coat and hung both garments in the mud room. "Oh, he's just a little excited," he said, chuckling.

Angie turned beet red, and Scott thought, *Wow. She does have a crush on him. And it's just a little obvious.*

"Zack does have a great idea. Why don't you tell them about it, honey?" Angie pulled out a chair and sat down, then looked at her son, who was standing in the middle of the room, still except for his fluttering fingers.

Sam pulled up a chair across from Angie. Scott was putting the dustpan away, and he turned back around and caught Jenny just about to stuff another Dorito into her mouth. Everyone else was staring at Zack.

"Umm," the boy said, his hands momentarily frozen. He looked down at the floor as though he wished he could bore a hole through it and slip out of the room. "I don't know, I don't know, I don't know." His hands began to flutter at his sides.

Chapter 33

Her son had frozen in front of people like this many times before, and Angie knew what to do. "It's okay, Zack. Take your time. No one's in a rush. We'll wait for you."

She sat still in the chair and looked around at everyone, putting a finger to her lips as if to say "shhh." They all remained silent. The only sounds in the room were Zack's labored breathing and the scraping of his fingers on his jeans. After several minutes he took a deeper breath, clenched his fingers and said, "Light up all the houses. We should light up all our houses for Mr. Cassidy. For when he comes home." He was still looking down at the floor. Angie let her breath out in relief.

Jenny was the first to speak. "Zack, that's a great idea! My dad would love that!"

"There's no reason why we can't, is there?" Angie asked. "I mean, the Selectmen didn't actually vote on anything."

"So why couldn't we light it up, as a surprise for my dad?" said Jenny.

Zack continued to look down, but he broke into a broad grin. "I can help. We can put lights on your house, Scott, and on my house, too. Blue, green, orange, red, white, yellow."

Sam looked at Angie. "Do you have any lights or decorations, Angie?"

She shook her head. "Guess I'll have to head down to the hardware store."

He leaned forward, hands on the table. "I've got some in the basement. We had our own, and then we inherited Stephanie's parents' collection when they passed away, so we've probably got enough for your house, too. I can come on over tomorrow morning and help you put them up, if you want."

Did she want Sam Anderson to come over to her house? That was a no-brainer. "Okay, that would be great." she said, sounding like a teenager. She couldn't help grinning at him. *I should have freshened my lipstick before coming in here.*

"Then, if you have time, maybe you can come over here and help us decorate our house, too," Sam said. "But before any of that, Scott and I will go over to your house first thing in the morning, Jenny, and make sure Santa and the reindeer are all set up securely on that roof. Your dad will be in for a great surprise when he gets home from the hospital."

"Oh, he'll be even more surprised when he sees what I've got up my sleeve," said Scott. "Want to take a ride down to Augusta with me after dinner, Jen? It's only a twenty minute drive. You'll be home in time to watch *The Bachelor* or whatever."

Jenny slugged him in the arm.

Chapter 34

Saturday dawned with a cloudless sky but there was a definite nip in the November air. Scott awoke to the whistle of a text from Jenny, and it took him a few minutes to come to the surface. He and his dad had stayed up pretty late the night before cleaning up the kitchen. It took a lot longer to really get it sparkling than Scott had anticipated, but it was kind of fun doing it with his dad as they listened to classic rock tunes blasting from his iPod dock.

He reached over and picked his phone up off the nightstand.

Hey. You up?

Yeah. I didn't sleep much. What's going on?

I told my Mom about what we're doing today. She was so happy. She said we should thank God for you.

What do you mean?

I mean she said a prayer out loud thanking God for you and asking Him to take care of you.

Me?

Well, you know, all you guys.

Scott had no idea how to respond to that, and he rested the phone on his chest while he pondered it. It was kind of weird. He wasn't religious, and they didn't really go to church any more since his mom died. The phone whistled with another text from Jenny.

???

"What am I supposed to say?" Scott mumbled to himself. "If I say the wrong thing..."

The phone whistled again.

Do you think that's weird or something?

"Oh, great. First time she texts me and I'm going to blow it," Scott whispered into his pillow. Then he typed furiously.

No! No! I'm just surprised, I guess. I never really thought about anybody praying for me, or us.

Well, that's my mom. She never takes anything for granted. :)

"Huh," Scott said. "That's interesting. Good way of looking at life, I guess."

Wow. Well, tell her thanks. That's really nice.

It's going to be hard keeping this a secret from my dad! I can't wait to see his reaction!!! <3 <3 <3

Do you know when he's coming home?

They're moving him to cardiac rehab today and Mom said he'll come home Tuesday or Wednesday. Think we'll have everything ready by then?

We'd better!

When are you coming over?

I don't know. Soon. I gotta get out of bed.

Well, hurry up, lazy bones. Mom's already got the coffee on.

As promised, Scott and Sam were knocking at the Cassidy's door at 9 a.m. Maggie answered the door wearing a blue flannel robe over her floor-length nightgown and Scooby Doo slippers on her feet. Scott couldn't help but laugh. "You like these?" she asked. "I won them in the gift swap at church last Christmas. They are so comfortable. And don't bother to ask, you can't have them." *She's a big kid just like her husband*, he thought.

Maggie invited them in for coffee and muffins. Jenny was in the kitchen, adding melon balls to a fruit salad as Angie set out plates and napkins. Zack was seated, staring at a box from Pierce's Pastry and Pie Shoppe downtown. Whatever was in there smelled really good.

The little group enjoyed breakfast and conversation around the table. The subject turned to Thanksgiving, and Sam told them all about Scott's brother, Brian, who would be coming home for the holiday. Everyone expressed a desire to meet him, especially Angie, who said she'd remembered seeing them all together, having fun in their yard, more than once. Images of fun and parties on the lawn flashed through Scott's mind, causing a tweak of pain in his gut.

Then he noticed how his father and Angie were looking at each other, and thought, *Mr. Cassidy's display is working its magic, just like he hoped. That's cool. Mom would be glad that Dad is happy again.*

When breakfast was finished, Sam and Scott went up on the roof and checked to make sure everything was secure. Jenny went into the living room to read up on the gizmo that she and Scott had purchased in Augusta the night before; the thing that was supposed to make the lights go all "blinky-flashy" in time to music.

After they climbed down off the roof, Scott walked into the street and took a look at the display in all its glory. He felt the stirrings of the little boy in him, and he smiled. Mr. Cassidy was right. He could just imagine the looks on the faces of all the little kids who might have passed by here in the weeks to come, and how happy they would have been to see all of these magical things. That thought filled him with joy, but it was quickly replaced by disappointment because it was only going to be lit up for just one night, and hardly any kids would see it.

But what a night that would be.

Angie could not believe Sam Anderson was here at her house, helping hang lights around the front porch of the bungalow. His attitude, the way he seemed to be enjoying himself—it all reminded her of the man she'd seen on those occasions when she saw him with his family as she'd passed by their house. It was great to see him like this again. Now, it would be even more wonderful if she had something to do with it, but it was way too early to think about that. She just really liked the way he looked, all bundled up in his winter gear, with his eyes twinkling and that gorgeous smile. Zack really seemed to be enjoying his company, and that was a big bonus.

Her mind was wandering through the possibilities when the Nadeaus' minivan pulled into their driveway next door. Andy jumped out and rushed around to open the back door as Angie, Sam and Zack approached the van. He carefully unfastened the baby carrier from its car seat mount, eager to show off the baby. While he was doing that, Jenny and Scott came across the driveway to join the group and offer congratulations. A tired-looking Esmerelda got out of the van and accepted hugs all around.

"Hey everybody," said Andy, beaming. "Meet Luisa Nicolette Nadeau!" He held up the baby carrier, as Esmerelda reached over and pulled the pink baby cap away from her daughter's eyes, where it had slid down during the ride from the hospital. Locks of jet-black hair peeked out from under the cap. The plump-cheeked baby looked like a little angel in her swaddle of pink, as she slept peacefully, in spite of the attention. Everyone marveled at her and agreed that she was the prettiest baby they'd ever seen.

Something in Angie stirred. She used to dream of having a little girl, and raising her with a loving and present father. Someone who would not just accept Zack, but love him, too. Just then, her son piped up.

"Is she real?"

"Yes, she's real," said Esmerelda. "You'll probably hear her crying all the way over from your house!"

"Is she sad? Will she be sad?"

"No, Zack, just hungry. She cries when she needs to be fed," said Esmerelda. "And speaking of that, it's great to see you guys, but I think I'm gonna take her in and feed her now, and then hopefully put her down and take a little nap myself."

"Need some help, Esme?" Andy asked.

"No, that's okay. I got it. I'm sure you have some stories to share." She smiled, kissed him on the cheek and took the baby carrier up the stairs to the porch.

"Something's missing here," said Angie, as she peeked through the van's back window. "Where are the boys?"

"Oh, they're at my mom and dad's house in Fairfield. They came to the hospital to meet their little sister, and then we thought it might be best if they spent the weekend with Mimi and Pépère, so we could have some quiet time at home with the baby for a few days. My folks are bringing them back on Monday morning." He paused. "So what are you guys up to?"

Angie took a breath. She'd been dreading telling Andy what had happened after he left Don up on the roof to take Esmerelda to the hospital. He looked exhausted, and there was a two-day growth of stubble on his chin and cheeks. "Um, Andy, there's something you should know," she said, putting a hand on his shoulder.

"About what happened to Don?" He looked at her, wide-eyed, and nodded. "I already know. I tried to call him Friday morning, and Maggie answered the phone."

As if on cue, Maggie and Jenny came out of their front door and bounded across the lawn. Catching up to the group, Maggie said, "Is there a beautiful new baby here? We want to see!"

"Hey, guys," said Andy. "Esme just took her into the house to feed her. Is it okay if we call you later when she's awake from her nap?

"Sure, that would be great," Maggie said.

"We can't wait to see her!" added Jenny.

Andy shifted his weight from foot-to-foot and said, "Listen, I know I told you already, Maggie, but I'm really, really sorry about what happened."

Maggie put a hand on his arm. "Andy, I told you, it wasn't your fault. You asked him to come down and he refused. He even told me that himself. My husband can be a very stubborn man when it comes to his display."

Andy shook his head and went on, "Well, anyway, Maggie told me on the phone that Don was also at Kennebec City Hospital, so when Esme and the baby were asleep I went to look in on him. He was sleeping, too, but Maggie was there, and she told me the whole story about how you found him, Sam, and I told her about how the boys came over to get me when Esmerelda's water broke." He shook his head and stuffed his hands in his pockets. "I should have made sure he got down off the roof before I left, but I was so nervous, and the baby was coming, and the twins were yelling and everything…"

Angie felt for him; he clearly felt at fault. "Hey, it's okay. How could you have known? Did you know he'd had a heart attack before?"

"That's the thing," said Andy. "No, I didn't."

Maggie interrupted. "Don really didn't want that to be common knowledge. He was hoping to move forward up here and not have everybody worrying about him all the time."

"Well, I never would have left him up there if I'd known that." He shook his head again.

"Don't beat yourself up, man," said Sam. "There's no way you could have predicted what would happen. You had to take care of your wife, after all."

"Well, I sure feel bad about it. I wish there was something I could do to make up for it."

Zack, who had been sitting on the bungalow porch rearranging a string of lights, called out. "Scott, look, I got this one done!" and he held up the string and waved it around.

"What are you guys doing?" said Andy. "Are you decorating? I thought you weren't supposed to do that. Didn't the Selectmen say Don couldn't have his display?"

Sam said, "Well, not exactly. They tabled the matter when Don had his accident. There's no actual law against it...yet. So we decided to finish the display and decorate our own houses, too, in solidarity. We're going to light up on Wednesday night, when Don comes home from the hospital."

"What about..." and he tilted his head toward the house across the street. Angie had to chuckle to herself. It was almost like Muriel Michaud had become "He Who Must Not Be Named" from the Harry Potter stories.

Maggie sighed. "That's a different story. I'm going to go talk to her, very gently, and explain things to her, and try to get her to see our side. I'm going to tell her we just want to light up that one night."

Sam shook his head. "You don't need to do that. The Selectmen didn't make any ruling, so we can light up the whole town if we want and keep the lights on until the next Selectmen's meeting. Who cares what that old bat thinks?"

Maggie put her hands on her hips and looked at him sternly. "*I* care what she thinks. I do. For whatever reason, this has become a big deal to her, and I think the kind and courteous thing would be to tell her what we plan to do. In fact, I actually think it was a big mistake that Don didn't talk to the neighbors about his display before he started setting it up. Maybe all this madness could have been avoided."

"Hmm. Well, maybe you have a point. Maybe we should only light up for that one night until the Selectmen have their say," said Sam.

"Do you think she'll be okay with it, Mom?" asked Jenny.

"I don't know, sweetheart, but I have to try. Maybe she's not just a mean old lady. She looked so fragile at the Selectmen's Meeting, I actually started to feel sorry for her."

Angie nodded. She'd had a few thoughts like that of her own over the last couple of days. "Want me to go with you?"

"No, that's okay. They're not home anyway. I went over there this morning after breakfast but there's no one around."

"Well, in any case, count me in on the decorating. Guess I'll have to make a trip down to the hardware store," said Andy.

"Have we got a deal for you!" said Sam, and he ushered him over to the porch where Zack was now replacing the lights in another string. A cardboard carton full of tangled lights sat there. "Help yourself, pardner!" said Sam, and Andy dug in.

Chapter 35

The Michauds spent a restful night in a comfortable four-poster bed with a fluffy down comforter at the White Mountain Bed and Breakfast in North Conway, New Hampshire. Muriel woke up feeling better than she had in a long time. *Must be something about the mountain air, she thought. It cleanses the brain.*

They enjoyed a late breakfast in the dining room—cranberry walnut muffins, omelets, and home fries, with fresh juice and hot coffee. It was a little more than Muriel usually ate, but what did that matter when one was on vacation? While waiting for the food to arrive, she had entertained their fellow travelers—a middle aged man and woman from down in Connecticut, a young couple on their honeymoon, and a family who had come up to the area to visit Santa's Village—with tales of the children, grandchildren, and Emma, the apple of her eye.

After the meal, they sat and enjoyed their coffee, and Muriel started in with the story of their "horrible" neighbor. The young couple and the family had excused themselves by the time she got to the part about the petition, and she noticed Ray giving her a look.

"Muriel," he said, "We're supposed to be here to put that behind us."

She felt sheepish. "I know, but he's just so inconsiderate."

Ray nodded. "Yes, but I'm sure our new friends here have heard quite enough. They have things to do, and so do we." She glanced at the only other people left at the table, the middle-aged couple. He had a really bad comb-over and she could have benefited from a dye job. Muriel wondered if they were married, and checked out their hands to search for wedding rings. That's when she noticed they were both getting a little fidgety.

Ray folded his napkin, put it on the table and stood up. "Time's a wastin'," he said, cheerfully. "Didn't you want to hit some of the antique barns around here?"

"Oh well, all right," she said, getting up. "It was awfully nice to meet you folks. Stop by if you're ever up in Central Maine."

"Oh, we sure will," said the man, smiling, but Muriel had a feeling he really didn't mean it. He rose from the table so fast his chair nearly fell over.

The woman nodded and said, "Have a nice day, now!" She picked up her purse and they scooted out of the dining room and up the stairs about as fast as they could go.

The rest of the day was filled with antiquing, good food and enjoying each other's company. Every once in a while, though, the thought of what was going on at home popped into Muriel's head. She had a sinking feeling she hadn't seen the last of those Christmas decorations.

Chapter 36

Angie smiled warmly at Zack as they stood on the sidewalk with Sam and Andy and admired their handiwork. Her bungalow porch was festooned with lights, as were the mailbox and the shrubs out front. Sam had found a couple of strings of candy cane path markers and placed them along the walk. Maggie had let them borrow a blow-mold Santa that hadn't made it out to Don's display this year, and he looked pretty jolly standing at the top of the porch stairs, his sack of toys slung over his back. It wasn't quite as magnificent as Don Cassidy's display, but Angie thought it was pretty festive, nonetheless.

"Looks pretty good, huh?" said Sam. "What do you think, Zack?"

"Fantastic!" Zack yelled. He clapped his hands several times and his smile was one of the biggest Angie had ever seen.

"Well, we couldn't have done it without you, you know." Sam reached over and tentatively patted Zack on the back. The boy suddenly jerked away, put his head down and tightened his shoulders, and Sam quickly removed his hand. After a second or two Zack looked up and smiled again, and Sam smiled back reassuringly.

He's good with my son, Angie thought. *And Zack seems to be warming up to him. But maybe I shouldn't read too much into this.*

It was after 1pm, and with the Nadeaus' and Angie and Zack's house looking great, the group decided to break for lunch before tackling the Anderson place.

"Sergeant Pepperoni's again?" suggested Sam.

"Sounds good to me," said Angie. "I could eat pizza for breakfast, lunch and dinner."

Oh great, she immediately thought. *What a dumb thing to say. As if my figure isn't bad enough, now I sound like a fast food glutton.*

"I'm gonna have to pass on that. I've got the new baby, plus a ton of school work to do. Thanks for helping me decorate the house, though," said Andy. "So I guess I'll see you guys later?"

"Would it help if we brought you some food? How about a couple of pizzas and a family-sized salad?" offered Sam.

"Oh, that would be great. A big help. I'll tell Esme, she'll be really happy. Let me go get you some cash," said Andy, as he turned to cross the driveway to his house.

"No, no," said Angie.

"Not necessary," said Sam at the same time.

Andy stopped and looked at them. "But—"

"Consider it a baby gift! I don't have time to make a casserole!"

"Yeah," said Sam. "That's great. A baby gift!"

Andy tilted his head and his lips formed a lopsided smile. "Are you sure? Cause I feel like I should pay—"

"Your money's no good here," said Sam and Angie at the same time, and they all burst into laughter, even Zack.

"I'll swing by with the food when we get back," said Sam.

"Well, okay then. Thanks a lot! I guess I'll see you guys later."

As Andy turned and strode across the lawn to his house, the others went next door to the Cassidy house.

Scott and Jenny were busy setting up the "Light-O-Rama" equipment purchased in Augusta the night before. There were two metal boxes on the ground, and Scott had his laptop set up on a card table nearby. They were plugging extension cords into the cables coming from one of the boxes and checking things on the computer as they did it. The boxes and wires all looked Greek to Angie, but from the way Zack stood by patiently and watched, she could tell he was fascinated.

"How's it going?" Sam asked.

Scott smiled up at his dad. "Great. It's easy. I don't know why Mr. Cassidy never did this before."

"Well, not everyone's as fluent in computers as you are, Scott," Sam said. Angie saw the pride on his face, and the happiness beaming from Scott.

"And you know what, Dad? Paul Wood, that guy in Augusta that I got this stuff from? He had a sequence for that song I told you about—'The House on Christmas Street.' I think that's the song we should have playing when Mr. Cassidy comes home."

"You guys ready for a lunch break?" asked Sam.

Scott and Jenny, engrossed in their project, declined the offer to go out to lunch, but Maggie took some cash out of her purse and asked Sam to bring something back for the young workers. "I'm heading over to the hospital, and I don't know when I'll be back." She paused for a minute, and looked over at the other houses, and all the decorations that had been put up that morning. "And, really, thanks for everything. You guys are great. You barely know us yet, and you've all been so kind."

Angie actually felt a lump in her throat. "We should be thanking you. Look at how your family has brought us all together. This is wonderful. It's what a neighborhood should be."

"Well, it seems like a great neighborhood to me," Maggie said. "Now I'm gonna scoot, and I really appreciate you feeding my daughter!"

"No problem. I'll make sure no one goes hungry," said Sam, waving away her cash. "And don't worry. I got it."

"You sure?" Maggie asked.

"You bet. Now go see your husband and tell him he'd better be minding the doctor's orders, because we all need him back here, pronto." He turned to Zack. "Come on Zack, it's pizza time!"

The boy stood still and looked at his mother. "Can I stay here, Mom? I want to stay here," he said. "I like this. I want, I want to watch."

"Oh, I don't know..." Angie looked at Scott.

He shrugged. "That would be okay."

Angie had great misgivings about this; at the same time, she realized this was her chance to be alone with Sam. Still, her son was so unpredictable. But shouldn't she give him a chance? After all, his doctor had been suggesting they test the boundaries a little and try to give him a little more independence now that he was a teenager, and he seemed to really like these folks. Maybe she ought to take the risk. She turned back to Zack. "Wow, must be pretty amazing if you're willing to give up Sergeant Pepperoni's. You sure you won't get in the way?" asked Angie.

"I won't. I promise," said Zack, fluttering his fingers under his chin in excitement.

"And no meltdowns?"

Zack rapidly shook his head, but Angie knew this promise was meaningless. Zack could no more control his meltdowns than she could control the wind. She could give them her number, and the pizza place wasn't really that far away.

Angie looked at Jenny. "Is this okay with you?"

"It's fine. We're buds, aren't we, Zack?" She chucked him lightly on the shoulder.

Zack nodded rapidly and played with his scarf fringe. "Yes, we are buds. We sure are buds." He giggled.

Angie gave Jenny her cell phone number, and made Zack promise one more time that he would try really hard to use his calming strategies if he felt himself getting upset. These were things they had been working on for quite a while, and he had shown some success in using them. She had to learn to trust him when she wasn't around.

Sam turned to Angie. "Shall we go?"

"We shall!" she said, feeling positively giddy as they headed across the lawn, but as they got in Sam's car, she felt a nervous clench in her stomach. She didn't really know Sam Anderson at all. *What the heck am I going to talk about with this man? There is absolutely nothing interesting about me!*

Alone in his car with a good-looking woman for the first time in a long time, Sam began to feel awkward. The ride to the pizza place was mercifully short, but quiet, as he struggled to say something interesting that wouldn't make him sound like a dork. He liked her. She was pretty, of course, but there was something else about her. Like that old song said, she was "sunshine on a cloudy day." She was also careful and loving with her son. He didn't know a lot about her, but he was definitely liking what he had seen so far and he was feeling something, some kind of spark. All he really knew was that he was glad to get the chance to be with her today for a little while, and get to know her better.

The restaurant was crowded with families. Angie and Sam only needed a table for two, though, so they didn't have to wait very long. They briefly considered just getting take-out, but Sam put the kibosh on that.

"Let's stay," he said. "With all you have to do every day, wouldn't it feel good to just sit down and take a breather?" He hoped he wasn't being too forward, but he really wanted to have some alone time with her.

Angie nodded. "Yes. And some grown-up conversation wouldn't be bad, either."

"Well, that might be asking a little too much, but I'll try," Sam said, winking. *Oh no. Did I really just wink? She's gonna think I'm a weirdo.*

The hostess led them to a booth near a four-foot standup of "Sergeant Pepperoni." His blue uniform had patches of pepperoni on the shoulders and he seemed to be winking devilishly at them as they approached. *Now* that *guy can wink and not seem like a jerk,* thought Sam.

Angie took off her coat, and as Sam stepped behind her to help, tugging on a sleeve, she whirled around. "Oh!" she said. "You surprised me there for a sec."

"I may be getting to be a rusty old man, but I haven't forgotten the manners my mama taught me." He hung her coat on the hook at the end of the booth and they both sat down.

"Well, guys like you are rare these days," she said, then quickly looked away and grabbed a menu from the stand near the napkin dispenser. She studied it intently. "Zack loves this place, but we don't come here very often," she said. "He can't handle it for long."

Looking around at the tables packed with families, Sam said, "I can see why." The noise and chaos were enough to drive anyone crazy.

At a birthday party in one corner of the large room, someone dressed as Sergeant Pepperoni was pretending to play an accordion and serenading the birthday girl. Children were hopping up and down and laughing hysterically. Over at another table, a baby and toddler were having full-fledged, simultaneous meltdowns. Their harried-looking mother tried to contain the situation while her male companion paid the bill. The noise from the electronic games in the back of the room rang through the air, and every once in a while a deep voice with an Italian accent blurted out "A-make-a mine-a pepperoni!"

They ordered a plain cheese pizza to share, along with a couple of colas, and gave the waitress their additional "to go" order and asked that it be ready about a half hour after theirs was served. A moment of uncomfortable silence occurred after the waitress left, and then Angie clasped her hands together, set them down on the table and said, "So, second trip here in a week. You must really like pizza."

Sam looked at her and couldn't help but break into a grin. He raised his eyebrows and said, in his best Curly voice, "Soitanly!"

Angie's reaction was instantaneous. "I love The Three Stooges!"

Sam's heart leapt. She liked the Stooges! It was rare to find a woman who enjoyed their distinctive brand of humor. "You do?"

"Yes! I used to watch them all the time with my dad when I was little. They still make me laugh. Zack and I spend every New Year's Eve watching The Three Stooges marathon on TV56. It's become something of a tradition."

This was too much. It was a secret known only to his family that he was a dyed-in-the-wool fan. "Okay...then I gotta ask you a question, although I'm a little afraid of the answer."

Angie's eyes twinkled merrily. "I know. Who's my favorite Stooge, right? Uh-oh, this is where it all falls apart."

"Why? Which one is it?"

"I don't want to say. You'll think I'm weird."

"And what would be wrong with that?" Sam asked. "Come on. I'm already blown away by the fact that you like them at all. Tell you what. I'll count to three, and then we'll each say our favorite Stooge, okay?"

Her smile was radiant. "Okay," she said.

He counted slowly. "One...two...three..."

"Shemp!" they both shouted at once.

Angie burst into gales of laughter as Sam's mouth dropped open. "Stop it! Really? Are you kidding? Is he really your favorite?"

"Yes! He is! I know it's odd, but my dad looked kind of like Shemp, so I've always been partial to him. The unsung Stooge." Then she stopped laughing and looked at him seriously. "Were you kidding?"

Sam shook his head in amazement. "No, I wasn't! I've just always thought he was hilarious. I mean, I know Curly is the one everyone loves, but to me, Shemp's humor was more...sophisticated."

"Sophisticated?" she said, and started laughing heartily again. It was like music to his ears. Those dimples of hers were so enchanting he wanted desperately to keep her laughing.

He put on a serious face and said, "Did your dad really look like Shemp? Cause if he did, I feel kinda sorry for him."

Angie cracked up to the point where tears were streaming down her face. If there was one thing Sam loved, it was being with people who knew how to laugh. It had been so very long since he'd had that in his life. Finally, her laughter faded into a giggle and she wiped her eyes with a napkin. She managed to look at him again without losing it.

The waitress brought their drinks and set them on the table, then quickly left and went to serve another customer.

Angie sighed. "Well, I guess we've broken the ice."

"I guess so," he said. "I knew my Three Stooges obsession would come in handy someday." Now that the laughter was over, Sam found himself stymied. He looked down at the paper menu on the table. "I haven't been much for conversation in quite some time." As if to prove the point, words failed him.

As the moment stretched out, Angie looked around awkwardly, then said, "Don's Christmas display sure is going to be something."

Sam seized on this. "Funny the effect it seems to have on people. And it isn't even lit up yet." *And funny the effect you're having on me,* he thought.

"I know. It sure has gotten Zack and me out of a rut. I can't believe how all this has affected him. It's really brought him out of himself, which is pretty amazing."

"He's pretty amazing," said Sam. "And from what I can see, so is his mom."

Angie blushed again, in a way that was absolutely endearing.

"You know," he said, "I wasn't even going to help out. I barely realized what was going on next door until the Michauds came to my door with that petition."

"Oh, I know. Isn't she something else? She hardly ever talks to anyone in the neighborhood and suddenly she's out knocking on doors."

"Oh, you don't know the half of it. When my wife—Stephanie— was alive, that woman called the cops on us a couple of times because we were having fun outdoors. But anyway, I guess I've been in kind of a fog since Stephanie died. I haven't even been paying attention to my own sons, let alone what's going on in the neighborhood. Drinking my sorrows away like some bad cliché. I just, you know, I just didn't know how to live without her."

He shook his head slowly from side-to-side. "I don't know why I'm talking about this. I'm sorry. I don't mean to be a downer."

Angie put her hand over his. "You don't have to talk about it if it makes you sad, but I really don't mind. I'm a pretty good listener, and like I said, I don't get enough adult conversation, so please don't stop on my account."

Sam put his glass down and wiped his mouth with a napkin. "The thing is, I guess I really do need to talk about it, because I haven't talked with anyone, really. I've just been going through the motions every day. It wasn't until they came to the door and I actually took a look around that it hit me. That display is just the kind of thing Stephanie would have loved. Loved? Hell, she would have been over there on the first day, helping them out, and here I was not even noticing what was going on. I was turning into a real jerk, too. I completely forgot about Scotty's birthday, and then when I did remember I felt like it was too late, and all I did was sit and watch old videos of his birthday party instead of celebrating with him. I haven't known how to deal with my grief, let alone his. I'm actually thinking about going to an AA meeting next week. I mean, it hasn't gotten out of control yet, but I don't want it to, either."

He stared into Angie's unwavering brown eyes, feeling the warmth of her hand on his. He was really unloading now, and wondering what was going on in her head. "Hmm," he said, shrugging. "You probably think I'm a loser."

Angie shook her head. "No, I would never think that. I think you're great." She blushed, and it was beautiful. *She thinks you're great. Okay, you haven't screwed it up yet.*

"I mean, I don't really know you very well, but you seem great to me. I mean, what I know of you…is great. I mean…oh, I sound ridiculous. What I'm trying to say is, you shouldn't feel bad. You've gone through a lot. Everybody handles grief differently. And the fact you're taking positive steps like considering to an AA meeting…well, that seems pretty brave to me."

Sam looked up and gazed into her eyes. She seemed so kind, and sweet, and yet so strong, raising her son all by herself. Yes, they hardly knew each other, but he felt like he'd known her all his life. There was only one other woman who'd ever had that effect on him. And those beautiful brown eyes. They made him feel safe again.

He took a deep breath and sighed. "I can't even believe it's already been over a year," he said. Then he felt himself starting to tear up, and he broke her gaze. This definitely wasn't like him. He cleared his throat, took another sip of soda, and shrugged. "Anyway, when the Michauds came to my door, at first I thought I'd go over and help with the display just out of spite. But the more I thought about it, the more I realized that helping out would be just what Steph would want me to do, and it would be a way to connect with Scotty again, and just get me out of my own way, you know? I thought about it all week long, and then when I saw everybody over there last Saturday it seemed as though my wife was giving me a sign."

Angie took her hand away from Sam's and fiddled with her necklace. "I wish I had known her. I've been so busy raising Zack that I've never really taken the time to stop and talk to anyone in the neighborhood. Whenever I drove by and saw her out in your yard with your boys it always made me smile, though. She seemed like such an adoring and fun-loving mom."

"Oh, she was. She loved our boys more than anything in the world. We weren't supposed to be able to have kids…she had something called polycystic ovarian syndrome."

"Oh, I know what that is. My sister has it," said Angie.

"Really? I'd never heard of it until Stephanie was diagnosed. That's too bad. Does your sister have kids?"

"No, she's not married. Hasn't met the right guy, I guess."

"Well I hope it works out for her. With us, just as we were about to start fertility treatments, Steph got pregnant with Brian. But Scotty was another story. She ended up going on fertility drugs and she got pregnant the very first month. If she hadn't, we might have ended up with twins, or maybe even more. She said it didn't matter. We could have had ten kids and she'd have loved them all the same."

Then, without hesitation or fear, Sam told her about Stephanie's fatal illness; what it was like when she was first diagnosed, and how hard it had been to lose her. He told Angie things he had never told another living person, and she listened.

It felt good, like a huge bag of sand was being lifted off his chest. As he spoke he noticed that she didn't interrupt, and when she did speak it was obvious that she had really heard him and had only thoughtful things to say. The two of them didn't even notice how long it was taking for their order to arrive on this exceptionally busy day.

When the pizza and drinks arrived, Sam served up a couple of slices to Angie, saying "Bon appétit!" as he placed the paper plate in front of her.

"Umm, that's French," she said, raising her eyebrows. "Shouldn't you be speaking Italian?"

"I don't know Italian. How's this?" he said, affecting an exaggerated accent. "Bon-a appetit-a! Make-a-mine-a pepperoni!"

Angie giggled.

Sam got serious again. "Enough about me," he said. "Tell me about you and Zack."

At first Angie spoke clinically; about Zack's autism, his talents and challenges, like she was reciting it by rote. But then she confided in Sam about the frustration, exhaustion, and unique joy of raising her special boy. Her voice filled with emotion as the words came tumbling out of her mouth. She talked about Zack's father, how they were supposed to get married but he left before their son was born. *What a creep,* Sam thought.

"Geez," Angie said after a while, "I don't know why I'm telling you all this!"

"It's okay," said Sam. "I guess both of us have really needed somebody to talk to. And here we are. Funny that we've been just up the street from each other all this time and never realized that what we needed was practically in our own backyard."

He stopped talking and just looked at her. That had been kind of a bombshell thing to say, and maybe he shouldn't have said it. He held his breath as she sat there, not saying anything for what seemed like forever. Then she said, "Well, I guess the timing just wasn't right."

Just then his cell phone beeped. He fished it out of his pocket and looked at the screen. It was a text from Scott:

Hey Dad, didya get lost? You've been gone almost an hour and a half. We're starving here!

"Oh shoot," he said, "It's nearly three. We'd better get out of here or we're gonna have some angry people on our hands!"

They had barely noticed when the waitress put their "to go" order on the table with a convenient box for their leftovers. "Oh, when did she bring this? I didn't even notice," said Angie.

"Neither did I," said Sam. "I guess I was kind of distracted." He wiggled his eyebrows up and down. Now he was officially flirting. Was it okay? Was it too hokey? *How are middle aged guys like me supposed to flirt? Jeez, I'm such a dork.*

Angie didn't respond. She just stood up and reached for her coat, a Mona Lisa smile on her face. Awkward, he thought. I've gone too far out on a limb. He helped her with her coat, and she scooped up her bag and the pizza boxes and started toward the door. Sam ushered her through the noisy crowd with his hand lightly on her back, and he didn't remove it when they walked out into the parking lot. In fact, he kept it there all the way to the car, where he politely opened the door for her. He figured he was out on that limb already; he may as well hang there.

Mercifully, she started talking as soon as he got in the car, and the ride home was completely different than the ride to the restaurant. They talked about the plan for Don's return, and the conversation was easy. No awkwardness at all; in fact, Sam actually wished it would take longer to get home.

When they pulled into the driveway at his house he was stunned to see that the front steps, front door, the windows and all the hedges were trimmed with the white lights Stephanie had loved. Her favorite lighted wreath was hanging on the front door, and her wooden snowman was staked in the ground by the front steps. On the other side was the sign she had hand-painted; a bright red stop sign trimmed in green, and on it was lettered "Santa—Please Stop Here."

Angie got out of the car right away; he was glad she didn't notice that he was just sitting there, forgetting to breathe. His stomach clenched and he felt tears burning in his eyes. *Stephanie. Oh, Stephanie, how I wish it was you who had put all of these things in their places,* he thought, and in his mind's eye he saw her, standing on the little front stoop and smiling at him. *What am I doing, thinking of Stephanie when I've just been flirting with Angie? Oh my God, I'm so confused.* He squeezed his eyes shut, and for the briefest of seconds he heard Stephanie's voice saying, "It's alright, my love. It's alright." Those were the very last words she'd ever spoken, as she lay in a hospice bed, her hand in his, before she slipped into oblivion.

He took a deep breath, let it out and realized that he felt a little better. It was as though Stephanie was giving him her blessing, and the momentary pain melted into a feeling of calm. He put his hand on the door handle.

Chapter 37

Carrying the containers of salad and utensils up the steps toward Sam's house, Angie felt like she was floating. Sam Anderson had been outright *flirting* with her. At least she thought he had. It had been so long she wasn't even sure what it was like anymore. In fact, she'd been so surprised that she didn't even react, and it had been awkward for just a minute there. Luckily, she was able to rescue things by talking about Don Cassidy on the way home. She owed *that* guy big-time.

Maggie was on a stepladder, hanging a ball of greenery from the roof of the small front porch. *Oh God*, Angie thought. *Is that a kissing ball?*

"Well, what took you guys so long? I've been to the hospital and back and you're just getting here now? Must've been crowded at Sergeant Pepperoni's." Angie detected a hint of friendly teasing in Maggie's voice.

"Yes, it was," said Angie. Then she looked up and pointed at the greenery in mock bewilderment. "What's that?"

"Oh, I have a feeling you'll find out soon enough," Maggie said, winking. Angie quickly looked down in embarrassment.

The car door slammed and Sam walked toward them with the pizza boxes. "Your boy is a certified genius," Maggie said, pointing to

Scott and Jenny on her lawn next door. "He figured out that synchronized lighting stuff in no time."

"Speaking of boys, where's mine?" asked Angie, looking around. She panicked for just a second until Maggie pointed across the street. Lo and behold, there was Zack, sitting on Eileen Ferris' porch with an old cardboard box, unscrewing light bulbs and screwing others back in a long string. Mrs. Ferris was wrapping a garland of plastic poinsettias and greenery around the porch posts and railings while her little dog capered on the front lawn, occasionally scampering up to Zack for a pet. "Wonders never cease!" said Angie.

She was startled out of her reverie by the shrill sound of Sam whistling, his fingers in his mouth. "Hey, you Christmas crew!" he yelled across the street. "We got hot pizza here! Everybody come over to our house and have some! You too, Mrs. Ferris!"

Within a few minutes the whole gang, including Mrs. Ferris, was gathered in the kitchen as they had been the previous evening, passing around drinks and paper plates and talking about the progress they'd made lighting up the neighborhood.

Sam ran over to Andy and Esme's house to deliver their food. When he returned, he reported back that the household was in chaos.

"What's going on?" asked Angie. "Do they need help?"

"No, I think they've got it under control. I just happened to walk in at the wrong time. The baby was screaming and the boys were fighting and Esmerelda was in the middle of it all. Andy was at the dining room table trying to study. He said the baby had been up most of the night."

Angie and Maggie exchanged sympathetic looks. "I remember those days of no sleep," said Angie.

"You feel like you're sleepwalking," Maggie added. "I can't imagine how hard it must be with preschooler twins to boot!"

"He offered me a tip," said Sam, "And said there'd be more if I could babysit for an hour or three. I don't even think he was joking."

"Hmm," said Angie. "I'll pop over there soon and see if there's any way I can help."

"Maybe we should bring them a meal," said Maggie. "Would you help me whip up a pasta bake tomorrow, Jenny?" Her daughter nodded.

Sam grabbed a can of soda and sat down across from Angie. "You know, it's great to have this place filled with people again. This is the first time the kitchen has felt so warm in a long time."

"And clean," added Scott.

"I noticed that!" Jenny winked.

"My dad and I stayed up half the night..."

Angie was startled when Sam reached out and gave her hand a squeeze. She turned and looked at him.

"I'm glad you're here," he said, in such a low voice that she wasn't sure anyone else could hear above the laughter and conversation. Those green eyes of his made her heart thump so loudly she could have sworn everyone in the kitchen could hear *that*. She felt her face flush, and she looked away quickly. She saw Maggie wink at her and mouth the words, "Kissing ball." That was it. She said, "Excuse me," and got up. "Uh, where's the...uh, powder room?"

"It's the second door down the hall, Ms. Ellis," said Scott.

Angie made a beeline for it, and didn't come back until the flush had gone out of her cheeks.

When the meal was finished, Maggie and Jenny excused themselves to head back to the hospital to visit Don. Sam walked them out to the driveway.

Scott gathered up the paper plates and boxes and took them out to the trash bin in the garage as Angie loaded the glasses into the dishwasher. Mrs. Ferris grabbed a sponge and wiped down the kitchen table. Zack stayed put in his chair and just watched everyone.

When Sam and Scott came back in the kitchen they were in the middle of a conversation. "...felt kind of like old times, didn't it, Dad?"

"It sure did, Scotty. It was great to have everybody here. We need to do this more often."

I'd love to come over more often, thought Angie.

Zack suddenly boomed out, "Finish the lights at Mrs. Ferris' house!"

Angie was a bit startled by this sudden outburst, but then Sam said, "You're right, Zack. We still have to do that." He looked at his watch. "We've only got an hour or so of daylight left, so we'd better hurry."

The five of them got back into their outdoor wear and went across the street to finish the job, which was completed in a snap. Then they all enjoyed a snack of vanilla cookies and cocoa, as Muffin ran around snarfing up the crumbs. Mrs. Ferris delighted them with stories of Christmases past on Franklin Street.

"You know," she said, "Muriel Michaud wasn't always the humbug she is now. When her kids were little, she spent many a cold day out there helping them make snow angels and build snowmen. She was a wonderful mother. And—oh yes, I almost forgot about this—she was the one who got the Christmas Parade started in Kennebec City."

"The Christmas Parade? What Christmas Parade?" asked Sam.

Angie brightened with the memory. "Oh, yeah. I remember that. I marched in that every year with the KCHS band. I played the trumpet."

"You did?" said Sam. "Wow! Do you still play?"

"Oh, no. I haven't touched that thing since high school. I think it's in my parents' attic, unless they sold it at a yard sale." Angie looked back at Mrs. Ferris and said, "I had no idea Mrs. Michaud was involved in that parade."

"Oh yes, she was, dear. When her kids were little, she and her husband had taken them up to Bangor to see the parade on Thanksgiving weekend, and she decided Kennebec City ought to have one, too. She got a committee of moms and dads together, they got the Rotary Club involved, and we had a parade every year. All three of her kids marched in it. Her son was in the Boy Scouts and her oldest daughter, when she got to high school, was a drum majorette. The youngest one, I think, played the glockenspiel or some such. That went on for years, until her kids grew up, and then she left the committee and things just petered out not long after that. There just wasn't any money or interest anymore, and then there was no parade anymore. It's too bad. It was a lot of fun."

"Wow, I had no idea," said Sam. "What the heck happened to make her so sour?"

"Oh, I don't know, dear. Sometimes it's just life, getting older. You know, it's so much fun to raise kids—oh, don't get me wrong, it has its challenges too—but when they leave, my goodness, it can leave a big hole in your life. Sometimes I wonder if Muriel is just lonely. I tried to stay friendly with her, but she turned me down for get-togethers so often I finally gave up."

Everyone went quiet for a minute, until Sam got up and said, "Well, we'd better be going. I still have papers to grade for Monday. Thank you, Mrs. Ferris, for your hospitality, and for agreeing to be a part of this little project."

Mrs. Ferris got up and brushed the crumbs off her skirt. "Oh I'm happy to do it, dear. You come over any time. Muffin and I just love to have visitors!"

They all said their good evenings, and Sam and Scott walked Angie and Zack back to their house. They could hear the baby wailing at the Nadeaus' house as they walked by, and Zack made an exaggerated "baby crying" face. Angie and Scott chuckled, but Sam didn't seem to notice.

When they got to Angie's door, she felt a little nervous. After such a wonderful day with everyone, and what seemed to be a big move forward in her relationship with Sam, she wasn't sure how their time together would end. And with Scott there…well, it seemed unlikely that there would be anything like a goodnight kiss. And besides, it was too soon for that, although she wouldn't turn her head if Sam leaned in.

"Well, uh, this has been a great day," Sam said. "And, um, guess we'll see you on Wednesday, huh?"

Angie was flustered at first, not knowing what he meant. *Did we make a date and I didn't realize it?*

"You know, for the big light-up, when Mr. Cassidy comes home?" Scott helpfully added.

"Oh, yes! Of course, yes!" she said. She felt suddenly very shy.

Sam said, "Yeah, yeah." He nodded rapidly. "Hey, thanks for having lunch with me. That was really, uh, nice." Suddenly he stopped. Angie noticed Scott looking down at the ground as time went ticking by. Then he raised his head suddenly.

"For gosh sakes, Dad, why don't you just ask her out? Everybody knows you two like each other!"

Angie was mortified. She couldn't believe that introverted Scott had just blurted this out. Sam looked as though he'd been backed into a corner, and she just wanted to run in the house, shut the door and never come out. Zack seemed oblivious to the whole thing.

After what felt like a million years, Sam cleared his throat and opened his mouth. "You know what? Scott is right. I do like you. Would you like to go out to dinner next weekend?"

She smiled. "Are you? I mean, I don't want…just because Scott…" She knew she was stumbling and felt foolish. But she *did* want to go out with him. She wanted that very much. Finally she swallowed, looked straight into his eyes and said, "Yes, I would. I would like that very much, as a matter of fact."

"Well alright," said Scott, and he tried to get Zack to high five him, but Zack just raised his hand in a salute.

Sam grinned and said, "How about Friday night, dinner and a movie? We can go anywhere you like, except Sergeant Pepperoni's."

"Ha!" Angie said, "Okay, how about Maria's?"

"That's-a-still-Italian!" said Sam in his goofy voice, and Scott looked at him like he came from Mars.

"Okay, then. How about the Kennebec City Steakhouse? I've heard it's very good and I've never been," said Angie.

"That sounds great. It's a date. I'll pick you up at six."

Then Sam gave her a quick hug, everyone said goodnight, and Sam and Scott headed back down the street to their house.

What the heck just happened? thought Angie. She didn't want this day to end. She wanted to believe it was the start of something for her and Sam. Feeling hopeful, she helped Zack through his bedtime routine, and then went into her own room and changed into her pajamas. She sat down at her mother's old vanity and began to brush her hair-100 strokes, just like she'd done as a child because her mom had told her it would make her hair shiny. As she looked at herself in the mirror, those old insecurities began to raise their ugly heads, and she started to question the possibility that Sam wanted anything more than friendship, even after the lovely time they'd had together. Scott *had* kind of put him on the spot. What could he do in that situation but ask her out? His wife had been a raving beauty. What could a handsome, intelligent man like him see in a plain Jane dental hygienist?

Chapter 38

The Michauds didn't arrive home until late Sunday night, long after sunset. During the ride home, Muriel said her stomach felt a little queasy and wondered if she was coming down with something. She eventually fell asleep and snoozed until Ray gently nudged her and helped her into the house and into bed.

Monday morning, the sky was partly cloudy and the radio weatherman was predicting a real snowstorm by Thanksgiving night. Other than the few flurries they'd had the night of the Selectmen's Meeting, Kennebec City had yet to see any lasting snow. Ray stepped outside to pick up the morning paper and hugged himself against the crisp breeze. The paper wasn't on the steps, and he had just spotted it on the driveway when something glittering across the street caught his eye. A ray of sunlight was glinting off the star at the top of one of those giant tree things they'd constructed at the Cassidys' house.

Hmmm, he thought, guess no one's had a chance to take all that stuff down yet. *Oh well, that's okay. If they leave it up until after Christmas no one will mind, as long as they don't light it up, and we'll have some peace and quiet around here.* Then he heard the jingling of bells coming from right next door.

To his utter astonishment, he noticed a string of sleigh bells hanging from Eileen Ferris' porch roof. And lights and garland wrapped all around the posts and bannister. And a plastic Santa Claus waving from the front stoop.

"What the heck?" he said out loud. Then he looked around slowly. All up and down the block, as far as he could see, most of the houses were decorated for Christmas, with plastic snowmen, angels, lights galore and Christmas banners waving in the breeze. "Oh my goodness," he said. "She is going to go out of her gourd when she sees this."

He snatched the newspaper off the driveway and rushed into the house, where, as far as he knew, his wife was still sleeping an untroubled sleep.

Ray was dismayed when Muriel woke up a while later, complaining of a headache and nausea. She immediately ran to the bathroom, and it wasn't good. He got her back into bed and brought her a large bowl in case she had to heave again. At some point it dawned on him that this might not be an entirely bad thing. If he could convince her she needed to lie in bed all day while he took care of her, maybe she wouldn't see what was going on in the neighborhood. He could at least buy some time and figure out what to do. He felt terrible thinking this way, but really, maybe this was a gift from God. He brought her tea and toast in bed, but she had no appetite. She asked him to keep the blinds closed because the light would hurt her eyes. Gladly, he thought. *It's not just the light out there that would hurt your eyes.* He sat on the bed with her and read the newspaper while she tried to go back to sleep.

When she finally nodded off, he waited just a little while, then he got up, went downstairs and called Paula and asked her to run an errand for him. When Muriel woke up a little while later, he was standing over her with a glass of water and two pills. "What's that?" she asked.

"Over-the-counter stomach flu medicine. The pharmacist recommended it. It will help you feel better."

"If I take that stuff I'll sleep the day away."

"And why would that be so bad?" said Ray, as he held out the pills. "Come on, sugar plum, open up."

Chapter 39

Don was sitting upright in bed, the untouched breakfast tray on the hospital table before him, when Maggie appeared in the doorway. He had been looking out the window, thinking about what a mess he'd made of everything. All his hopes for the Christmas season, all the smiling children's faces he'd imagined, all the happy families and the good feelings, all up in smoke because he was too stubborn to come down off that roof when he should have. Then he heard the sweet voice he knew so well say, "Well, hi there. That looks like a yummy breakfast. I can't understand why you aren't chowing down." He turned and saw her, a sight for sore eyes. She was wearing jeans and an oversized green cowl-neck sweater that reflected in her hazel eyes. Her shiny brown hair was down around her shoulders, and she didn't look a day older than the first time he'd laid eyes on her all those years earlier. She approached him and inspected the congealed scrambled eggs and cup of applesauce on the tray, then leaned over and kissed his head. He looked up at her, but didn't say anything. He was glad to see her, but just couldn't find the words.

"What's the matter? Cat got your tongue?"

"Eh, I'm just not hungry, I guess. I really don't feel like eating, or doing anything." He pushed the tray table away. "I really messed things up, Mags. I should have gone over there the very first day we looked at the house and introduced myself. I shouldn't have just assumed that everyone was going to love my display the way the people in Punta Gorda did."

Maggie rolled the tray table over to the side of the room and sat down on the bed with him. She said, "Honey, it's not going to do you any good to dwell on this. You know the doctor said you need to de-stress. Just put it all aside for now and maybe we can patch things up with them in the new year. Maybe next year this will all be just a bad memory."

He barely heard her; he was stuck on a train of thought and had to ride it until the end of the line. "And I was just an idiot to stay up on that roof after Andy left. I should have gone down and left it for another day. Now there's no way it's going to get finished, and it doesn't even matter that they didn't actually shut it down. Who needs Mrs. Michaud and the Selectmen when I could colossally mess up the plan all by myself?"

Maggie patted his knee. "You know," she said, "If you insist on talking about this I'm going to ask the doctor to give you a sedative. You really need to focus on getting better."

Don heaved a heavy sigh and said, "All right. I'll do my best." But he knew it was no use. He couldn't recall a time when he'd been so depressed during the holiday season.

"Here," said Maggie, reaching behind him. "Lift up your head and I'll fluff up your pillows."

"No, don't bother. I'm fine," he said in a tired voice. He turned his head away from her and looked out the window again. An image of his father flashed in his mind. "I feel as though I'm letting my father down. I promised him I'd always keep the display tradition going."

At this, Maggie pulled the guest chair over to the side of the bed, sat down and took his hand. She said, "I was wondering when you were going to get to that. So much of this decorating stuff is centered on your father." She paused for a second to gather her thoughts. "Sweetheart, I know the decorating thing was important to your father, and that it was the one thing during the year that you guys really did together, with him being so busy with work the rest of the time."

Don shook his head. "No, not all the time, but, I guess so, yeah. We never went fishing, or worked on cars, or anything like that. I've told you before that the display was the thing that we enjoyed doing most."

"But do you really think he'd be let down, knowing you risked your life staying up on that roof after Andy left?"

Don thought about this. Perhaps he had spoken hastily, but then again, he wasn't sure. His father actually had been kind of obsessive about the decorating hobby.

He rubbed his hands over the sandpapery stubble on his chin. "I don't know, Maggie. I really don't. It was really important to him that I carry on the tradition."

Maggie took a sip from his water glass. "Look, I'm going to say something, and I really want you to hear me, okay? Don't say anything until I've finished, because I think this is something you need to think about."

He was taken aback. Here was he, at his lowest point, and here was she, about to give him a lecture? "Maggie, I feel bad enough as it is. I don't need you to make me feel worse."

"That's not my intention. I just...now that I've got your attention, so to speak, and you can't get away, I think we should talk about this." She let out a nervous laugh.

Don shrugged and said, "Go ahead, then." He had no idea what she was about to say, but her beautiful eyes were kind, as always.

"I loved your father, you know I did, but he was a rather demanding man. Sometimes I think you still feel the pressure of his expectations—not just about the Christmas display—but about everything. After all, it was he who made you go to school to study electrical engineering when you wanted to be a carpenter, wasn't it? And he who wanted you to not only follow in his footsteps with decorating, but also in life. He always had something to say about your decisions, whether they were financial or about raising our child. I loved him, but like I said, he was demanding."

This was frustrating. "Is there a point here, Mags? Because I can't change the way my father was."

"Yes, I'm getting to that right now. I know you loved—and still love—your father, but you are not like him, and that's good. Where he could be harsh, you are gentle. Where he was demanding, you are laid back. Where he was brash, you are more introverted. All these things are the qualities that made me fall in love with you."

"But…"

"No, wait a second before you interrupt. I'm getting to the point, and you're supposed to be listening." She smiled her most patient smile at him, and he made a motion of zipping his lips.

"Now that we've looked at your relationship with your father, let's look at your relationship with Jenny."

Don bit his lower lip and looked away. "Oh, boy," he muttered.

"Jenny loves you more than anything in the world, but she's not into the decorating thing, and I think she sees it as the complete opposite of the how it was with your father. Instead of bringing you together, I think she thinks the decorating thing comes between you."

He turned back toward her. "What?" This was something he had never considered.

"Yes, that's what I think. I mean, remember when she was younger and she loved to do whatever *you* wanted to do, and she'd always help with the yearly outdoor projects? And as the years have passed, she's stopped doing that and just done the little decorating things inside the house with me? She just doesn't like the outdoor decorating. She's not into it, and she won't do it just to please you, because she is her own person, and you don't force her to do it the way your father insisted with you."

"But I liked decorating with my father."

"And yet, every year, from September to January, it takes you away from her, away from us."

"I've tried to include her, I really have."

"Don, are you listening to me? She doesn't want to be included. She wants to be involved with you, not with decorating. She wants you to help her with her homework, talk with her about the stuff she's into, and now she's starting to think about colleges and I'll bet you don't even know where she wants to go, do you?"

Don sighed. As the reality of what his wife was saying permeated his brain, he realized she was right. He had no idea what Jenny's new life at her new school was like, what she was thinking about studying in college, or...anything. He'd been so focused on his display for several months every year that he had missed out on a lot of his daughter's life.

"No," he said in a small voice. "I don't know what colleges she's thinking about."

He felt tears begin to well up in his eyes, and he looked out the window. "What an idiot I've been. I've been so worried about trying to please my dead father that I've let down my own child."

Maggie rubbed his arm. "That's not what I'm saying. I'm just trying to get you to see that maybe this, this whole accident and the disagreement with Muriel Michaud, is a blessing in disguise. It will give you a chance to reassess. Connect with Jenny...and not to throw away the display, necessarily, but maybe downsize a little bit. After all, she only has two more Christmas seasons here, and then she's off to college."

Don nodded vigorously, unable to speak lest the tears begin falling. As if she knew this were an embarrassing possibility, Maggie walked over to the windowsill and gently sniffed a bright floral arrangement sitting there. "Who sent the flowers?" she asked, reaching for the small envelope next to the vase.

"Oh, hah. You'll get a kick out of that."

She opened the envelope, pulled out the card, and gasped. "Oh, you've got to be kidding me. Well, I guess they must've felt bad. Maybe they're not so awful after all." She pulled a chair up next to the bed, sat down, and took her husband's hand. "Don, come on. You have to try to think positive. You're going to have rehab today and we're going to learn how to use the wheelchair. I've got a guy coming to put up a ramp."

He turned his head. "A ramp? You can't have anybody build a ramp. It will ruin the display! I'm not going to be in that dumb wheelchair forever." Then he looked at her, his eyes wide as the recognition dawned on him that it didn't matter what happened with the display. "Oh," he said. "That's right."

"Hey," she put both of her hands on his. "No worries. The ramp is going to be in the garage, and it's only temporary, so it won't get in the way of anything."

"It doesn't matter, I guess," Don said, as Maggie sat down and took his hand again.

Chapter 40

Elmo was yowling in the kitchen when Ray Michaud walked back into the house. Muriel had woken up a few times to use the bathroom, and then he'd given her another, smaller dose of the medication and she'd gone back to dreamland soon after. With his wife sound asleep, he'd decided to take a little walk around the neighborhood to see who'd put up decorations. Even the Cables had gotten into the act. Hadn't Nick Cable been one of the people on Muriel's side at the meeting?

"Hey, buddy. You hungry? Guess I forgot to feed you since your Mama usually does it." He reached down and picked up the yellow ceramic bowl marked "Hungry Kitty," filled it from the bag of cat food in the cupboard, and placed it back down on its placemat on the floor.

"Come to think of it, I'm hungry, too." He looked at the clock. "No wonder. It's almost one-thirty. I missed my lunch." He opened a can of chicken noodle soup, poured it into a pot and put it on the stove to heat up.

He was just finishing up his soup and munching on some crackers when he heard the sound of his wife running to the bathroom.

"Ray? Raymond? Are you there?" she yelled.

He walked to the bottom of the stairs. "I'm here, sugar plum. I'm just feeding Elmo. Can I get you something?"

She moaned. Then, "Yes. Please, may I have some water?"

"Sure thing. I'll bring it up."

"Oh, thank you." She moaned some more. Poor thing, she really was having a hard time of it. He poured a glass of ice water from the pitcher in the refrigerator as the cat rubbed up against his leg. "What are we gonna do, Elmo? Should we tell her, or just let her see it for herself? Oh, buddy, are we in for it. No matter what we do, it's just not going to be good."

He walked up the stairs with the glass of cold water and set it down on the nightstand. Muriel was back in bed with her eyes shut, but he could tell she was not asleep. He placed a hand on her forehead. "You've got a little fever. Want some more medicine?"

"That stuff isn't working."

"You have to keep taking it for it to work properly. The directions say you may take one more dose today. Maybe I should call Dr. Dalton. You might need to be seen," he said, and then immediately regretted it. She'd see those decorations for sure if he took her to the doctor's office.

He got another pill out of the package. "Down the hatch," he said. "Have a drink of water to chase that down."

He waited patiently. She swallowed and said, "Oh no. I don't want to go to the doctor. I just need to rest today and I'll be fine tomorrow. This is just some 24-hour bug. We need to pick up the turkey we ordered from the butcher shop and do some baking tomorrow. I can't be sick."

"Oh, don't worry about that now. I'm sure, if need be, Paula will be happy to do the cooking for Thursday. You just rest now, okay?" He patted her head. "I'll sit here with you if you want. Want me to turn on the TV?"

"Yes, please," she said, and settled back down into the pillow.

He pressed the button on the remote and flipped through the channels until he found a talk show.

"I like Ellen," Muriel said drowsily. She was asleep before the first guest came on, but he still sat there, watching the show but not really thinking about it. The feeling of dread in his stomach was growing.

Monday night was quiet. Muriel didn't get up at all, but on Tuesday morning her fever was gone and she was able to keep down some toast and tea for breakfast. Ray convinced her to stay in bed most of the day, however, as she was still weak. Turned out he didn't need to give her any more of the medicine. She slept most of the day away anyway, and when she was awake she was content to have him bring her soup and crackers and tea and generally make a fuss over her.

He still hadn't come up with a solution to the problem in the neighborhood.

A visit across the street might be in order, but with Don Cassidy still in the hospital, he didn't see the point, and he really didn't want to bother the man even if he did come home. This had all been just too much. He decided to wait and see what happened.

Chapter 41

Scott and Jenny walked home from the bus together. He was feeling pretty good, and hoped this would become a regular thing now. He didn't really know what being in love was like, but this sure felt pretty awesome. He just wished she felt the same, as unlikely as that was. Still, he told himself, she'd been choosing to spend time with him instead of any of the guys at school, so that had to count for something.

"That you, Jen?" called Mrs. Cassidy from upstairs.

"Yes. Scott's with me," Jenny yelled back. "Did you go grocery shopping today?"

There came the sound of footsteps hurrying down the stairs, and Jenny's mom popped through the kitchen doorway. "Yes, I did. You've got yogurt in the fridge and plenty of fruit, and there's some organic granola bars in the cupboard. Hi, Scott."

"Hi Mrs. Cassidy. I see the guy got started with the ramp out in the garage."

"Yes, he was able to get a head start today. Tomorrow he's going to move it over to the door and finish it, so it will be done before Don comes home on Thanksgiving."

"Thanks for everything, Mom," said Jenny. She gave her mom a quick hug. "Scott, want a snack?"

He made a sour face. Granola bars and yogurt were not really his first choices in after-school treats. "Uh, no thanks. I'll grab something when I get home."

Mrs. Cassidy laughed. "Not a health food fan, huh? Well, you're in luck, I also made some brownies this afternoon when I got home from the hospital. They're still in the pan. I haven't had time to cut them."

"You did not?! When did you have time to do that?" asked Jenny, as Scott zipped by her to reach for the pan, which sat cooling on a rack by the breadbox. The treats looked amazing. He couldn't remember the last time he'd had a warm homemade brownie. He grabbed a bread knife from the dish drainer and began cutting through the moist treats. His stomach was rumbling, and he hoped the women couldn't hear it.

"Oh, don't get too excited. They're just from a mix. It took me about five minutes. I just thought you'd like something chocolatey today."

Jenny cocked her head, then a smile broke across her face. "Oh, I get it. Don't you mean YOU wanted something chocolatey today? Scott, was there already a brownie missing from that pan?"

Scott was chewing on the huge chunk he'd jammed into his mouth, and couldn't answer her, so he just shook his head. He may not have known much about girls, but he was smart enough to figure out that you don't get into a dispute between a daughter and mother. After a few seconds he swallowed and said, "I don't know. I'm not getting involved in this."

Jenny looked exasperated. He just shrugged and looked at her mother. "These are delicious, Mrs. Cassidy. If you haven't had one, then you should."

The woman threw her arms up. "Alright! I confess. I wanted brownies. But I thought you might like some too. Otherwise I would have just stopped at the bakery and bought one of those giant frosted ones," she said, sitting down at the table. "I just wanted a treat after the exhausting day."

Jenny opened the refrigerator and took out a container of yogurt. "Why? What happened?"

"Oh, Daddy's just feeling blue. He's sad about the display, and everything. Feeling discouraged, you know. It was really hard not to tell him about our surprise."

The familiar notes of Beethoven's Fifth Symphony filled the air, and Mrs. Cassidy reached into her handbag on the table to fish out her cell phone. She looked at it. "It's Daddy," she said, and then, "Hi Sweetheart! How are you doing?" A pause. "Oh really? Really? That's great! That's more than great, that's terrific!" Another pause. "I'm so happy! Let me tell the kids." Pause. "Oh, Scott is here with Jenny. Let me tell them the good news."

While she had been talking on the phone Scott couldn't resist taking a second brownie from the pan. Jenny was focused on her mother and didn't seem to notice. Maybe she'd think he was still working on the first brownie. He didn't want her to think he was a pig, after all. Then again, she looked like she was really into that yogurt. Maybe he should try that sometime. It wouldn't hurt him to lose a few pounds.

"Daddy's coming home tomorrow!" said Mrs. Cassidy. "They said he did so well in rehab, and using the wheelchair, that if he has a good night he can come home tomorrow after he sees the doctor."

Scott and Jenny both said, "That's great!" at the same time. She punched him in the arm and said, "You owe me a root beer!" God, he loved the sound of her laugh.

"That's wonderful, honey. I'm so happy you'll be home before Thanksgiving. The turkey is thawing and I'm going to cook us a fantastic meal. Mom and Dad are coming up from Portland, too, and so is Holly, for a little while. They really want to see you. Mom's bringing her famous apricot Grand Marnier stuffing."

Jenny rose, grabbed Scott's arm and led him into the living room. "My dad's coming home tomorrow. That means we have to test everything tonight as soon as it gets dark to make sure everything is working right." He almost didn't even hear what she said, he was so thrilled to feel her touch.

"That's right," he said, looking at his cell phone. "It's almost four o'clock. My dad'll be home around five, and then we can go around and check everything. We can't forget to include Zack. He'll definitely wanna see this."

Chapter 42

It was just before seven o'clock when Mark DiSalvatore turned his Camry onto Franklin Street and gasped. It looked like the Las Vegas strip. Not just the Cassidy house, but four or five other houses were lit up and twinkling, with plastic Santa Clauses waving everywhere, stars blinking on and off, and those giant blowup things. He barely noticed the cars parked on the side of the street as he pulled around them and into his driveway, because he was looking across the way at that young couple's house...the couple with the wild twin boys. Their decorations had sprung up just today, and they were almost as crazy as the ones next door to them. There was a huge blowup Santa popping out of a Christmas gift, and a giant green blowup Grinch, and a pair of giant snowmen.

Muriel Michaud must be having a regular fit, he thought. Then he noticed a twinkling, multi-colored wreath on his own front door. He walked around the side of the house to see Tommy, dressed in his orange down vest circa 1985, plugging in a heavy-duty extension cord attached to a string of white lights that looked about a hundred feet long. "Hey, Marty McFly," said Mark. "What are you doing?"

"Hi," said Tommy, with a sheepish grin. "If you can't beat 'em, join 'em!"

Chapter 43

Scott, his dad, Mrs. Cassidy, and Jenny were waiting for seven o'clock as they sat in the car in front of the Cassidy house. The other houses were already lit up, and they cast a pretty glow on the lawns and streets. They had the radio tuned to 99.1, the frequency of the low FM transmitter Scott had purchased from the man in Augusta, along with all the other equipment that would make the lights dance in time to the music. Scott was so nervous he was practically shaking. His stomach was in knots. He knew he'd set everything up just as it should be, but still he was worried there would be some glitch in the system and he'd end up looking like a bonehead. Looking like a bonehead in front of the most beautiful girl in the world would definitely be a bummer.

At seven on the dot, the opening strains of "Jingle Bells" by Bing Crosby and the Andrews Sisters came chiming out of the car radio. The lights and decorations at 40 Franklin Street lit up in time with the music, the arches leaped, and the mega-tree appeared to swirl and twirl. Scott breathed a sigh of relief as everyone gasped, and he could hear the cheers coming from the SUV parked in front of them, where Angie, Zack, Andy, Esmerelda and the kids were sitting. It was a light and sound extravaganza unlike anything Kennebec City had ever seen before. The other houses were festive, but this was the crown jewel that topped them all.

Jenny turned to Scott and flashed a thousand-watt grin. "My father is going to go absolutely bananas when he sees this!"

"He's going to love, love, love it! I can't wait to see the look on his face," Mrs. Cassidy said. "How can we ever thank you enough, Scott?"

"No thanks necessary."

"This street is so bright we should rename it Christmas Street!" said Jenny, and then she launched across the seat and squeezed Scott so tightly he could barely breathe. *This is the best way to die ever, he thought.*

Chapter 44

Ray Michaud was in the kitchen fixing himself a bite to eat when the lights came on. His wife had been solidly asleep for hours, and he had been thanking his lucky stars she'd slept through the daylight. He figured they weren't planning on turning on any of those lights until at least Thanksgiving night, but here it was, only Tuesday, and boom! The lights were illuminating the whole neighborhood. He stepped out onto the side porch, leaving the door ajar, walked down to the driveway and looked around.

It is kinda pretty, he thought. *Too bad it's going to give Muriel a heart attack.* He noticed the two cars parked directly in front of his house and recognized them as belonging to Sam Anderson and that woman up the street. *Must be checking out their handiwork. Hopefully they won't keep them on for long.*

Then he heard it. "Raymond!! Raaaaaaaaaaaaay-moooooooooonnn-nnnd!" coming all the way from upstairs. *Uh oh*, he thought, here we go, and rushed back into the house.

Sam was mesmerized by the light show, and was just thinking how proud he was of his son for putting it all together, when Jenny said, "Did you see that? I just saw Mr. Michaud come walking down his driveway and look around, and then he turned around and bolted back inside."

"Oh, no. I hope he's not calling the police," said Maggie.

Sam shrugged. "Let him. There's not a thing they can do about it. No ordinance was passed and we aren't breaking any laws." He wasn't going to let anything stand in the way of this great event. This was the best thing he'd been a part of in years, and it was going to go off without a hitch if he had any say in it.

"Why can't that lady just chill out and be happy?" Scott added, frustrated.

"I don't know," said Maggie. "Maybe she's not a happy person. It would be a wonderful thing if she saw these lights and they actually cheered her up somehow. We can say a prayer for that to happen."

Scott frowned. "I'm sorry, Mrs. Cassidy, but I have a hard time picturing that. We've known her a lot longer than you have. It really would take a miracle for her to change."

Maggie nodded. "Well, that's what prayer is for. Miracles."

Sam turned the car around in the Nadeaus' driveway and headed back home. It was time to turn everything off for the night. Tomorrow night, when Don came home, would be something to look forward to after all the hard work. He felt the best he'd felt in a long, long, time.

Ray rushed up the stairs. Muriel was still calling his name, and sobbing now, too. "Raymond! Raymond! How could they do this?" she asked as he came into the room, out of breath and panting. She was standing at the window, disheveled in her nightgown, her hair going every which way. She was holding the curtain aside and had lifted the blinds so the entire vista of lights and decorations could be seen. Lights were reflecting off the wall behind her, giving the room a disco ball effect.

"I thought that man was still in the hospital? Who did this? Why?" she sobbed.

"Sweetheart, you need to rest," he said, and led her back to the bed. "I don't know why they did it, but I suspect they wanted to cheer up Mr. Cassidy. He's been through an awful lot. Maybe they thought it would lift his spirits."

She looked at him, tears sliding down her wrinkled cheeks. "Lift his spirits? *His spirits?* What about the rest of us? What about me? Nobody asked me what I thought about this, and I'm the one who brought the petition. Nobody cares what I think."

He held her hand in his. "Now, now, sugar plum. I care what you think."

She looked at him, pleading in her eyes. "You do?"

"Yes, of course. You know I do."

"Then call the police and make a complaint. This is over the line. Now it's not just one house, it's the whole darned block."

His jaw dropped as he stared at her, incredulous. He'd thought the weekend had been a success, and they were off to a fresh start. Now it was all falling apart again. "What? No. I'm not calling the police. They can't do anything about it. No one is breaking any laws."

For an ailing woman, Muriel got up pretty fast and marched back to the window. She took a long look outside and turned back to her husband. "You know what? Now I get it. I think this whole thing, this "heart attack," was a hoax. Oh, the timing was too convenient. It was all just a trick to get the petition set aside."

Ray shook his head. He could not believe what his wife was saying. "You know, I've tried to be patient with you, Muriel, but now you're just being ridiculous."

Just then the twinkling lights and decorations shut off, house-by-house, and the neighborhood was dark again.

Ray headed downstairs and turned on the TV, leaving Muriel to sit alone and stew. He had reached the end of his rope.

Chapter 45

Despite her restless night, Muriel was up by eight on Wednesday morning. Her fever was gone, and the digestive issues had subsided, but she still didn't feel like her normal self. It wasn't just the residual effects of the bug; she was miffed about the sneaky goings-on in the neighborhood while she and Ray had been in New Hampshire. Still, nothing could keep her from her plans for the day. "Come on, Ray, get your behind out of bed. We've got a lot to do today. We have to clean this place up, pick up the turkey, put together the stuffing, bake—"

"Oh come on. It's early yet. Just twenty more minutes," said Ray, pulling the covers over his head. "Besides, maybe you need another day of rest."

Muriel slapped him on the buttocks through the covers. "No! Get up! We don't even have ten minutes to spare. You're taking me out to breakfast, and then we're going over to City Hall."

The covers came down and Ray's head popped out. "Breakfast? Where?"

"Blake's. They've got their pumpkin pancakes on the menu again."

"Oh really? If I remember correctly, those are pretty good," he said, pulling back the rest of the covers and swinging his legs out of bed. "Guess you got your appetite back, huh?" He didn't say anything about City Hall.

Fifteen minutes later they were pulling out of the driveway. Muriel scowled as she looked from house to house, but Ray didn't say a word.

At ten sharp, Muriel was striding into the City Hall with her husband behind her, doing his best to keep up. When they reached the elevator, she furiously punched the button for the second floor, where the Selectmen's Office was located. The more she thought about what had transpired while they were in New Hampshire, the more upset she became.

"I don't know why we're doing this, Muriel," said Ray. "They can't do anything until their next meeting."

"They can do something. A temporary injunction or whatever it's called."

Just then the elevator door opened, and Muriel charged out into the second floor lobby, where the receptionist sat behind a large mahogany desk. The last time they'd been here, there was no one seated at the desk and they'd just gone straight into Roger Girard's office. Muriel was loaded for bear and she wasn't about to stop for anybody.

"Excuse me," said the young lady as Muriel strode past her. "Excuse me, may I help you?"

"Muriel, wait." Ray grabbed his wife by the arm and held her there, much to her dismay. "There's no need to be rude to this woman."

The receptionist, a cheerful-looking woman with curly bottle-blonde hair cut in a short bob, had sparkling green eyes and cutie-pie dimples, and the name plate on her desk read "Janet Ellis." Muriel zeroed in on the Christmas light earrings dangling beneath that golden hair and automatically disliked the woman.

Without any concern for formalities, Muriel pursed her lips, stepped up to the desk and said, "A little early for Christmas earrings, wouldn't you say?"

"Excuse me?"

"Never mind. We're here to see Roger Girard. It's an emergency."

Janet Ellis looked at her with those big green eyes and smiled. "Well, good morning to you! Mr. Girard has left for the holiday weekend. What is the emergency? Perhaps I can help."

"Left for the holiday weekend already?" Muriel looked at her watch. "It's only ten o'clock!"

"Well, you know, ma'am, being a Selectman is only a part-time job, and Mr. Girard has other responsibilities. What is the nature of your emergency?" As she spoke, the earrings seemed to twinkle with every move of her head. It drove Muriel to distraction.

She clutched her purse tightly. "Are there any other people in charge here?" That smile was beginning to irritate her too, and those dimples!

"I'm afraid not. I'm the only one in the office today, and we are closing at three. I'd be happy to help, if you would tell me the nature of the emergency." Her smile seemed to grow wider, if that was possible. Muriel had had it. She didn't want to have to explain the situation to this overgrown Shirley Temple.

"I...I...oh, never mind. It's useless...and it's too early for Christmas earrings!" With that, the old woman wheeled around and marched past her husband out into the hallway, without even checking to see if he was following.

Ray caught up with his wife by the elevator. She turned to him and said, "This is ridiculous. If they turn those lights on tonight I'm calling the police and I don't care what you say."

At a little after ten, Angie got a text from her sister Janet. The two were thick as thieves, and Janet knew all about what had been happening on Franklin Street.

Just wanted to give you a heads up. Your crabby neighbor was just here. She's even worse than you said. I guess she noticed the lights. She's all worked up.

Angie replied,

Thanks for the warning.

Then she immediately texted Maggie.

Muriel sat stiff as a board on the ride home, fidgeting with her jewelry. Eventually, Ray spoke. "Muriel, I know you haven't listened much to me during this whole mess, but I'm just going to say this. Our family is coming home tomorrow, and I, for one, don't want Thanksgiving to be ruined by this thing with the Cassidys. So please, can you just try to put it aside for the next few days? Can you do that for me?"

Muriel didn't respond right away, still twisting her rings as she contemplated what he'd said. Frustrated as she was, she knew he was right; she had to get this Christmas light debacle out of her mind. *The kids are coming home*, she thought. *I don't want this stupidity to ruin our time together.*

"I'll try," she said. "I really will."

She remembered the calming exercises the therapist had taught her, and she breathed in slowly through her nose and out through her mouth a few times, but she couldn't concentrate for long. Distraction was another skill the therapist had suggested, so she resolved to spend the rest of the day attending to her to-do list for the holiday.

As they pulled into the driveway, Muriel had an idea. While Ray was getting out of the car, she reached into one of the grocery sacks, opened a box, and pulled out one of the masks she'd purchased in the pharmacy section. They were the kind they gave you at the doctor's office to prevent the spreading of germs when you were sick. She put it on and got out of the car.

She sidled up to her husband and tapped him on the shoulder. He turned around and let out a surprised laugh when he saw her.

"See," she said, "I'm already trying to lighten up the mood."

Ray took the grocery sack out of her hand. "Terrific! Now let's get in the house and you can lie down and rest a bit."

"You go on in," she said. "I just want to check the mail for the Black Friday sales flyers and then I'll be in to start baking." She turned and headed down the driveway toward the mail box.

"Are you really sure you should be baking? You were awfully sick. Why don't you let me do the baking?"

"Ha! Don't be silly. It was just a 24-hour thing and I wasn't even sick yesterday. Besides, I've got these, just in case." She snapped the cloth mask. "I'm fine. I'll be right in."

She knew she didn't need this ridiculous mask. She was feeling healthy as ever, if a bit weak. But it was funny to see the look on Ray's face when she put it on.

Muriel was absentmindedly looking through the stack of flyers and assorted junk in the mailbox when a shrill scream suddenly split the air, and she looked up in time to see one of the twins across the street galumphing down his porch steps as the door slammed behind him. He came running down the sidewalk in her direction, wailing loudly. He didn't seem to be taking notice of his surroundings, especially not the red pickup truck that was headed his way. But Muriel was paying attention.

She dropped the mail and ran across the street, sweeping the boy up in her arms just as he left the curb, the pickup's brakes squealing as the driver veered around them. The truck came to a stop just a couple of yards away from Muriel, who was standing there just inside the white line at the side of the road, her arms wrapped around the child.

She pulled the boy on to the sidewalk and scooched down to look him in the eye, keeping her hands on his shoulders. "Just what do you think you're doing?" she said, out of breath. "I'm sure your parents taught you to stop and look both ways before you cross the street. You must never do that again!" She tried to keep the panic out of her voice for the boy's sake.

The boy struggled to get out of her grip. "Let go of me. I'm running away. Let go!" he whined. Muriel held him tighter.

The driver of the pickup rolled down the passenger side window and shouted, "Everything okay over there?"

Muriel gave him her steeliest stare, although she could feel her entire body trembling. "We're alright. You need to slow down. This is a residential neighborhood. As you can see, there are children here."

The man nodded his head sheepishly, then drove off very slowly.

Suddenly there was the screech of a screen door flying open and, and Esmerelda came out onto the porch and down the stairs.

"Oh my god! Matteo!" she yelled, running toward them with the baby bundled in her arms and the other twin trailing behind her. "Matteo, what are you doing out here?" When she reached them, Muriel stood up, still keeping tight hold of the boy, feeling every nerve in her body vibrate. "It's alright, Mrs. Nadeau. I caught him before he ran out into the street."

Muriel was about to give the woman a stern talking to for neglecting her child when she noticed that Esmerelda was a frazzled mess. Her hair looked like a rat's nest, and she was wearing an old, stained track suit that had seen better days. She looked like she hadn't slept in a week.

"Dios Mio!" cried Esmerelda. "Oh my God, thank you! Thank you! I'm so sorry. The baby was crying and I didn't know he'd gone out, and then I heard that truck—"

"Muriel, what the heck is going on over there?" It was Ray. He'd heard the noise of the truck and rushed out the front door.

The boy began struggling again. "Let go of me! I'm running away. Nobody cares about me no more."

"That's not true! We love you, Matteo!" said Esmerelda. She held out the baby to Muriel. "Would you mind taking her?" The old woman instinctively reached for the soft bundle and held her carefully. She was glad she was wearing the mask; she wouldn't want to breathe germs onto the infant.

Esmerelda knelt down to speak to her son. "I'm sorry I was harsh with you, mijo."

The boy looked at her, tears streaking his cheeks. "I didn't do anything and you yelled at me. You don't care about nobody but Lulu anymore." He eyed his brother, who was just standing there, kicking at some dirt on the sidewalk and looking worried.

Esmerelda pulled him close. "I'm so sorry. I didn't mean to upset you." She stroked his hair. "I know it's been hard since Luisa was born, but she's just little and she needs me more. She needs all of us. It won't always be this hard, but I need your help and I'll try to be more patient with you, okay? We love both you guys just the same as we always have." She reached out her arm to her other son and hugged them both tightly. "Now come on, it's cold out here. Let's go back in the house."

While Esmerelda was comforting Matteo, Muriel was rocking the baby slowly. She vaguely heard what Esmerelda was saying, but she was also concentrating on the little human being in her arms. *It's true what they say*, she thought. *It all comes back to you.*

The baby started to stir. "There, there, little one," she cooed. "It's alright. Nothing going on here you need to fuss about."

Suddenly she felt Ray nudging her. "Muriel, Mrs. Nadeau is speaking to you." Startled, she looked up and saw that Esmerelda was now standing up across from her, looking at her expectantly.

"I'm sorry," Muriel said. "What's that you said?"

"I was just thanking you again, Mrs. Michaud. You must think I'm the worst mother in the world. I'm so grateful you happened to be there to catch Matteo." Tears welled in her eyes. "I don't know how to tell you how much I appreciate it." She wiped an errant strand of hair away from her eyes and then paused, as if a new idea had popped into her head. "Would you like to come in the house for a cup of coffee?"

It had been a very long time since any neighbor had invited Muriel over for coffee, and she was caught off-guard, not sure what to do. Holding that baby had done something to her. For a minute there, she'd forgotten all about her troubles and was lost in the moment. She hadn't been interested in visiting with neighbors for years, but she wanted to accept this invitation. Still, she had been sick, and even though she was feeling better, this might not be a good idea. She looked at Ray for his approval. Then she nodded. "I sure would like that. But I had some sort of 24-hour bug earlier this week. That's why I'm wearing this ridiculous mask on my face. I probably shouldn't even be holding the baby."

Esmerelda waved a hand. "Oh, don't worry about that. The boys both came home from my in-laws' with runny noses. I called the pediatrician and she said not to worry about it as long as they don't get too close to her and we all wash our hands and disinfect surfaces frequently. And you have that mask. I'm sure it's fine. You're feeling better now?"

Muriel nodded. "Yes, I am. Much better."

"Then please, come on over. I'd like some adult company, even for just a little while." She looked at Ray. "Would you like to come over, too, Mr. Michaud?"

"Oh, no, thank you anyway," he said. "But you go over, Muriel. You deserve a little break." He patted her on the back. "After all, you just probably saved that little boy's life."

Muriel felt her face flushing. "Oh, don't be silly, Raymond," she said. "It all just happened so fast. I only did what anyone would have done." Then she turned back to Esmerelda, forgetting all about the baking and cleaning she had planned. "Well, okay then, if you think it will be alright. I sure would like that."

Ray smiled. "I'll see you when you get home. Take your time. I'll start the baking." He winked and chuckled. "See you later, Mrs. Nadeau." He turned and started back across the street, looking both ways before he crossed.

Muriel, Esmerelda, and the twins walked up to the house, the old woman still carrying the warm bundle of joy in her arms.

Chapter 46

Muriel had never seen a home in such disarray since her own children were little. Toys were strewn everywhere; dishes were piled in the sink and on the sideboard. Bowls of half-eaten cereal and glasses of juice sat on the kitchen table. She could see into the dining room, where an old oak table was covered with books and papers, pencils and pens. What a mess, she thought. She forgot all about the comments she had made about the Nadeaus not being ready for a third child. Being in the middle of it touched her memories of being a young mother herself. *This poor girl is overwhelmed.*

"I'm sorry for the mess," said Esmerelda. "I'm having a hard time keeping up, as you can see." Then, as she whisked about the room, picking up clutter, Muriel heard her mumble, "I should have cleaned up before inviting anyone over." Then she turned to the boys. "Matty, Ricky, why don't I put in a movie for you in the play room? Would you like that?"

"*Cars!*"

"*Batman!*"

"How about *The Brave Little Toaster*? You haven't watched that in a while," said their mother, and both boys nodded and scrambled down the hall, their mom bringing up the rear.

"But after, I want to watch Batman!" Muriel heard one of them say.

She took a couple of toy cars off a kitchen chair and made a space for them on the table. She looked down at the baby, content in her arms. That perfect little face, and the sweet baby smell, had her completely entranced. "You are a little cutie pie, aren't you? I'd love to kiss your pudgy cheeks, but I've been sick, so I'm not going to," she whispered.

In her pleasure, she began to breathe much more calmly. Her stress was melting away.

The baby's eyelids were starting to flutter, and she yawned, her little hands balled into fists. Muriel began to sing softly. "Hush little baby, don't you cry... "

Through the archway to the living room she could see an old-fashioned cradle. She stood up and walked toward it, still singing. After rocking the baby a little while longer, she laid her down. When she stood upright again, her attention was attracted to a colorful oil painting on the opposite wall. It was done in that Impressionistic style, like Monet, and it was of a carnival on a riverbank. Muriel was captivated.

Esmerelda peeked around the corner and seemed relieved that the baby was sleeping. Muriel went to join her in the kitchen.

"That painting is just gorgeous. Where did you get it?"

Esmerelda pulled out a chair, swept a baby bib off it onto the floor and plopped down. "Oh, that was me. I painted that." She sounded exhausted, as though she couldn't care less about her accomplishment.

Muriel could not hide her amazement. "You did? It's wonderful. You are incredibly talented. When do you find time to paint?"

"That's just it. I don't. I painted that when I still lived in the Dominican. In fact, I won a few prizes for my works there. I was still painting when we moved here, but then I got pregnant with the twins, and you can pretty much guess what happened to my free time."

Before Muriel had a chance to respond, Esmerelda continued. "I honestly think I'm losing my mind," she said, her voice breaking. She put her arms on the table, dropped her head down onto them, and began to weep.

Muriel hadn't expected this. She paused a minute, then reached out and tentatively patted Esmerelda's shoulder. "It's okay, now, it's all right," she said.

The young mother spoke through tears. "I can't do it. It's too much. The holidays are coming and everyone is cheerful and I just feel so overwhelmed and lonely. Andy is gone all the time, and when he is here, there's so much going on with the boys and the baby and oh, I just…I just…I'm so gosh darn tired all the time. Forget about painting; I can't even keep up with life."

Muriel sat down, overcome, as a memory came flooding into her mind. There she was, a young mother herself, crying in Lucy Wyman's kitchen. It was so long ago, and yet the event was as fresh in her mind as if it had happened yesterday. She recalled Lucy's kindness, and how she had been like a second mother to her, guiding and helping her through the trials and tribulations of motherhood. Could she help this woman the way Lucy helped her? What harm could there be in trying?

What if she rejects me? Everyone in this neighborhood thinks I'm a crazy old lady…

She decided to try.

"This happens to all of us with the second baby," she said. "And in your case it's actually the third, so you really have your hands full. How can I help you, dear?"

"I just really need somebody to talk to," Esmerelda sobbed, and Muriel realized why she was there.

"Then talk. I'm here to listen, and I've got all the time in the world."

Esmerelda told her that her own mother was in the Dominican Republic, and Andy's had a full-time job and not much time to spend with them and the kids. She went through whole days when she didn't speak to another adult except Andy, and he was always busy. She had gone to hairdressing school in the Dominican so she could earn a steady paycheck to support her art, and when she moved to the U.S. with Andy, she'd taken a job in a salon. She took time off to have the twins, and then went back to work, and now she was on maternity leave again.

Aha! She's a hairdresser, Muriel thought. *So that's where she goes.*

Barely taking a breath, Esmerelda went on about how hard it was to nurse the baby and care for her properly when the twins seemed to need her for something every second of the day. She was worried Luisa wouldn't get the attention she needed, and she felt guilty about that. The end of her maternity leave was circled in red on her calendar; she didn't want to go back to work full-time until the twins were ready for kindergarten. And painting? That seemed like a lifetime ago.

"I know it was a poor decision to have another baby at this time, but somehow I got pregnant, even though we were…careful," she said. "So Andy and I figured God wanted us to have another child."

Muriel nodded. "I see. And look, you have a beautiful little angel there. I think you were right." She reached over and patted Esmerelda's hand. "Don't worry, dear, all this is overwhelming because she is a newborn. This time will pass quickly and things will get better. You know they will."

As she spoke, Muriel felt sure that her instincts to come over had been right. She was meant to be there. It was more than just the nostalgic feeling about Lucy Wyman. This was a place where she could help, a place where she was needed. She hadn't been able to help Paula much when her children were born because she'd been a full-time teacher then, and now she wasn't needed to help with little Emma because there were two grandmothers to do that. But here, right in her own neighborhood, somebody needed her.

I could help her the way Lucy helped me, she thought. *I've got plenty of time, and I'm right across the street.*

"Esme," she said, "Is it okay if I call you Esme?"

Esmerelda nodded. "Of course."

Muriel smiled. "And you may call me Muriel. You know, I'm just across the way, and I have plenty of time on my hands. I know a thing or two about raising children. I'd love to help you, if you'll let me."

Esmerelda looked at her with wide eyes. "Really? You'd be willing to do that? I thought...I thought..." She abruptly stopped speaking, a mortified look on her face.

"Oh, I know. You thought I was a mean old lady," Muriel said. And then her own tears began to stream down her face. "But I'm not. I'm really not, even though I know the whole neighborhood thinks I am."

"I never..." said Esme, but Muriel interrupted, shaking her head.

"It's just that, since my own children grew up and left the nest... well, I guess I just have too much time on my hands, you know? And you know what they say, 'Idle hands are the devil's workshop.' Maybe I've somewhat lost myself over these past few years." She swallowed and swiped at her tears, and Esme got up and got her a glass of tap water. Muriel took a sip and continued. "So that's why I'd like to help you. We can help each other, you know?" she, grabbing a tissue from the box on the table and blowing her nose.

Esme's own tears had begun to trickle again. She reached out, and the two women grasped hands. "I never thought you were a mean old lady. I just had no idea what was going on. Now you are telling me, I'm so sorry I didn't reach out to you. I could have been friendlier. I just never thought that was what you wanted. I should have made the effort to get to know you instead of just assuming."

"Nor have I made the effort to get to know you. And I'm sorry, too. But I hope we can start now, if it's not too late."

The two women comforted each other. After a time Muriel convinced Esme to take a nap upstairs while she handled things downstairs. With the baby sound asleep in the cradle, she cajoled the Ricky and Matty into helping her tidy the kitchen with the promise of a game of Candyland after lunch.

Muriel made peanut butter and jelly sandwiches with carrot sticks and a glass of milk for each of them, then sat with them while they ate. She told them the story of Bum-de-Bo the giant, a story she'd made up for her children long ago. The boys loved it so much they wanted another, and she made one up on the spot. It was fun to resurrect her old pretend pal from the woods and give him a new adventure.

After lunch and Candyland, which she purposely made shorter by hiding all the "go back" cards as they came up, she left them having fun in their play room while she tackled the dirty dishes, found the broom, and gave the kitchen a good sweeping.

When she was just finishing up with the dustpan the boys appeared in the doorway, each carrying a book. "Will you read to us?" they asked, together.

"I'd love to," she said.

The trio sat on the sofa and time flew by as Muriel read the classic *The Cat in the Hat* and some new books about characters she didn't know. It was around two o'clock when the baby woke up crying. Esme, hearing the baby monitor, came downstairs and sleepily took Luisa from Muriel's arms and settled down to nurse her. The twins scrambled up on the couch with her and bombarded her with a replay of their time with Muriel.

Muriel said, "Now boys, remember what we talked about. You give Mommy some peace and quiet while she's feeding your sister. Why don't you make something with your Legos? When it's done, maybe your Mom will send me a picture of it so I can see."

They scrambled off the couch and dumped the bin of Legos on the carpet. Esme smiled gratefully at Muriel and turned her attention back to the baby.

Muriel slipped back into the kitchen. She prepared a peanut butter and jelly sandwich and a glass of milk and set it on the end table for Esme. Then she crept out of the room. Before she left the house, she scribbled a note that said, "I'm just across the street. Call me any time. I love playing Candyland. And thank you for letting me help." Then she added her phone number and at the bottom, "P.S. I'd love to see what they make with their Legos."

As she made her way across the street to her house she found herself humming a Christmas carol. *Maybe I will do some baking after all,* she thought. *If Ray hasn't made a disaster in the kitchen already.*

She went over to pick up the mail she'd dropped and saw that it was gone. Ray must've picked it up when he went back to the house.

Suddenly, the sound of a car door closing broke her reverie, and she looked up to see the Cassidy woman marching across the street. She was smiling, but it looked forced, and Muriel stiffened. When she reached Muriel she stuck out her hand and said "Hello, Mrs. Michaud, I'm Maggie Cassidy. I thought it was about time we met."

Muriel, flustered, automatically shook Maggie's hand. "Hello," she said, pulling her coat tighter against herself. What was going on here?

Ray came out of the house so fast you'd have been forgiven for thinking he'd been peeking through the curtains.

Maggie turned to face him. "Hello, Mr. Michaud. I'm Maggie Cassidy. I believe you've met my husband." There was a quaver in her voice as she spoke rapidly. "I've just come home from seeing my husband at the hospital, and I wanted to talk to you folks about what's going on here. I'm assuming you've noticed the lights on the other houses besides ours?"

Muriel was taken aback. This woman had quite a bit of nerve coming over here like this. It almost made her forget how good she'd felt just a few minutes earlier. She straightened her back, squared her shoulders and said, "Yes, as a matter of fact, we have. We saw them all lit up last night. Just what do you aim to do?"

Maggie Cassidy pulled in a sharp breath. She looked nervous. *That's why her voice is quavering.* Then it dawned on Muriel. *Is she actually scared of me?* She thought back to her conversation with Es-merelda. It seemed this Cassidy woman did think she was a "mean old lady."

"Well, as you probably know, my husband had a serious heart attack and then an accident. He's been in the hospital since Thursday night, but in addition to the medical problems, he's been very de-pressed." She sounded as though she might burst into tears at any moment.

Muriel was startled to hear about Don Cassidy's depression, but she didn't comment as her neighbor continued.

"Well, we...myself and my daughter, and some of the neighbors... we wanted to do something special to welcome him home. We wanted to surprise him."

Ray stepped forward. "That's understandable. But it seems you and your friends have done kind of a...kind of an end run around the Se-lectmen, haven't you? They tabled the matter because it seemed your husband would be in no shape to continue with his display plans."

Maggie leveled her gaze at him. "Well, no, it's not our intention to circumvent the Selectmen. They didn't actually make any ruling, so legally we can do whatever we want."

Muriel, aghast at this disrespect, blurted out, "Now just wait a minute..."

Maggie was quick to interrupt. She made a "calm down" motion with her hands. "But we're not trying to be sneaky. We just wanted to surprise Don. Just for one night. And out of respect for you, I came here asking for your blessing."

Before Muriel had a chance to respond to this turn of events, Maggie sighed and clasped her gloved hands together. Her face, which had been so composed, broke into a mask of worry. "Look, none of this went the way he was hoping. He sincerely thought he was doing something nice for the community. He wasn't prepared for all the opposition with your petition and everything. He's not a contentious man; he's a peaceful man. A good man."

"All right. But that doesn't change the fact that some people around here might not enjoy the lights and all of the hoopla that goes along with them. He should have talked to us about it before just jumping right in and setting it up," said Muriel.

Maggie was wringing her hands. "We agree with you. Don knows he went about it the wrong way. To be honest with you, he's never been a very outgoing person. He expresses himself through his Christmas display. His dad did the same thing. But it wasn't malicious. Don just didn't consider that anyone would be opposed. In Florida, where we used to live, everyone loved his display."

Muriel had a hard time believing that, but she didn't say anything.

"And we were prepared to let the Selectmen make the decision, and abide by it, but then Don had the accident..."

Muriel interrupted. "And I'm sorry about that, Mrs. Cassidy, I truly am..."

Now it was Ray's turn to interrupt. "Did your husband get our flowers?"

Maggie looked surprised; she had forgotten about their gift. "Yes, he did. That was very kind of you."

"...but that really doesn't change anything. A lot of people signed that petition. Not just us," Muriel continued, as if no one else had spoken. She wasn't about to let her efforts be swept under the rug.

Maggie Cassidy looked exasperated, and she sighed again. "Look, I just came over here to ask you out of courtesy. Just one night. Just tonight. Last night was a test. We just want to surprise Don when he comes home from the hospital and cheer him up this one night, and then we won't turn them on again unless the Selectmen say it's okay at their next meeting. That might not even be until after Christmas, and then it's all moot anyway. So would that be okay with you? I mean, you won't call the police or anything?"

Muriel looked at Ray, who shrugged and made a facial expression that said, "Why not?"

Then she remembered little Lulu's sweet face, and the sound of the boys' laughter as they played Candyland. How good it had felt to be needed. It had been an unexpectedly pleasant afternoon, and she decided then and there not to let anything ruin it. After all, she'd promised Ray not to let these Christmas light shenanigans affect Thanksgiving with the family. She turned back to the woman. "Mrs. Cassidy, I'm not the evil old lady you probably think I am, and I am not unreasonable."

She held up her right index finger. "One night. Tonight, and that's it. I can be understanding, Mrs. Cassidy."

Maggie smiled and spread her arms wide in surprise. "Really? Oh, thank you, Mrs. Michaud, thank you so much. I appreciate your understanding, and I promise it will be just tonight, and then we will abide by whatever the Selectmen decide." She stepped forward and hugged the old lady briefly. Flustered, she allowed herself to be hugged but did not hug back. As soon as Maggie's arms were free of her, Muriel stepped back. She noticed tears in the other woman's eyes.

"Goodbye now, Mrs. Cassidy. I hope your husband continues to recover," Muriel said.

"You have a nice Thanksgiving," said Ray, "And thank you for coming over."

"Oh, you too, and thanks again!" said Maggie, and she turned around and jogged back across the street to where her daughter and the Anderson boy were waiting in the driveway, gawking.

Chapter 47

The University closed for Thanksgiving break at noon on Wednesday, and Sam Anderson was driving to Portland to pick up his older son. He had to admit, he was nervous. He hadn't heard much from Brian this semester, and he knew why. The previous summer had been filled with sadness, their first summer without Stephanie, and Sam had been ineffective in helping his sons grieve. That's when his drinking had begun to accelerate. Sam hoped that this weekend, he would be able to show Brian a new beginning. But he wouldn't know how much damage had been done until they spent some time together.

Sam pulled up at the Greyhound station and saw Brian waiting on the sidewalk, his backpack on one shoulder, a duffle bag over the other, and his ever-present smartphone in hand. Everyone said Brian was the spitting image of his Dad, while Scott clearly took after Stephanie.

Brian stood there in an Army jacket, something he'd no doubt picked up at a thrift shop. His blonde hair was covered by a black knit cap and he'd let his beard grow—it was coming out reddish-blond, just like his father's had done. Suddenly he looked like a man.

Sam experienced a thrill as he pulled up to the curb, left the car in park, and jumped out to grab his son in a bear hug.

"Woah! Hi Dad! Wow!" said Brian, laughing nervously. He seemed slightly embarrassed by his father's enthusiasm. He sniffed exaggeratedly. "Polo, Dad? What's going on? Scott texted me that good stuff had been happening lately, but I didn't expect you to wear your best aftershave to pick me up!"

Sam laughed and slapped him on the back several times. "Great to see you, Brian!" He pulled back, keeping his hands on his son's shoulders and studying him for a moment. "You look terrific! How was your trip?"

"It was okay," he said, as Sam grabbed his duffle and threw it into the back seat. "I had to sit next to a guy with really bad breath, though. And some kid was screaming in the back for the whole ride."

"Ah, the joys of public transportation. Well, maybe it's about time we got you your own wheels."

Brian looked at him, a suspicious expression on his face. "Really, Dad?"

Sam smirked. "No, Bri, I haven't been drinking. But yes, really. It is almost Christmas, after all, and a guy your age needs his own ride. Let's go look around this weekend and see what's out there for good used cars. But for now, are you hungry? Want to find someplace in the Old Port to eat?"

"Sounds good to me!" said Brian. "Where's Scott? I thought he'd be coming with you to get me."

"Oh, that's a whole story in itself. Your little brother has met a girl," Sam said, smiling.

Brian snapped upright. "A *girl?* Scott? Wow!"

"I'll tell you all about it over lunch. Hurrle's?"

"Let's go! I'm starved!"

Lunch was delicious. They ordered overstuffed sandwiches, sweet potato fries and mozzarella sticks, and managed to pack away every crumb. As the time passed, Brian became less and less defensive. On the way home he confided in his father about the struggles of going back to school, roommate trials and tribulations, and his thoughts about declaring a major.

Sam made a few suggestions, but mostly listened to what his son had to say. Brian was making major life decisions, and he was determined to be the best father he could be, now that he had finally figured out that Stephanie would live on through their boys.

They arrived home in Kennebec City to find a note on the side door:

> Hi Sam,
>
> Scott is hanging out at our house and wants you to come over as soon as you guys get home. We can't wait to meet Brian! If I'm not here when you come over, it means I've gone to fetch Don at the hospital. I'm so excited to see his reaction when he sees what everyone's done. And I was thinking…if you guys aren't doing anything tomorrow, you are welcome to join us for Thanksgiving. We're planning to eat around 2pm and we'd love to have you!
>
> Maggie C.

Sam put his things down, looked at the mail and walked over to the fridge as Brian went upstairs to put his bags in his room. There was the measly Cornish hen he'd bought to prepare for the next day's meal, and the cheesecake he'd picked up at Pierce's Pastry and Pie Shoppe the day before as a treat for Scott and Brian. He could bring that over as his contribution to the meal. *I wonder if Angie and Zack will be there,* he thought.

Don Cassidy sat in his hospital bed, waiting for Maggie and Jenny, or Doctor Zembruski, whoever arrived first. He noticed the first snowflakes sticking to the window, and then melting away as quickly as they'd appeared. He knew he should be excited at the sight of the snow, but all it did was remind him of the snow that had fallen on the roof that dreadful night. What a stupid thing he'd done, putting his life at risk like that. All for what? For a Christmas display that nobody wanted. Now he'd have to go home and watch it sit there during the whole Christmas season, and then, when he got the go-ahead from the doctor, take it all down and put it away. And never put it back up again. It just wasn't worth the hassle to fight with the neighbors.

Never in his life had he been so depressed. He knew it was ridiculous; after all, his family was healthy, he was okay and they had a roof over their heads. But deep inside, he felt as though he'd failed his father, and he'd failed this community. And now, because of Maggie, he knew he'd let Jenny down, too, in a completely different way. It was all too much.

He hadn't made a good case for why his display mattered. Sitting here in the hospital for the past few days, he'd been kicking himself over and over again for not going to that Selectmen's meeting. If he hadn't been such a coward, none of this would have happened, and he was sure Muriel Michaud's so-called Ordinance would have been voted down. As it turned out, the matter was tabled because of his accident, and even if the Selectmen met again before Christmas he couldn't even work on it now. He just didn't have the heart to fight her anymore.

Chapter 48

"Sittoo! You look beautiful as usual!"

Eileen Ferris' grandson, Joe, and his teenage son, Francis, came through her kitchen door and gave her a big hug. Joe came to Maine twice a year to visit his Sittoo-the Lebanese word for Grandmother. And every January, he flew her (and Muffin) out to stay with him in Vegas for four months.

Eileen bustled around them. "Oh I'm so happy to see you two! Did you have a good flight? How is the hotel? You're staying in that new one up by the college, right? I have so much to tell you."

"Sittoo! We haven't even got our coats off yet. What's got into you tonight?"

"Yeah, Grans, I don't think I've ever seen you this excited," said Francis, reaching down to pet Muffin. His smile filled Eileen's heart with joy.

"Oh just you wait and see. There are going to be big doings in this neighborhood tonight for the first time in years. And surprise! Even your cousins from Shawmut are coming up for this."

Joe lit up. "Really? That's great! I can't remember the last time we all got together here."

Even Muffin seemed to sense something different was in the air;

he was having a hard time settling down. This was something special, and it was all because of Don Cassidy and his obsession with Christmas lights.

Chapter 49

Angie saw her last patient at one. She went to the grocery store to pick up the fixings for tossed salad and a pumpkin pie, which were going to be her contribution to her sister's Thanksgiving table. Then she picked up Zack, and when they got home, she went to work on the pie while he watched his favorite cartoons.

They had been invited to the Cassidys' for the holiday, but she'd already made her commitment to her sister's annual feast, and it was too late to back out now. This was the first time in years that she didn't want to go to Janet's. What she really wanted to do was go to Don and Maggie's and flirt with Sam Anderson. She had been thinking about him ever since Saturday, but she hadn't seen him around the neighborhood—and she had her radar tuned in.

She was beginning to think she had imagined what had gone on between them at Sergeant Pepperoni's. *I probably read too much into it,* she thought. *As usual. And this date is only happening because Scott put him on the spot.*

Maggie called around four to let her know that the doctor would be in within an hour or so to give Don the all-clear and formally discharge him. She wanted to be there for that, so she was heading over to the hospital with Jenny.

"Can you get the word out to everyone that we'll be rolling up around six?" Maggie said. "Scott will be waiting at our house to start everything, but tell everybody else to make sure their lights are on by five forty-five."

"You bet," said Angie. "I'm so glad to hear he is definitely coming home." Zack, hearing this, broke out in a mile-wide grin and began fluttering his fingers.

Maggie promised that they'd text when they left the hospital with Don.

Maggie and Jenny had been waiting for nearly an hour when Dr. Zembruski finally showed up. Don was tired and he just wanted to get this discharge thing over with and get back home to his own bed. Dr. Zembruski said a perfunctory "hello," and took a look at the iPad he was carrying.

"That my husband's chart, Doc, or are you watching a movie?" asked Maggie, with a nervous laugh. That was his wife … she always had to try to make a bad situation better with a little joke.

But Dr. Zembruski didn't laugh, or even crack a smile. "What?"

"Oh, nothing," Maggie said, blushing. "How's my husband doing?"

The doctor looked at Don. "Well, as you know, the surgeries on your heart, and on your ankle, went well and there were no issues. After rehab, you should be on your way to resuming a normal life, with some dietary restrictions, of course. I don't know why we really call them that. It's just common sense eating that most people who want to live a long life should do."

He went on without a pause. "Now, after your first cardiac event, I don't know what kind of instructions you got from your doctor in …was it Florida?" Don nodded. "But I'm sure he or she told you that stress would always be a risk factor for someone with heart disease."

Don could sense what was coming. Maggie must've told the doctor about the stress he had been under since their neighbor had decided to oppose his display. He involuntarily twisted the sheets in his hands.

"Under normal circumstances, I would applaud the fact that you resumed regular activities and were enjoying creating your display, but I'd have to say that climbing up on a roof and lifting fifty pound sandbags while experiencing the kind of stress you've been under was perhaps not the wisest choice."

Don felt like an idiot. Suddenly he was back in school, being chastised by the principal for participating in the stupid prank of taking the classroom skeleton out of biology class and setting it up by the front door to greet students on Halloween morning. He didn't usually do that kind of thing, but he'd let a new friend—who he wanted to impress—talk him into it.

Then Maggie interrupted. "But you're not saying that it was putting up the display that caused his heart to malfunction, right?"

The doctor looked at her and said, "No, I'm not saying that at all," as though he were talking to a child. He looked back at Don. "What I'm saying is the combination of stress, hard work, some poor dietary choices—yes, your wife told me about your questionable gastronomic adventures—all of these factors combined to make your heart muscle seize." A picture of a delicious Yocco's hot dog flashed in Don's mind.

"You will be able to work on your display again, but not this year. This year you need to work on your rehab during the next six to eight weeks. But next year, if you find yourself in a stressful situation with your neighbor again, I'd advise you to hold off on any decorating until you have things worked out. Now, lie back and let me do a quick exam."

Don was unhappy Maggie had ratted on him about the food he'd been eating and about the ruckus in the neighborhood. But, oh well, she did what she had to do. He certainly wasn't going to say anything about it to her; he just didn't have the energy. Now he knew for sure that any ideas of trying to complete his display this year were out of the question. To think he'd actually been starting to picture himself wheeling around the front walkway, giving Scott and Andy directions about putting the finishing touches on things. Nope. Not while Mrs. Scrooge was watching from across the street. It didn't matter what the Selectmen decided; he was sure she wasn't going to take it lying down if they gave him the go-ahead, and he just couldn't bear her hostility any more.

After Don received his post-op instructions and was officially discharged, Maggie helped him get dressed and then went out to bring the car around. Jenny accompanied him as a nurse wheeled him down to the hospital main entrance.

As Maggie drove the Woodie back through the streets of Kennebec City, Don sat in the car, watching the snow come down gently but steadily. Thoughts swirled in his drug-addled mind. He had to get his priorities straight, and put this childish Christmas decorating stuff aside, maybe for good. He'd been pondering what Maggie had said about Jenny resenting the time he spent on the display, and the thought struck him that perhaps all this had happened for a reason. He needed to repair his bond with his daughter, and he had to do what he could to still make this a merry Christmas season for the family. But boy, it sure would've been cool to see his display lit up in the falling snow.

As they drove, Jenny kept a running commentary about school and the drama club, filling her father in on everything that had been happening in her life since he'd been in the hospital. He loved it, but she was chattering so fast that he had a hard time keeping up with her. He could see her in the door mirror, sitting behind him and wildly texting as she spoke, a masterful demonstration of multi-task-ing that only teens can perfect.

When they pulled up to the red light to make the left turn onto Franklin, Don closed his eyes, his hands clasped tightly in his lap. He really didn't want to see his display, sitting there incomplete, dark and forlorn. He felt the car turn and stop at the first intersection... and then he felt Maggie gently touching his shoulder. "Don, open your eyes, hon."

"Mm hmm," he mumbled, keeping his eyes closed. "I'm sleepy. Wake me when we get there."

"No honey, you need to open your eyes n—"

She was cut off by Jenny, her voice suddenly an octave higher than usual. "For goodness sake, Daddy, open your eyes!"

"Jenny!" Maggie said, "Don't surprise your father like that."

Don's eyes flew open. "What's...?" Then he saw the lights. His jaw dropped, and he was stunned into silence.

Jenny laughed. "So, Dad, what's up?"

"I...oh...what's going on here?" Don shook his head to clear the cobwebs and rubbed his eyes. He couldn't believe what he was seeing. Practically the entire block was lit up. Only the Michauds' house and, curiously, his own, were dark.

Maggie's smile lit up the car nearly as brightly as the lights on their neighbors' houses lit up Franklin Street. "You ain't seen nothin' yet, my love." She slowly drove up the street and stopped in front of their house.

As they pulled up, their neighbors came spilling out of their houses and into the street, heading toward the car. There was Sam Anderson with a young man Don didn't recognize. *Where's Scott?* And there was little old Eileen Ferris bundled up in her faux fur coat with her tiny dog sporting a festive Christmas sweater, and a group of people gathered around who all bore a strong resemblance to her.

Zack Ellis ran toward the car, his mother doing her best to catch up with him, while Andy and Esme Nadeau came across the street with the baby in a stroller and the twins doing a madcap dance, carrying a hand-lettered sign that boldly proclaimed "Welcum Home DON!" in bright red magic marker. Nick and Paula Cable were standing on their lawn, holding gloved hands by a fir tree ablaze in multi-colored lights—the big old fashioned C9s that Don remembered from his childhood. Next door to them, he saw the two guys from number forty-three standing in their driveway, looking toward the Cassidys' car. There were lights at their house, too. Everyone was smiling and laughing.

Don grabbed the door handle, momentarily forgetting that he couldn't walk by himself, and Maggie grabbed his arm. "Hold on a minute," she said. "Just sit tight." She turned to Jenny. "Did you text Scott?"

"Yup! He's all set."

Maggie rolled down the windows and Jenny yelled out, "Okay everybody. Here we go! Ten, nine… "

Everyone joined in the countdown while Maggie turned on the radio.

"ONE!" At that moment, the jolly sounds of the new holiday hit, "The House on Christmas Street," came pouring out of the radio and Don's display came to life. The lights blazed and began to dance. When the singer sang, "Santa Claus up on the roof," Santa and all the reindeer blinked on and off, and when she sang "a band of merry snowmen," the snowmen did the same thing, and on it went as the song listed almost all the elements of Don's display. Everywhere he looked there was something amazing happening, all of it choreographed in time to the rousing music. It was truly a sight to behold, and Don was speechless. Tears sprang to his eyes and the lights became blurry, but still overwhelmingly beautiful.

Someone had brought a battery-powered radio, and on the sidewalk everyone was whooping and cheering, and Muffin was yapping. Andy began a crazy dance with Zack, the twins were bouncing up and down, and Sam Anderson had his arm around Angie Ellis as they gazed at the lights together. What the heck was going on around here?

At that moment Scott Anderson came bounding across the street. Jenny jumped out of the car and met him halfway, almost careening into him, and he raised his hand for a high five. To Don's surprise, she threw her arms around Scott's neck. Looking completely out of his mind with joy, Scott picked the girl up and twirled her around as she laughed with all her heart and soul. Now Don knew he must be dreaming.

"So, what do you think, sweetheart?" asked Maggie as the song finished.

"Oh...my...gosh!" Don said, as "Jingle Bells" by Bing Crosby and the Andrews Sisters started up. "Ohmygosh, ohmygosh!" He was now weeping openly. "It's beautiful. It's fantastic. It's out of this world! How did you...?"

Maggie put a finger to her lips. "Shhh," she said. "Don't ask questions. Just enjoy."

Chapter 50

Just yards from where the Cassidys sat in their car, Muriel Michaud stood behind her picture window curtain and peeked out. *Those lights could give someone a stroke,* she thought, *but they are kind of pretty.* As she watched the people in the street, laughing and dancing and carrying on, another old memory flashed into her mind. She and Ray and the children were out in the yard, and all the neighbors were gathered with them. It was an impromptu block party to watch the annual Fourth of July fireworks display that was going off up at the municipal airport and making a show right over the neighborhood. Everyone had brought food and they were enjoying each other's company. The children were dancing and folks were laughing; everyone was happy.

Somewhere along the line those community events had stopped happening, and Muriel realized that, deep down, she had missed them. She was somewhat shocked to realize that this was exactly what was happening right now, in front of her very eyes. This would be the memory those young mothers would have. Why wasn't she a part of it? If she was honest with herself, she'd admit she wished she were out there having fun, too. But she could never go out there now, not after all the fuss she'd made.

"How's it going, sugar plum?" asked Ray, sneaking up behind her.

Muriel jumped. "How many times do I have to tell you not to surprise me like that?" She whacked him on the bum as she made her way over to the end table where she'd left her cup of peppermint tea. She picked it up gingerly and sat down on the couch, took a sip and settled herself. "Well, I hope they're happy."

Ray sat down in his recliner. "You did a good thing, Muriel. I'm sure Mr. Cassidy needed that after all he's been through." He picked up the remote and aimed it at the television.

"Hmph," said his wife. "Well, like I told her, I'm not an evil woman. I just don't think...well, you know how I feel about it."

The doorbell rang and Ray and Muriel looked at each other. They got up in tandem and walked to the front door. Ray opened it to find the Nadeau twins bouncing up and down on the stoop. "Mrs. Michaud! Mrs. Michaud!" they yelled.

Ricky stepped forward and grabbed Muriel's arm. "Come out and see the lights!" he said.

Matty added, "You gotta come out. Everybody's out here but you!"

"What the dickens?" Muriel said. This was a surprise.

Ray burst into a hearty laugh.

"Well what do you know? That's right, Muriel. You can't let the boys down. We gotta go see the lights! I'll get our coats."

Muriel didn't have a chance to protest before Ray was putting her coat around her shoulders and the boys were pulling her through the door. "Hold on, hold on!" she laughed. "Let me button my coat!" The boys were giggling and tugging madly at her.

She saw Andy Nadeau running up the walkway, looking appalled. "Ricardo! Matteo! Come over here! Leave those people alone!"

"It's okay, Mr. Nadeau," said Ray. "Muriel and your boys are pals now. Didn't they tell you they creamed her at Candyland today?"

Muriel thought this was a hoot. A hoot! When was the last time she'd used that word? She was laughing right out loud as she struggled to button her coat while the boys attempted to pull her down the steps.

"Hey, be careful guys," said Andy, and he stepped forward to help the Michauds down the stairs and the walkway.

Esme Nadeau came over and put an arm on the old woman's shoulder, leaning in. "Thank you so much for everything you did today. I don't know how I can repay you."

"Oh, don't be silly. You can repay me by letting me do it again. It made me happier than I've felt in a long time, believe it or not."

The Michauds stepped out into the street and watched the light show as the twins danced around them. She was mesmerized by the way the lights went with the music.

"Isn't that something?" Ray said, over and over.

Eileen Ferris wandered over with two male companions. "Muriel," she said, taking the younger woman's arm, "It's good to see you out here. You remember my grandson, Joe, but I don't believe you've ever met my great-grandson. Francis, meet my neighbors, Mr. and Mrs. Michaud."

Francis shook her hand, and then Ray's. Then to her surprise, Joe reached out and gave Muriel a brief hug. "Of course I remember you, Mrs. Michaud. I was in Boy Scouts with Mike, and you and your husband helped us on a community Christmas project. Remember? We brought presents and candy to all the folks at the Kennebec Valley Nursing Home. And then we sang Christmas carols with them? None of us really wanted to do it, but you told us how much joy it would bring to the old people, so we went along. It went so well the first time that we did it for several years after that."

Muriel nodded. She didn't remember that at all, but she supposed it must be true since it meant so much to this gentleman.

"And I always thought you were super cool because you kept up with the music and TV shows that we boys liked," he added.

Yes, she had been like that once, a long time ago, when the kids were still around to keep her up-to-date. "Well, I'm so happy to see you again," she said. "Will and his family will be here tomorrow, if you want to come by and say hello. We'd love to have you."

They were chatting in the glow of the lights when Muriel noticed Mrs. Cassidy pushing her husband toward them in his wheelchair. As they rolled up, she felt herself stiffen.

Don looked up at Muriel and she could see the glow of the lights twinkling in his eyes. He reached out and took her hand. "Mrs. Michaud, Maggie told me that you two chatted, and I want you to know that it really means a lot to me to see it all lit up, even if it is only for one night. I know how you feel about the display, so I want to thank you for giving her your blessing."

Muriel felt a hot flush begin creeping up her neck, and she didn't know what to say. Instead of feeling good about Don Cassidy's kind words, she felt sheepish. It was beginning to dawn on her that this display wasn't such a monstrosity after all. It was beautiful. And yes, although it may cause traffic problems, there were ways to deal with that.

Don continued. "I know I handled this whole thing all wrong. I should've introduced myself when we first moved in, talked with you about it. I'm so sorry. But again, thank you. This is really wonderful." Muriel gulped. This man's sincere gratitude was a little overwhelming, and she felt stinging tears begin to swell in her eyes. Just then, Ray chimed in.

"It's beautiful, young feller," he said. "Really beautiful." He chuckled heartily and shook his head in wonderment, as Maggie, Don and even Muriel joined in the laughter.

In the midst of the laughter Muriel felt a tap on her shoulder, and turned around to see that woman from up the street; she didn't know her name but had seen her many times walking with her boy.

Then she noticed Sam Anderson standing there with her. She immediately stepped back, remembering their last encounter at his door.

"Mrs. Michaud," Sam said. His voice was soft and low. "Please, don't be afraid. I just wanted to speak to you for a second. Is that okay?" The woman next to him grabbed his hand and smiled at him encouragingly.

"I...I want to apologize for being so rude to you when you came to my door." He shook his head as though he were ashamed of his behavior. "That's really not my nature, and I'm hoping we can just let bygones be bygones and start over as neighbors. It's just...it's been a hard year."

Muriel didn't know what to say. She just stood there with her mouth agape. It sure had been a night filled with surprises. Then she looked at the woman standing beside Sam. This was the first time she had really seen her up close, and Muriel was instantly taken by her genuine smile and the light in her eyes. This light wasn't from the display; it seemed to be glowing from within.

"Mrs. Michaud, I'm Angie Ellis. I don't believe we've ever really met. I live over there, in the bungalow, with my son." She pointed toward the house. "It's really great to see you and your husband out here. I heard you spent some time over at Esme's house today. She was so grateful for everything you did for her she just couldn't stop talking about it."

Muriel smiled. "Oh, that wasn't anything. She needed a helping hand, is all."

"Well, of all of us, you were the only one around who saw what she needed, and reached out. That's really something. She said you were her guardian angel, coming along when she needed you most."

"She did?" No one had ever called her an angel before.

"She truly did," said Angie.

"So, can we start over, Mrs. Michaud? I'd really love to get to know a guardian angel," said Sam. "In fact, I could use one myself."

He laughed, and he sounded so sincere that Muriel couldn't help but warm to him.

"Well, I guess so," she said. "And," She cleared her throat. "I want you to know that I really thought about what you said when we came to your door. I know I haven't always been the most understanding neighbor."

Sam started to speak, but she cut him off. "No, no, it is my turn to apologize. I'm sorry I caused you so much trouble. Believe it or not, I always thought highly of your wife; every time I saw her she was either playing with your boys or working outside in the yard. I wanted to talk with her but...well, I just didn't think she'd be interested in talking to an old lady like me. I should have, though. I should have said something when she was still with us to hear it. And so...well...I'd welcome the chance to start over. And if you ever need anything, I'm right across the street."

Sam just stood there, nodding.

Oh for goodness sake, Muriel thought, *now this one has tears in his eyes.* Then she felt her own floodgates beginning to open. Ray reached over and put his arms around his wife, patting her back. "I know that was hard, sugar plum," he whispered in her ear, "But you did the right thing, and I'm so proud of you."

Just then Mark DiSalvatore sidled up to her, seemingly out of nowhere. "Muriel!" he shouted. "Will wonders never cease? Look at you in the glow of the Christmas lights!" He grabbed her and gave her a big squeeze, and as he did, he whispered in her ear, "These lights make you look twenty years younger, Muriel. You should be begging him to keep them up year-round!"

She batted him on the shoulder. "Don't be ridiculous, you," she said.

"What's going on here?" said Ray. "Are you flirting with my wife?" Now it was his turn to get batted by Muriel. She was having a downright grand time out here.

As the crowd milled in the street and watched the lights, Muriel was amazed that so many people talked to her, and oh, how good it felt to be a part of the neighborhood again. She truly felt better than she had in years. Then the light show ended and the crowd began to split up, everyone wishing each other a good night and wandering off to their homes. As Muriel and Ray walked up their driveway, they noticed Angie Ellis' boy standing on their lawn, staring.

"Hello there, young man," said Ray. "Can we help you with something?"

The boy didn't look at them, but his mittened hands started fluttering at his sides. He said nothing.

"What's going on, son? Do you need something?" Ray asked again.

Zack didn't look up. "No lights," he mumbled. "You should have lights. Like all the other houses."

Muriel and Ray exchanged glances as Angie walked briskly up the walk toward them. "Zack, come on now. We have to go home. I'm sorry, Mr. and Mrs. Michaud." She placed a hand on her son's back and began quickly guiding him down the walk.

"Oh, that's okay. No trouble at all. You have a nice night, now," Ray said, but Angie and Zack were already well on their way down the street.

"Now remember, we've got to get up early in the morning and put the turkey in the oven, so don't get too involved in watching a movie or anything," said Muriel. "I'm pooped and I want to get to bed by eight."

She sat on the couch, picked her knitting basket from the floor, and set to work on the Christmas sweater she'd been knitting for Emma. She'd already finished a matching one for Elmo, which would be quite a surprise on Christmas morning.

Just as Vanna White was waving goodbye, Ray clicked off the TV and he and his wife made their way up the stairs. After their nightly ministrations, Muriel called Paula to briefly discuss the plans for the next morning, and Ray set the alarm clock for five a.m.

Nestled under the covers, Muriel found herself staring at a single white light she could see twinkling through the gap in the bedroom curtains. *Must be the star at the top of that big tree. Somehow it didn't turn off with the rest of the lights,* she thought as she drifted off to sleep, smiling.

Angie had a difficult time settling Zack down to bed, but she didn't mind. This had been an amazing evening. Everyone on the block had joined together like one big family, and even the Michauds had participated in the fun. And Sam Anderson, of course. He had made a point of introducing her to his older son, Brian, and then they'd all had a ball out there in the glow of the lights. She'd seen him clap Scott on the back, and she couldn't help but overhear him enthuse about how proud he was, and how thrilled Scott's mother would have been. At one point, he said she was watching from heaven, and as tears rolled down Scott's face, they hugged for a long time. It was such a special moment that Angie had felt she was intruding, so she'd moved away and found Zack dancing with Andy and the twins, and joined in. Later, she'd seen Scott introducing his brother to Jenny, and wondered if there was young love blooming as a result of all of this. She sure knew she was falling fast and hard. And she was happy.

She was in the kitchen putting together the salad to take to her sister's house the next day when she heard a soft knock on the back door. She opened it to find Sam standing in her doorway with a potted poinsettia.

"I couldn't find roses, and these were the only red flowers at the grocery store," he said, shrugging. He put the plant down on the kitchen floor, then stood up, a serious expression on his face. "I just gotta do this," he said, and he swept her into his arms and kissed her tenderly.

Chapter 51

Muriel sat up in bed, feeling refreshed and invigorated. She had the turkey stuffed and in the oven by quarter of six, then set to work preparing the green bean casserole.

Will and his wife Emily arrived from Hartford a little after eleven, and before too long the rest of the guests joined them. Finally, the house was filled with noise again, and Muriel was at the center of it all. How she had missed this—and oh, how she basked in it now.

At one point, alone in the kitchen, Ray whispered to Muriel, "It's grand to see you so happy today, sugar plum. Maybe doing a kind deed yesterday did your heart some good."

She shooed him away. "Don't be ridiculous. You make me sound like an old fool. I'm just happy because most of our children are here."

But it was true that the visit with Esmerelda Nadeau and her children had begun to lift her cares, and now, thanks to the events of the previous evening, she finally felt like part of the neighborhood again. Having her precious family here with her, she envisioned the troubles of the past year or so floating away, as if in a big soap bubble. Her heart was growing warm again, and she wanted to share the feeling with everyone around her.

She went back into the living room with a tray of coffee and soft drinks and asked Paula to join her in the kitchen. "I just need some help bringing in the appetizers."

"What's up, Mom?" asked Paula. "Is everything okay?"

"Yes, yes, everything is fine," she said, then she took Paula's hand and looked into her eyes. "I just want you to know that I love you and Will and Nancy more than anything in the world."

"I know that, Mom. We all know that. You don't need to say it," said Paula.

"No, I do. I used to tell you all the time when you were little, but now, well, I don't think I say it enough. Your father and I are so proud of all of you, and we love you with all our hearts. You are the reason our lives have been so full, and I just think you should know that. We were not only blessed to have you, but to have lived long enough to see what wonderful people you've become."

"Oh, Mom." Paula threw her arms around her mother. "You'll always be my Mommy, no matter how old we get," she whispered. "I love you too, Mom,"

Later, Muriel, Paula and Karen were setting the dining room table when Muriel felt the cat brush against her leg. She scooched down and gave him a pet. "It's wonderful, isn't it, Elmo? The house feels alive again." Then Emma came running in from the living room, barreling toward her, and she opened her arms and gathered the little girl into a giant hug.

"Grand-Mémère, I wanted to hug Elmo!" said Emma, wriggling to get free.

"But Grand-Mémère wanted to hug YOU!" Muriel said, as the cat fled into the relative safety of the living room.

Just before they all sat down to their Thanksgiving feast, Nancy and Levi called from Pennsylvania. Muriel passed the phone around, everyone wishing the couple a long-distance happy day. When everyone had had a turn, Muriel took the phone back, and Nancy surprised her with the news that she and Levi were planning to come to visit for Christmas. "You are? That's wonderful!" she said. "Let me tell Dad." She held the phone away from her ear and walked over to her husband. "Nancy and Levi are coming home for Christmas!"

"Terrific!" said Ray with a big smile. "Can't wait to see you!" he yelled toward the phone.

Once the telephone conversation had ended, everyone sat down at the table and marveled at the perfectly roasted turkey on its platter. Muriel was quite pleased with herself and, though she was modest in accepting the praise, she agreed it was one of the finest Thanksgiving birds she'd ever cooked.

All went silent and Ray, at the head of the table, reached out and grasped Muriel and Emily's hands. Everyone else did the same with the people sitting next to them.

"Lord," Ray said. "Thank you for our wonderful family, and the many blessings you have given all of us. Thank you for once again bringing us together. We ask for your favor on Nancy and Levi, and for all of our loved ones who aren't here with us today. And please bless Mr. Cassidy with a full recovery. Thank you for this bountiful meal. Amen."

Ray rose to carve the turkey as the adults began passing the side dishes around the table.

"This all looks great Mom, as usual," said Will.

"Oh, it's just the same old thing every year. You know, with the thermometer in the turkey, you hardly have to do anything!"

Emily nodded. "That's true, but this stuffing of yours is quite a project. I tried it at Christmas last year and it came out good, but not quite as tasty as yours. Did you add something extra to the recipe?"

Muriel leaned over and whispered in her ear. "I use a whole cup of Grand Marnier, not just a half cup."

"Well! So that's the secret! I'll have to try that next time." Emily winked.

"What's for dessert?" asked Emma, and everyone laughed. Karen gestured toward the little girl's plate and said, "Eat your meal first before thinking about dessert."

"I know, I just want to know what to look forward to."

"Dig into one of Grand-Mémère's homemade rolls and you won't even think about dessert anymore," said Will, handing her the basket of bread.

"And we've got honey butter from Reph Farms too," said Ray, passing over the butter dish.

"Yummy!" Emma said, and stuffed a roll into her mouth without waiting for the butter.

It was a positively delightful dinner, and Muriel was filled with joy. Ray caught her eye and said, "What are you thinking about, sugar plum? You've got a mischievous twinkle in your eye all of a sudden."

His wife leaned forward, hands in her lap. "Well," she said, "As I told Paula on the phone this morning, I've had somewhat of a … well, I guess you could say a change of heart. And I need all of you to pitch in and help me."

"A change of heart?" said Emma, still chewing on her roll. "Is that like what happens to the Grinch, Grand-Mémère?"

A few guests around the table gasped, but Muriel just smiled at Emma. "Yes, sweetheart, now that you mention it, that's exactly what it is. Now everyone listen up. Here's what we're going to do… "

Scott was his usual quiet self as he sat in the Cassidy's living room and watched the various people milling about the house. Jenny's grandparents and her aunt Holly were here, and he had been introduced to them all. They were very nice, but he felt awkward and didn't know what he should be doing. It was weird being at someone else's house for the celebrations. Last year they didn't even have Thanksgiving. The three Anderson guys had just retreated to their own rooms and pretended the holiday wasn't happening. Now, here he was, in the home of a family he hadn't even known last year, with a girl he was falling hard and fast for, and he was worried about doing or saying the wrong thing. It was a miracle he'd even gotten to be friends with her, and holding her in his arms and twirling her around last night...did he dream that? Whoa. That had made his heart almost pound right out of his chest. Should he make a move today? Maybe try to kiss her? He hadn't ever kissed a girl for real.

As if on cue, Jenny walked into the living room. "Hey, do you like cranberry sauce?

"Uh...what?" he said, shaking his head a little. That had come out of the blue.

Jenny spoke a little louder. "I said, do you like cranberry sauce? And if you do, do you like the jellied kind or whole berry?"

"Um, I never really thought about it before. Cranberry sauce. Is that like beets?"

"Oh my Lord. You are so weird," Jenny said, and left the room.

Ohhhh. I've ruined things already!

"Scott, can you come help me set the table?" asked Maggie. Where had she come from? She'd seemed to appear out of nowhere.

"Sure, I'd be glad to. I'm not really any good at it, though."

"I'll tell you what to do. Come on in the dining room."

He was attempting to fold the napkins the way Maggie had demonstrated when he noticed her pass by his dad and whisper, "Angie and Zack are at her sister's house. She said they might stop by later. I'm guessing that since she knows you're here, that's a pretty safe bet." She winked and walked on by, leaving his dad looking embarrassed by the dining room table. Scott had to smile to himself.

"What was that all about?" asked Jenny, stepping up beside her mother. They walked into the kitchen together, but Scott could still hear them.

"Oh, let's just say there's more than one Anderson man who may have his heart stolen this holiday season," said Maggie, and she swept on back into the dining room, carrying the pilgrim salt and pepper shakers. Now Scott could feel himself blushing, and he couldn't look anyone in the eye as he took his place by his brother at the table.

Mr. Cassidy said a short prayer before the meal, thanking God for everyone and for his health, and then they all tucked into the delicious dinner. Scott wasn't used to all the praying stuff that this family did, but he guessed it was okay. They weren't weird about it; in fact it just seemed natural to them, like part of their daily lives. During the prayer, it occurred to him that it might be a good thing to have faith in some sort of higher power. That could've helped him a lot in the past year. It was something he'd like to talk with Jenny about.

The food was great. Scott had heard Maggie say that everything was low sodium, per doctor's orders, but he didn't notice any difference at all. It all tasted delicious, and definitely better than the Anderson guys would have had at home. The other day his dad had come home with a chicken and some Stove Top stuffing mix and said he was going to make a Thanksgiving meal for them this year. That's when Scott knew things really were turning around, but still, he was glad they were having this tasty meal instead of his father's efforts.

They ate until the plates were clean and they were stuffed. Afterwards, Scott stayed in the kitchen and helped Maggie, Jenny and Aunt Holly clean up while everyone else took coffee and pie into the living room and tuned in to watch the football game on TV.

The other folks got into the game right away, but Don's mind wandered off before long. Football had never really been his thing, but he understood the tradition and tried to be a genial and accommodating host. Still, he couldn't help but feel a tiny wince of regret that he wouldn't be outside, turning on his light show and greeting the folks who'd come to see it tonight. He sighed and tried to remain positive.

Suddenly, everyone started shouting at something that was happening in the game, and Don looked up, but it wasn't the television that caught his eye first. His attention was drawn to the picture window and the commotion going on across the street.

Not believing his eyes, he rolled his wheelchair across the room to the window. "Hey," he said, pointing toward the street. "Hey, you guys. Look at this. Look at what's going on at the Michaud's."

Maggie was wiping her hands with a dishtowel as she walked up to stand beside her husband. "Well, I'll be."

There was a flurry of activity going on at 39 Franklin Street. A man was up on a ladder, attaching a string of icicle lights to the gutters. A couple were placing nets of lights over the front hedges, and Ray was setting up a row of snowman path lights along the driveway. On either side of the walkway, a younger guy was pounding a row of stakes into the ground, and a woman placed a four-foot angel on top of each one. There were eight in all, each blowing a golden trumpet. There was a lady pulling a child around in a blue plastic sled over the two inches of snow that had fallen the previous night. And Muriel Michaud was standing in the center of the walkway, looking as though she were conducting an orchestra, directing each person at their task.

Don was sitting there stunned when he was further surprised to see Sam outside walking across the street. He hadn't even noticed him leave the room. Through the window he heard him yell, "Hey folks, need a hand?"

Don looked at Maggie. "Hey," he said. "If this is some kind of miracle on Franklin Street, I want to be involved, too. I mean, it was me that started this whole thing, after all."

Maggie smiled, and gave her husband a big hug and a kiss. "You sure did, honey," she said. "You've always been my miracle man." She turned to Jenny and said, "Will you help Dad get over there? I'm not sure how this wheelchair will handle in the snow, and I want to stay here and spend some time catching up with Gramma and Grandpa and Aunt Holly."

"Sure," said Jenny. "Will this count as hours on my practice driving log?" Her smile was winsome.

"Maybe I'd better come with you," said Scott. "Wouldn't want you running any red lights."

She shook her head. "Oh no, I don't need a backseat driver! I'll get my jacket."

As Jenny was opening the hall coat closet, Don suddenly had an epiphany. He plainly saw that this, right here, was the time to make a choice, and he knew what that choice had to be. "You know what, Jen," he said. "Let's not go over. Sam can handle it. Why don't you and I get out the cribbage board and play a game. It's been a long time since we've done that."

Jenny stuck her head out from the behind the closet door and said, "Are you sure, Dad? Cause I really don't mind."

He nodded firmly. "I'm sure. I'd rather spend some time with you." Then he thought for a second and said, "Or we could really go old school and play a game of Clue, and Scott could play, too."

Jenny's face lit up. "Oh, my gosh, we haven't played Clue in years. I'd love to do that!" She whirled around to Scott. "You want to play it with us? Let's go get my game. It's up in my closet."

As the two kids went upstairs, Don smiled to himself. There would be many opportunities for Christmas displays, but Maggie was right —there were only a couple more years left with Jenny before she went to college. The time to repair their bond was now.

Sometime later the doorbell rang, and when Maggie opened it, Don was surprised to see Muriel Michaud standing there. "May I come in for a second, Mrs. Cassidy?" the old woman asked. I'd like to speak with your husband."

Maggie welcomed her in and she walked straight up to Don, who was sitting at the dining room table with Jenny, Scott and Holly. They'd been engrossed in their game and the inevitable reveal of who killed Mr. Boddy was coming any minute.

Muriel looked him square in the eye and said, "Mr. Cassidy, I've been wrong, and I'm so sorry. What you've been doing here is helping this neighborhood get back to what it once was, a long, long time ago. I didn't understand that until last night, and I want to be a part of it. Can you forgive a foolish old lady?"

Before Don could respond, Maggie said, "Of course, Mrs. Michaud," and reached out to give her a hug. To his astonishment, Muriel actually hugged her back, then looked down again at him.

"Mr. Cassidy, if my callous behavior had anything to do with your accident, please know that I—"

Don interrupted her. "No, no, no, Mrs. Michaud. It was my own fault that I was too darned stubborn to get down off that roof when I should have." He gestured toward the window and the view of her house. "But what's all that? Where have you been hiding all those Christmas decorations?"

Muriel winked. "It helps to have a daughter and son-in-law who own a hardware store, Mr. Cassidy." She smiled a mischievous smile.

Don sat full upright in his chair. "Well, what do you know? And by the way, you're not going to believe this, but I've still got plenty of decorations in the garage that I haven't used this year. So if you want to make your display even grander…"

The sun was setting, and the neighbors—and Muriel knew they all truly were neighbors now—were standing in the street, waiting for Will to throw the switch that would set her home aglow. All day long her heart had been growing fuller and fuller, and she chuckled to herself as she thought of what Emma had said at dinner about The Grinch. Maybe it was true. She had been the Grinch. But now she was going to make up for it. And just like the Grinch, she was going to see to it that Christmas from now on would be filled with love and kindness. For as long as she could, she was going to make sure Franklin Street had the best Christmas displays in all of Kennebec City.

The group had been joined by Mr. and Mrs. Cassidy and their daughter, the Anderson boy, Mark and Tommy, Eileen, Francis and Joe. To Muriel's delight, Will was delighted to see his old friend Joe, and they'd spent a few minutes catching up during the decorating. Now everyone was counting down. "Ten...nine...eight...seven... six...five...four...three...two...one!"

The house was ablaze with hundreds of red, white and green lights, and the angels appeared to be trumpeting their song for all to hear. Don had overseen the placing of his smaller blow mold Nativity set in the center of one side of the lawn; the figures of Joseph, Mary and Baby Jesus in the manger glowed softly in the winter air.

Suddenly half of the bunting lights that were set along the fence between the Michauds' and Mrs. Ferris' house went out. The crowd let out a collective, "Oh!"

"Oh drat!" Muriel said, exasperated. Why did this have to go wrong?

Don, who was seated in his chair next to her, said, "No worries, no worries, Mrs. Michaud. This is a simple problem and I've got just the tool to fix it." He turned to his trusty assistant. "Scott, will you please go into the garage and get something for me? On the work desk in the back you'll see a tool—it looks kind of like a Star Trek phaser."

"A what?" Scott said, looking confused.

"Okay. Generational reference problem. Uh, it looks kind of like a red water pistol. It says Light Keeper Pro on it. Can you get that for me?"

"I know where it is. I'll help you find it," said Jenny, and they bounded off into the garage together.

The garage still had that new pine smell, and Scott appreciated the warmth after being out in the cold for a while. As they made their way around the cars to the back of the room Jenny said, "I really owe you. You helped me get interested in my dad's display again. Doing the light synchronization thing was really fun. Next year I'm going to try to program some of the songs myself."

"That would be great. Maybe I could learn how to do it with you, if you want."

He'd had a lot of fun playing Clue with Jenny and her family, but now, here they were, alone together in the garage. There was a bit of fading winter light still filtering through the garage windows, so Jenny hadn't switched on the overhead light, just a smaller lamp that sat on her father's workbench. Crazy as it seemed, the garage actually felt kind of romantic. But maybe anywhere Jenny was would feel that way. She was so beautiful and vivacious. He wanted so badly to know if she felt the same way about him. He wanted to kiss her, but what a risk! He could ruin their friendship with the wrong move. Should he throw caution to the wind and try to kiss her here? Among all her father's Christmas decorations? Or should he just ask her out? "Here it is," Jenny said, as she reached for the tool her father had been talking about. "Dad got this at one of those decorating conventions. He calls it the decorator's miracle tool."

"Cool," said Scott, who had sidled up beside her. Though his mind was racing, he pretended to be looking at the assortment of light bulbs, fuses and other electronic doodads that were littering the work table. Suddenly, Jenny moved in front of him, placed her hands behind his neck and pull his head down. Her lips brushed his in a soft kiss. He caught the scent of her lip gloss. It was peppermint. Somehow he knew he would never forget this. Then it was all over before he'd even had a chance to enjoy it. Well, at least he didn't have to wonder what to do anymore.

She pulled away quickly, that radiant smile beaming from her face. "I've been thinking about doing that since last night, but I didn't want to do it where everybody could see us."

Scott was stunned. "You just kissed me," he said, dazed.

"I sure did. And it wasn't bad for our first kiss. Hopefully we'll have lots of chances to practice and get better at it, but right now we'd better get back outside or everyone will wonder what's going on in here." She grabbed the Light Keeper Pro and headed for the door.

Chapter 52

One December evening many years later, Muriel was sitting in a rocking chair by the fire with Emma. They'd been baking cookies all afternoon, one of their favorite holiday traditions. Emma had grown up so pretty, with long blonde hair and a dancer's figure and the talent to match. She was smart as a whip, too. Muriel liked to think those brains came from her side of the family.

Now, feeling inspired, the old woman said, "As you go through life, Emma, don't ever give up on living. When you get older you may start to feel useless, but remember that it's a big world with a lot of people in it, and there's always somebody who needs you. When you were little, I felt that way for a while, until somewhat of a miracle happened, right here on Franklin Street." Muriel thought perhaps she'd said this to Emma before, but her memory wasn't what it used to be, and she wasn't quite sure.

"Tell me about it, Grand-Mémère," said Emma, and Muriel knew the teen was humoring her. She'd heard this tale a million times, but if she wanted to hear it again, she would be glad to tell it.

Before she had a chance to go on with the story, the door burst open and in came Karen with two good-looking young men, surrounded by a gust of wind and snow. "Mémère!" Karen said. "Look what the wind blew in."

At once, the two boys shouted, "Nana Muriel!" and rushed over to give the old woman a hug.

Muriel was thrilled and reached her arms out to grasp both of them at once. "Matteo! Ricky! Where have you been? I haven't seen you since Thanksgiving."

"We've been really busy," said Matteo, now a tall, dark, and handsome teen. "High school is *hard.*"

"But we baked you some cookies this afternoon," said Ricky. He had also grown up tall and handsome, though he didn't have quite the athletic build of his brother. Ricky was more of the studious sort while Matteo had excelled at athletics and was playing Junior Varsity football.

Ricky placed a festively decorated Christmas container on the end table, then turned to Emma. "Hey, Emma."

"Hi Ricky," she replied, and Muriel detected a bit of a blush in her great-granddaughter's cheeks.

Karen brought in a tray of mugs filled with cocoa piled high with whipped cream. She placed it on the coffee table, then sat in an easy chair and took up her knitting as the lads got comfy on the sofa. They spent a few minutes telling Muriel about their first semester of high school.

"I met a nice girl," said Matteo. "Her name is Patti, and she even has a twin sister named Cassie, but Ricky's not into her."

"She's just not my type," said Ricky. "I like more athletic girls."

Matteo glanced over at Emma. "Oh, you mean like dancers?" He cracked a wicked grin as Ricky instantly turned fire-engine red.

Then Matteo said, "Mom wanted us to give you her love. She and Dad are in New York this weekend for the opening of her big show at that gallery. She's so excited about her first Manhattan show."

"Well, it's about time," said Muriel. "She has such a gift."

Ricky leaned forward on the couch, resting his chin on his hands. He looked as though he might be in the mood for a story. Sure enough, he said, "Tell us again how Franklin Street got to be known as Christmas Street, Nana Muriel."

Muriel waved her hands at him. "Oh, you've heard that story a thousand times."

"But we love hearing it!" Ricky said.

"She was just about to tell it, weren't you, Grand-Mémère? We always love hearing that story, every Christmas," said Emma. "It's a tradition."

Muriel pulled her sweater around her shoulders and took a sip of her cocoa. She settled back in her chair and searched her memory for that fall and winter from so many years before. Then she launched into the time-worn story about the little feud she'd had with Don Cassidy, and how she was so unhappy about growing old and feeling unwanted and useless. And then how she'd had a change of heart about everything because she found out she was needed after all. It was true that her memory wasn't what it used to be, but she'd never forgotten that Christmas season on Franklin Street.

And she never would.

"That's where we come in!" said Ricky.

The old woman nodded and continued the story of how she came to be their "Nana Muriel."

"And then," she continued, "the Sunday after that very first Thanksgiving evening, Roger Girard visited the displays and I asked him to file that petition in the shredder. Before we knew it, word had spread about the marvelous lights on our street, and Franklin Street became a destination for families, sweethearts, and lonely folks, and everyone who saw it had their hearts lifted by the sound of the music and the beauty of the lights. We were so busy we had the Knights of Columbus out here every night directing traffic, just like they do now.

"Year after year, more and more of our neighbors got into the act of decorating their houses for the holidays. Eventually the Kennebec City Selectmen voted to symbolically rename our street 'Christmas Street' for the month of December, and Don Cassidy made those very street signs you still see at the ends of the road from Thanksgiving to Christmas."

"It's always been Christmas Street, for as long as I can remember," said Emma. "In fact, I thought they wrote that song, The House on Christmas Street, about Franklin Street!"

"No, no," said Matteo. "I remember that song was playing in the street when we were little, the very first time they lit up the lights. Ricky and I went and got you, Nana. I remember."

Muriel shook her head. "You can't possibly remember that. You two were just little boys back then."

"But I do, Nana Muriel, I do. I remember that you didn't want to come out, but Papa Ray got your coat on for you and made you come out with us."

"Yeah, I remember that too. We were all dancing in the street. It was really something!" added Ricky.

What beautiful memories these are, thought Muriel. *And to think I almost missed out on all of it.*

"What are you guys doing?" said a voice from the kitchen. "It's time to bundle up, sugar plum." Ray came out, with a huge thermos in one hand and a bowl of cookies in the other. "We've got the cocoa all ready and I've already brought out the candy canes. We can't shirk our annual responsibilities!"

Ray helped his wife with her coat and hat, then she put on her mittens and let the kids lead her out into the frosty night, just as they had done all those years ago. The traffic was already lining the street to see the lights as she and Ray took up their position at the hot chocolate table. For years, they had been at their post on the sidewalk for at least one hour every night, handing out treats and directing folks to the donation box for the Kennebec City Food Pantry. It was an important job in the grand scheme of things, and Muriel and Ray loved doing it together. Tonight she was feeling particularly sentimental.

She smiled and waved at Don and Maggie Cassidy and Scott Anderson, who were standing on the sidewalk across the street. Muriel guessed that Jenny Cassidy—now Jenny Anderson—was in the house with the baby. Scott and Jenny had stayed together through college, started a business together designing video games, and had even invited Muriel and Ray to their wedding.

Angie and Zack—who were now also Andersons—wove through the traffic to come over and say hello, and Muriel saw Mark and Tommy greeting visitors up the street.

The Nadeau family had moved to a bigger house in Augusta a couple of years earlier, and they'd brought Muriel down to see it. It had a beautiful, light-filled studio for Esme. She'd even done a portrait of her best friend Muriel. They'd actually sold their house to the newlyweds, and now Jenny and Scott and the baby —Muriel couldn't seem to remember his name—lived right next door to Don and Maggie.

Eileen had joined Muriel and Ray at the hot chocolate stand for as long as she had been able, and Muriel was grateful she'd had the opportunity to rekindle her relationship with her old friend. Then Eileen and Muffin had moved to Las Vegas to stay with her grandson, and several months later Joe had phoned to say that Eileen had passed peacefully in her sleep. Not long after, Muffin had gone over the Rainbow Bridge to be with his beloved mistress.

There were new families living in Eileen Ferris' house and the bungalow, and they all got into the spirit of decorating, too.

Muriel watched her husband, who was happily handing a paper cup of hot chocolate to a little girl standing at the table with her parents. Then she saw Matteo, Ricky and Emma walking together from car to car and handing out candy canes. She took it all in, looking around at all the smiling faces in the glow of the lights. Everyone was jolly, but no one enjoyed the festivities more than she did.

She'd had many more Christmases than she'd ever dreamed possible, and on this night, basking once again in the warmth in spite of the cold temperature, Muriel thought the house at 40 Franklin Street—*the* House on Christmas Street—had never looked more beautiful.

Epilogue

One winter night, a lonely woman was driving back to her new apartment in Kennebec City after her shift as a deejay at the local radio station. She'd just moved to the city to start the job a week earlier, after a difficult divorce from an abusive husband. Still unfamiliar with the neighborhoods, she accidentally missed the turn for her street, and instead, ended up driving down Franklin Street.

At the sight of the magnificent light displays shining in the winter night, she had to pull over. She sat alone in her car for a long time, just looking at the lights. Seeing them shining and sparkling in the dark filled her sad heart with hope and joy. The next day she went out and bought a little tree for her apartment, and decorated it gaily. It was her first real step toward starting a happier life.

In spite of what hardships they faced during the rest of the year, all hearts were filled with hope when visiting that neighborhood of lights, and memories were made that lasted for lifetimes. No matter their differences, at Christmas time there was one place where everyone could meet and enjoy the spirit of the season together, a place where all hearts would join in the true spirit of Christmas, and that was The House on Christmas Street.

THE END

Afterword

This story was first conceived after a long drive home to New Hampshire from Gatlinburg, Tennessee, where I had attended the Planet Christmas Lights UP Expo in 2007. Therefore my first "thank you" goes to Chuck Smith, who began the Planet Christmas website and first welcomed me into the Christmas decorating community with open arms.

I owe a great debt of gratitude to the first decorating enthusiast who found my song in some corner of the internet and synchronized his Christmas display to it. I don't know who you are, but you brought my song the kind of worldwide attention most songwriters only dream of, and I thank you from the bottom of my heart.

As I said in the Dedication, the Christmas decorating community worldwide has been an inspiration and a blessing to me. I would love to thank each and every one of you by name, but if I tried to do that I would invariably leave someone out and feelings would be hurt. Some of you have probably already found your names in this book. For the rest of you, there just aren't enough characters in a book to fill it with all the people who have extended their kindness to me over the years. You will always have a special place in my heart.

A very heartfelt "thank you" goes to my dear friend, the late *New*

York Times best-selling author, Rick Hautala. Rick sat on his deck one summer afternoon and listened to me pour out the beginnings of this story, and he fashioned a screenplay out of it. Unfortunately, Rick passed suddenly before the screenplay had a chance to get "out there," and so I continued his work by using the screenplay as an outline for the novel you have just read. It took me many years and I don't know if I would have done it without what Rick had first done. I miss you every day, my friend.

Thanks to my writing coach, Jon McGoran, and my editors, Linda Nagle and Louisa Pancoast. I am very appreciative of all the folks who read this book in its various stages, including Holly Newstein Hautala, Emma Pancoast, Diane Galutia, Deb Noack, Maxine Puleo, and Michael Pierce. Your input has been invaluable and I thank you so much for all of the encouragement.

Last but never least, thank you Philip Pancoast. You know why.

-Judy Pancoast Goffstown, NH
July 7, 2019